The Reason
for Wings

The Reason for Wings

A NOVEL

Joyce Reiser Kornblatt

Fic = 9/99

SYRACUSE UNIVERSITY PRESS
in association with DRYAD PRESS

Cover art: *Brief Intent to Fly,* fresco on paper by Claudia Bernardi, is in the collection of William Pettis. Reproduced with permission of the artist.

Text and cover design by Sandy Rodgers.
Text is set in Bembo 11.5/15.5

The paper used in this publication meets the minimum requirements of American National Standard for Information Sciences — Permanence of Paper for Printed Library Materials, ANSI Z39.48-1984 ∞

Library of Congress Cataloging-in-Publication Data

Kornblatt, Joyce Reiser.
    The reason for wings / by Joyce Reiser Kornblatt. — 1st ed.
        p. cm. — (Library of modern Jewish literature)
    ISBN 0-8156-0578-1 (alk. paper)
    1. Jews — Danube River Delta (Romania and Ukraine) — History — 20th century Fiction. 2. Jews — Argentina — History — 20th century — Fiction. 3. Holocaust, Jewish (1939 — 1945) Fiction. I. Title. II. Series.
PS3561.0622R42 1999
813' .54 — dc21   99-25075

Manufactured in the United States of America

for Sara, Miriam-Rose and Erin

1

ONE MORNING, LONG BEFORE I was born, my grandfather left his home in the port of Tulcea and disappeared into the unmapped labyrinth of the Danube Delta. He went in his rowboat, as always. He was not the first in our line to vanish — and surely not the last — but his is the first such story to survive in any detail, entrusted to me as I entrust it now to you. For eighty years, my mother had kept the memory of her father's disappearance buried within her, but in her last days, she emerged suddenly from delirium and summoned me to her bedside here in Buenos Aires, to which we had fled decades ago, after the war. She was finally old enough, she said, to understand the duties of the witness: she could not die without leaving me her narrative. She insisted that I take down her words as she spoke them, and, with a medium's clarity, she began the recitation with which my chronicle begins. In her voice I found my own. Each generation cradles the next with a tale and the family that loses its legends orphans the souls of it progeny.

She rose with him at dawn to help him assemble the provisions he would need for the day: goat's cheese, bread, apples, two full canteens, a compass, binoculars, a sack of seed for the birds whose habits he studied with a scholar's passionate diligence and recorded in leather-bound notebooks he made himself. All her life my mother Sonia would treasure the seven volumes he filled over the years with his observations of pelicans, egrets, ibis and herons, words and drawings fine as a trained ornithologist might have rendered, though

her father was a cobbler by trade. An unschooled, Yiddish-speaking
Jew who never travelled beyond the region of Dobrujda, Dov
Landau kept his notebooks in French, a language he had mastered
himself, in secret, much as he learned the various declensions of
birdcall on his solitary excursions into the vast Delta sanctuary. She
might always have assumed him a natural casualty of that watery
wilderness — those infinite miles of reed beds, marshes, lakes, ser-
pentine channels, forests so dense the sun seemed unable to penetrate those dark arboreal pockets — had not the gypsy named Ovid
brought her distraught mother the news, many days later, that her
husband was still alive in the Delta, not dead as the search party had
concluded — as likely murdered as drowned, they'd said, soldiers
killing Jews these days with the ease of hunters out for rabbits or
ducks. "Alive," Ovid insisted, Dov inhabiting a nest much like a pelican's which Ovid believed the cobbler had appropriated, or, more
likely, constructed himself — in his last notebook, in fact, he had
made a detailed diagram of such a nest, its materials and design. It
was, Ovid suggested, as if his friend believed he had actually been
transformed into that female bird whose legendary patterns of
maternal devotion Dov so revered, he whose own mother had died
during his birth.

"I spoke to Dov Landau for more than an hour," Ovid said in
the halting Yiddish he had learned over the years, "but he wouldn't
make a sound." He put a finger to his lips, the gesture part of an
improvised sign language with which he augmented his speech.
"Pelicans are almost mute, you know."

Reba Landau stared at the man who announced to her her husband's madness. He was blind in one eye, and the gaze of the other
carried within it the scorching intensity of compensation, that fire
in the faculties which survive an affliction. She was afraid of that
fiery eye. She was afraid of the sharp bones in his beardless face.

Over his embroidered smock hung a hammered silver chain and the sun glinted off each link like a blade, so that Ovid appeared to be wearing a necklace of knives. Reba picked up Sonia as if she were an infant — actually, she was five years old — and put a shielding hand over her eyes, the woman's touch turned cold as the carp Dov often brought back from his day-long Delta sojourns. Reba had never talked to a gypsy before. Once she had warned her husband, "They put spells on children, they take them away in their wagons."

"Don't inflict your superstitions on me," Dov had said. "Human beings make themselves mad with their hatreds. Sometimes I wish I had been born a bird."

Was it the memory of that remark, a certain disquieting fervor that kept her from sending away the agitated Ovid? Or was it the simple fact of hope where none had existed? She was already wearing a black dress, the funeral was scheduled for the next day. "What will we put in the coffin?" the casket-maker had asked her when she had gone to his shop to order the plain pine box. "My happiness," Reba Landau had said, surprised to hear from her own mouth the kind of epigrammatic response Dov would have made, were he still alive. How could she send away the gypsy and bury the empty coffin and mourn a man who might not be dead at all? Every night, for the rest of her life, she would dream of Dov in his nest, coming out of his pelican silence to call her name — "Reba! Reba!" — and she would wander the Delta's maze alone, never finding him, husband and wife lost to each other forever.

"Take me there," she said at last to Ovid. She was trembling badly. Still on Reba's hip, Sonia feared the two of them would topple; she clung to her mother as if they were in a storm from which there was no protection, a quake about which they could do nothing, could simply endure, until the tremors finally subsided of their own accord. "Take me to where he is."

They went in Ovid's wagon. When neighbors saw them that morning inside the weathered birchwood carriage, leaving Tulcea in the shower of dust the hooves of the driven horse stirred up, they ran into the dry dirt road like chickens loosed from their pens, they squawked "Reba, stop!" and "Let them go!" and "God in Heaven!" and Reba waved them back to their yards, shouting assurances to herself as well as to them: "He's found Dov! Don't worry! It's God's will!"

Hearing her mother's assertions, Sonia's fear — which had battered her insides since the day of her father's disappearance — left her body like a flock of entrapped birds riding the current of her exhalation. She felt bird-like herself, buoyant. So her father was playing some kind of game with them! Well, wasn't he always making up games for her at home, hiding from her in the root cellar, under the porch, high up in the sycamore from which he would swoop down to surprise her with his crane-whoops or hawkish shrieks? And now he was hiding in the Delta, pretending to be a pelican, waiting all these days for them to discover him — who else could have contrived such a marvellous adventure, such a thrilling charade? Riding in the gypsy's carriage! All her life my mother would remember this ecstatic reprieve from grief as a gift her father had bequeathed her, and in times of sorrow she would return to that mental state as if to an actual place she had inherited: the town turning to mist behind them, the world they entered a fecund paradise, song-thralled and shimmering and green.

Did Reba derive similar consolations from this journey? None. Years later she would tell Sonia how she had submitted to three possibilities, all of them terrible: she and Sonia were Ovid's hostages, the news about Dov a ruse devised by the kidnapper who would kill them both when he discovered there was no one in this world from whom he could extract a ransom; or, Dov was dead as their neighbors had informed her, his nesting just a gypsy dream Ovid took for truth; or, Dov did believe himself to be a bird, in which case the man as she had known him no longer existed and Reba's bereavement would continue, even as she claimed as her own the deranged cobbler whose differences from other men had always confused her, Dov's mental life a maze through which she tracked him, exactly as the horse now threaded its way along the twisting moss-laced road. Her husband's mind, this strange landscape: how were they different? In both terrains she was a stranger, though she had been Dov Landau's wife for twelve years, had lived a mile from here for the same length of time. Who had ever felt so lost as Reba Landau did right now, the mist that rose from the marsh grass obscuring even further her dwindling sense of location?

"Here," said Ovid, as if intuiting her need for some kind of landmark, "is where I left his boat."

The gypsy brought the wagon to a halt, descended, tied the horse to a tree, its roots breaking like gnarled bones through the bank of the channel whose route they had been following awhile by land. They watched Ovid drag a vessel out from behind a stand of reeds. They knew immediately it was Dov's: on each side of the rowboat, he had painted a white wing, the feathers silvering over the years so that they had nearly vanished into the gray wood on which he had so carefully replicated their construction. Why wings on a boat? Reba had asked him, though Sonia had found the paradox delightful and had no need for explanation.

"Legend has it," he had said, "that, long ago, pelicans forgot how to fly and that is why they build their nest on the ground. One by one they are recalling the reason for wings. When the last pelican remembers how to fly, I want to be ready to follow it into the heavens."

Later, Reba claimed that there in the Delta she heard Dov
uttering the same words again — "When the last pelican remembers how to fly, I want to be ready to follow it into the heavens."
— so clearly she sensed this was not a memory she was experienc-
ing at all, but the moment itself, returned as if there were no past
from which to retrieve it, no present in which to recall it, no future
in which she might imagine herself granted some fragment of
understanding about it. In the Delta, time collapsed, she seemed to
hear it falling like a town razed to its foundations, all the rubble
sinking to the bottom of streams, disappearing forever into the
Danube. She felt dizzy, sick. How had she allowed herself to come
here with a mad gypsy? She would take her child and run from
him! She would retrace on foot the distance they had covered from
Tulcea — but how, how? The road had forked so often, and sometimes vegetation obscured it entirely — she could never find her
way alone. Ovid was beckoning to them from the winged boat.
Reba closed her eyes: perhaps if she listened with the superior concentration of a blind woman, she could catch sounds from Tulcea
toward which she could direct their escape. Did she hear the voices of neighbors haggling over prices in the central market, or were
those geese honking in the distance? A fisherman seemed to drag
his day's netted catch across the splintered deck of his trawler, but
then she feared the sound was actually one of those giant turtles she
had seen earlier pulling its body out of the pond and up a pebbled
bank. And was that the great bell of the Orthodox Church clang-
ing miles away in the town square, or could she be confusing the
semblance of familiar music with the song of some Delta bird she
had never heard before in her life? She opened her eyes and yielded to it fully: in this timeless world they had entered, the one-eyed
gypsy was their only guide.

It was noon when they set out on the water. They travelled
beneath a canopy of branches, and the sunlight lay like twig-edged

scales upon the stream, as if it were a snake or a lizard on whose back they rode. What for her mother was a nightmare to which she had assented was for Sonia a dream whose beauty she would never again in her life approach. Ovid sang as he rowed, a gypsy serenade that joined itself to the larger chorus that surrounded them. In the Delta, everything was music, they were part of a great orchestra in which the instruments cawed and twittered and scuttled and hummed, some parts crescendo, others hush, Ovid's tenor rising like the sweet flute her father had made for her from reeds he'd brought back once from this very place.

"How much longer?" her mother said, nothing melodic in the tone she struck. Sonia had nearly forgotten that Reba was there beside her, so soothed was the child by Ovid's song and the fluid transit they were making through the water. Reba sat so stiffly there in the boat, Sonia had lost nearly all sense of her organic presence: the woman barely breathed, she clutched her hands together in her lap, she kept her eyes closed as they travelled, as if to deny as much of this journey as she could, as if keeping it outside the range of her senses might lessen the claim it could make on her mind. If she submitted to the Delta's spell, perhaps she, too, would begin to think herself a bird, or a fish, or a purple thistle rising from the mud; perhaps she, too, would succumb to the confusion that might have stricken her husband, perched somewhere in these wilds, all memory of his life in Tulcea vanished as if it had never existed at all.

"Soon," Ovid said, and as if the word were an incantation, the stream they travelled opened suddenly into a lake so vast Sonia could not see its shores, the mirroring water a kind of rippled sky in which the counterparts of clouds above them floated in the lake's surface, and then a bit further the sun, too, doubled itself, and there the twin suns melted into each other's element, boundaries vanished, sky and lake became a single incandescent span, light meeting light at that place one would have called the horizon, had it not

been utterly absorbed by that luminosity toward which their tiny
winged rowboat travelled. Oh God, the radiance! When would
Sonia ever again see such a shining?

Just as it seemed to her that they would disappear into that
brightness — who could imagine anything beyond it? — Ovid
shifted course, shadows fell across the lake, geography returned, a
shoreline rose, an island swallowed by the brightness emerged, birds
she had been blinded to dove to the water for fish and soared off
with the catch in their beaks, and in the wafting grasses at the
island's edge, a family of pelicans rested on the rocks in the mid-day
warmth.

"Here?" said Reba.

Sonia looked at her mother's face and saw she had been weeping, awed as much by that unfathomable light as her child had been,
though Reba would never admit that she had even noticed it at all.

"Here," Ovid said, and tied Dov's rowboat to one of the pines
near the pelican's resting-place.

He lifted Sonia to shore, then took Reba's hand and helped her
from the boat. Sonia was staring at the long-billed birds, at the
pouches where they stored their food, at the twig-topped earthen
nest on which a female perched. Was that her father? Was he wearing a disguise so convincing she could not tell him from a true
pelican?

"Papa?" she said.

"Where, where?" Reba cried, wheeling like a bird herself, her
arms outstretched like wings that might fly her to her missing husband's side.

"There," the gypsy said, pointing a ring-laden finger farther
down-shore.

Reba grabbed Sonia's hand and pulled her along the island's
edge, the ground like sponge under their feet, so that their shoes

made a sucking noise as they went, and it felt as if they were sinking even as they covered ground.

Could Ovid fly? How else did he manage to run twice the distance mother and child had managed, circling the island to meet them at the spot to which he'd pointed, greeting them there like a chieftain into whose realm they had stumbled?

"Here," the gypsy said. "Dov Landau was right here."

They looked down. What had become a pelican's nest lay among the reeds and rocks, chunks of packed sandy gravel-veined earth scattered like the rubble of a fallen house, the top layer of twigs strewn across the ground. Reba knelt and sifted the debris through her hands. On her heels, she rocked. She was murmuring her husband's name over and over and over. Dov, Dov, Dov.

And Ovid? From the site of the nest, he walked ten paces to the shoreline and found the cobbler's clothes folded neatly in a pile weighted down with a rock. There Ovid stood, holding his friend's cap, gazing out at the water as if he knew exactly where Dov had given himself to the lake.

What did Sonia do? She fled from her mother and the gypsy, too, she ran inland, through a thicket of shoulder-high grass, through moss-crusted woods, over shallows streaking the island's center like veins and up a sudden rise, then down its rocky slope to a clearing, almost a meadow, through woods again and out to the shoreline of the far side of the island where, because of how the sun had moved or the the way the water caught its glow at this location of the lake or because she yearned to see it again, the magical light appeared to her, its magnitude even brighter this time, and toward that infinite illumination a pelican soared, its black-tipped wings growing smaller, its pouch shrinking, its long beak piercing the light into which, finally, the bird's entire body passed. What was it Ovid had said? "Pelicans are almost mute, you know." But this one spoke before it vanished, and it was her father's voice, travelling a distance she could never begin to calculate: "Take care of your mother for me, *maydele*, and never forget that I love you." Then the light took him in, he was gone, and she was the only one, until now, who would ever know the true story of Dov Landau's disappearance.

Why did she keep it a secret so long?

Who would have believed her?

Who?

2

THE DEAD ARE EASIER to believe than the living.

As I took it down, my mother's tale seemed to me most likely a dream she'd had in order to make her own imminent death less frightening; but once she was gone, the story she had given me grew so convincing that I continued to record it on my own. I was the medium now, writing down in a kind of trance the fates of my grandmother Reba, my mother Sonia, and Ovid, the gypsy who knew the Delta's interior as well as he knew my mother's palm which he would read for her, in secret, under the sycamore in whose leafy architecture Dov Landau used to hide.

When a loved one disappears and there is no body from which the answer is always the same — Yes, dear ones, I am dead — the entire family falls sick. Vacillating each moment between grief and hope, kin lose their equilibrium, suffer from dizziness, stumble and fall in the midst of the simplest tasks. It is a universal illness. Relatives left behind grow impatient with each other, so exhausted is each one from the constant effort required to stay erect, to move across a room, to get to the market and back without dropping the fruit in the road or tripping over one's own feet. Children fall asleep over their lessons; parents forget the birthdays of sons and daughters who remain at home; grandparents spend so much time in bed that coming to the kitchen for a meal seems like a journey that they will never complete.

Sometimes waiting becomes one's vocation, as surely as if one were schooled in its stages, ordained to carry out its lonely tasks. It is not simply for the loved one's return that one waits. Reba waited for Dov's soul to speak; she waited for his ghost at the door; she even imagined him a bigamist gone to a different wife in Cluj who, upon his death, would write to Reba and tell her the truth of her husband's disappearance, how he had feigned in the Delta his madness and drowning in order to flee hundreds of miles to another woman who bore him six sons: Reba waited for this news, too.

Here in Buenos Aires, I have waited for a phone call in which my daughter might have been allowed to utter my name, for a note in her hand smuggled out by a cell-mate or a comrade-in-hiding, for the names of others waiting like me, for the first meeting of a dozen such mothers, for the placards to be made, for the marches to begin in the Plaza de Mayo, for the funds to open an office, for the bombing threats, for the leads that went nowhere, for someone's child's bloodied shirt, for all the graves to be discovered, for exhumations, for dental records, for pathology reports, for the collapse of the military government, for free elections, for the trials of the generals, for the convictions, for the testimony published by the National Commission — "After that day, I never saw my daughter again," is how I began my own tale of loss, and will tell yet again as these stories unfold, chapter after chapter of family history I write in your name, as if I were still under oath.

And so I understand exactly how Dov's unconfirmable death pitched Reba into that vertigo from which there is no final rescue. She refused to be convinced, as Ovid was, that Dov had drowned himself (accidentally or on purpose, Ovid would not say), the neatly-piled clothes at the water's edge evidence enough for him. He believed that someday fishermen would find the cobbler's body washed up on land, or snared by a net in search of giant tuna, but if Dov's corpse was ever found, no one in Tulcea heard the news.

Finally consenting to the funeral, Reba had placed in the empty coffin some of her husband's most cherished possessions: a blank notebook, a drawing pen, binoculars, one of the oars from his beloved rowboat, a French dictionary, a lock of her own hair, a sketch he had made of Sonia days after her birth. At the gravesite, Reba prayed that Dov would send his wife a message only she could decipher, a kind of husbandly communique private as the words he used to whisper to her at night in their bed: "I'm in the new world now, dearest," or "What a paradise!" or "Yesterday, Reba, I found my mother, can you imagine that? I had never met her before, but I knew her immediately! How we wept!."

But no such messages came. Or if they did, Reba Landau did not trust that they were truly Dov's, and finally after many months of keeping herself so alert for his voice, she doubted if she'd slept more than two hours at a time since his disappearance, or had a single conversation with anyone into which her pain did not intrude, the room spinning around her or the earth seeming to tilt at an angle that rendered gravity helpless, she gave up her inner vigil for him as I will give up my own for you, once these tales are properly recorded, once the stories have all been set down.

After the funeral, Ovid volunteered to reside for a time in the backyard shed where Dov had conducted his cobbler's trade. Reba was worried about bandits who would take advantage of a widow and child living alone, and the gypsy offered his presence as protection. Reba's family was far away, in Jassy, where her husband, too, had spent his youth, waiting for years to flee the village in which every single person knew his mother had died birthing him, treated him with pity, sighed in his presence, his very face half-ghost to every Jew in Jassy. In Tulcea, he had heard, a man could make a living in the thriving port, and it was rumored that Jews and gentiles lived easily together there, as they did in America, that Eden half way around the world. Well, the Delta was a kind of Eden, was it not? A vast aquatic garden that stirred in its inhabitants some sort of ancient innocence. In Tulcea, people would not tremble in his presence or lower their eyes or turn away from that ghost-burdened face. Reba remembered what Dov had said to her the day they'd arrived in the strange town: "Today I am born. Today Dov Landau starts his true life. This is my birthplace." Who would have imagined that he would vanish forever twelve years later, a gypsy offering himself as protector to Dov's widow and child, Reba and Sonia now the ones on whom a whole town's sorrow fell like unending rain?

Thinking that Ovid had taken over Dov's business, townspeople brought the gypsy their shoes and boots and leather valises, and he repaired the items as if he had been Dov's apprentice. Perhaps he had been, absorbing the cobbler's skill without knowing it, all those hours they had talked together while Dov had worked, wonderful conversations — half Yiddish, half Romany — Ovid remembered now to ease the pain of Dov's absence. At first the gypsy turned Dov's customers away, then he did a job here and there for the ones he personally knew, and finally he realized that Reba could stop baking the hundred loaves of bread a week she sold for pennies at a stall in the market, worrying half of each night how she and her child could live much longer on such a meager income.

"A gypsy needs very little money," Ovid told the widow. "Pay me a small salary each week, bring supper to me in the shed, and the rest of the profits are yours. Your husband had a loyal clientele; they trust me because I was his friend."

Reba did not have to ask him to repeat what he'd said; once he had accepted Dov's death, the gypsy's Yiddish had grown increasingly fluent, as if the cobbler had bequeathed Ovid his language as well as his work. What else had Dov meant for his friend to inherit? Ovid would wait, ready for signs.

"I need time to consider this proposition," Reba said. "I will decide by morning."

That night, long after she had given up hoping it would happen, Dov's ghost appeared to her. She had been struggling for hours with Ovid's offer — what did she know about business? was Ovid trustworthy, as he claimed? should she leave Tulcea altogether and return with Sonia to Jassy, and where would she live if she did? how could she burden her sister's family, who had already taken in Reba's elderly parents? should she take her child and go to this mysterious America, wherever that was? how would she find the strength to endure this lonely confusion for all the years ahead of her?

Just at that time when worries were gathering before her with the swirling intensity of a tornado from which she could imagine no possible shelter, and it seemed to Reba that life itself was the disaster from which she would never recover; at that instant when despair might have claimed her — a sudden heart attack, an accidental fall, a swig of poison mistaken for medicine — at that very moment she felt Dov's arm around her and this time she did not distrust its presence, she let herself be comforted, she surrendered to her need. She did not know why God had taken Dov away and she doubted she would be consoled should he be willing to explain. But at least her husband's spirit, for which she had abandoned conscious hope, had come to her at last.

"Why did you wait so long?" she cried.

"I was not the one who waited," Dov said. "I was not the one."

If she needed verification, which she did not, that her husband's ghost was truly in the room with her, that riddle of an answer would have been proof enough. Who else but Dov Landau spoke to her that way? Who else offered her answers more perplexing than any question she might have asked?

In the morning she sought out Ovid in the shed. "Dov says the job is yours. My child and I are very grateful." She turned to leave, then faced him again. "And you will take your suppers with us, at our table," Reba said and felt her cheeks flush. What had made her say that to the gypsy? It had not come up at all in her talk with Dov, but said it she had. If she did not withdraw the invitation now, in three hours he would be at their table. She opened her mouth to speak, but instead of saying what she had intended, Reba told Ovid, "I hope you like boiled chicken," shook his outstretched hand — why did a man wear so many rings? — and walked back across the dusty yard to the house in which a gypsy — a gypsy! — would be taking his evening meals.

For Sonia, Ovid's presence was a blessing. In the Delta, she had promised her father she would carry out his mandate to her — "Take care of your mother for me" — but she had no idea how a child should fulfill this charge. Was she supposed to cook the meals now instead of Reba and make sure the grief-drained woman ate enough to sustain herself? Should Sonia soothe her mother when Reba cried out at night from the depths of a fearful dream? Was it the child's job to wash and iron and fold the clothes, to sweep the wooden floors, to take on each task that her mother seemed too tired to do, so that the songs Reba used to hum while she went about her daily work turned into a dirge of sighs? When Reba had to spend a day in bed — a blinding headache, stomach cramps, a terrible pain in the small of her back — was it Sonia's job to know which remedies to try — cool compresses for her mother's brow, steamed towels for the cramps, pillows under Reba's knees to ease the spasm in her spine? How should the child decide when to go for the doctor? Her mother knew at a touch whether or not Sonia had a fever, when a cold was coming on, what to do for rashes and how to treat a cough. Who would teach the girl how to be a mother, if not her mother herself? How Sonia wished her father would appear to her again, coming for both his daughter and his wife to turn them into pelicans, too — if he had transformed himself, surely he could work his magic on them — and take them deep into the Delta, where the three of them would live together as a family. So what if they were birds now? Would that be any less normal than this fatherless life?

Instead of magic, Dov produced Ovid. Sonia was sure the gypsy's offer was her father's doing, his response to her ceaseless worry about Reba, his realization that he had asked too much of a five-year-old, however smart she was, however obedient she tried to be. One night she had lain awake and felt rage gather in her like a storm about to break. How dare Dov Landau take her childhood from her! He was soaring through the clouds, practicing his loops and dives, eating fish that did not even have to be cooked! Here was Sonia left behind with endless chores and a mother who seemed soothed by nothing her child did. If Dov returned as bird or man, Sonia would beat him and beat him and beat him with the fists she pounded now into her feather-stuffed pillow.

The very next day, Ovid brought Reba his proposal. A day after that he affixed to the shed a sign which read "Open for Business," took his supper with them in the kitchen, and read Sonia's palm for the first time under the sycamore in the front yard. "Long life," Ovid told her. "Many escapes from danger. A sea journey." From the house, Sonia could hear her mother humming again the melodies that had been her repertoire before Dov had vanished. And that night, Reba sat down on the edge of her daughter's bed.

"You know," said the woman, "your father used to tell you wonderful stories before you went to sleep. Would you like to hear some of mine?"

"Where did you learn stories, Mama? You never — "

"I never did a lot of things," Reba said. She brushed her daughter's hair from her eyes. "When her husband disappears, a woman is forced to discover herself. It is the one good thing to come from such sorrow."

"Do you know any stories about pelicans?"

"Once," Reba began, closing her eyes in the manner of one chanting a sacred text, "all the pelicans in the world forgot how to fly. That is why they build their nests on the ground, or in the lowest limb of a tree. . . ."

Dov had vanished in the springtime, and the next year that season was the driest anyone in Tulcea could recall. By June, not a drop had fallen or would until October. Even in the Delta, streams evaporated, riverbeds turned to muddy roads you could cross by foot, ponds became puddles and whole schools of fish travelled like refugees to any water they could find, algae-depleted lakes now graveyards for the fish they could not feed. Haul up nets and find them filled with rotting flounder, decomposing pike, starved salmon. "And the birds are dying as well," the fishermen moaned. Drought. Turn the cracked earth for a garden and all you had were bone-dry clods that crumbled to the touch, leaving a large pile of dust in which nothing could thrive. Farmers' fields lay fallow; those who had plowed and planted watched their crops die at the seedling stage. Cattle expired in the parched pastures. Chickens fought each other for spaces at the waterless troughs, and the hens that survived stopped laying eggs. Marketplaces closed down — there was nothing to sell; peddlers went broke — no one had the money to buy a cast-iron pot or a washboard or a straw basket good for shopping; craftsmen — cobblers, knife-sharpeners, tailors, carpenters — lost most of their customers. When the people started dying — dehydration, jaundice typhus — a royal proclamation denounced the Jews for bringing famine to the land, Jews were banished from whole districts of the country, and the mayor of Jassy ordered a pogrom in his town.

How did Reba and Sonia survive? In a time of plague, who knows why some are spared?

The word about the Jassy massacre reached Reba on the first overcast morning in months. When she opened the door to the messenger's knock, she saw masses of bruise-colored clouds moving in from the west, the sun bleeding here and there through the darkening sky. In spite of her daily prayers for rain, the thunder she heard in the distance frightened her, as if one ordeal would replace another, famine giving way to flood, heat abating just as fields sank from sight beneath the deluge. And the young bearded man on her doorstep: weren't his eyes glazed with fear, as if he already knew knew the next way in which nature would ravage them, as if he had travelled through towns already under water, arriving in Tulcea to warn its residents about this new catastrophe for which they must prepare?

"What is it?" she said. Her hand was over her mouth, ready to catch the scream that gathered in her throat.

The messenger lowered his eyes and delivered his news: the King's soldiers had killed all of her relatives and all of Dov's, may they rest in Heaven; the dead had already been buried by the few survivors and he, the messenger, had brought with him the few family possessions that had not been destroyed by the arsonists and pillagers who had turned Jassy's Jewish quarter into a pile of acrid rubble. On the ground beside his feet, a wooden crate in which she would find her sister's cast-iron soup tureen, her father's prayer shawl, her father-in-law's spectacles, his second wife's sewing basket, and — most unbearable of all — her sweet mother's mortar-and-pestle with which she had chopped nuts for Passover feasts she had prepared each spring for the last fifty years.

If Reba had realized that such disaster would repeat itself in her daughter's life, and then in mine, and then my daughter's, and now again in yours for whom this narrative exists, and in fact had ravaged generations before her as well, so that the history of our family had been and would continue to be a genealogy *in extremis*, would she have followed through on her pain-forged vow, delivered to the messenger who took it for a curse and fled, to kill herself and Sonia both, hope a sentimental idiocy from which she would rescue them and all those descendants for whom further suffering surely lay in store?

How fortunate that Reba Landau was no seer.

For eight days, she lay in delirious collapse, and Ovid ministered to his lost friend's wife as if he, the gypsy, were the husband, and the child Sonia his as well. Finally, Reba's fever broke and she rose from her sick-bed like a woman leaving the grave itself. Before she even took a drop of water from the cup Ovid held out to her, she called to her daughter. Ovid had not let Sonia come closer than the doorway all the days of Reba's illness, but now he took her hand and led her to her mother's side. "The crisis is over," he said. "The worst is past."

Perhaps it was. And not simply in physical terms. Perhaps in her fever-driven dreams, as she passed many times from the living world to the other and back again, she came to see how, after death, the soul remembers earthly blessings no less vividly than sorrows, joy

no less than catastrophe. She came to love her life without condition, and her daughter's, and although she may not have realized it
then, my life and your mother's, and yours as well. This time the
knowledge she needed came to her without the agency of her husband's ghost, and as all true knowledge does, it humbled her. Who
was Reba Landau to steal from herself and her child their time on
earth? How would that be different from the massacre in Jassy, all
those lives vanquished by one man's murderous decision?

I would never meet my mother's mother, and there have been
times when I have wished our line had, in fact, ended in Tulcea, so
that I would not be sitting here day after day at my desk taking
down for you like a court stenographer this testimony of survivors.
But in the evenings, when I move to the veranda where your mother played as a child with the toys she would have bequeathed to you
whose birth she awaited with such fierce impatience — I have
never dismantled the nursery she'd readied for you in this house to
which she'd returned in the last months of her pregnancy — and
there in the dwindling light I read the pages I have written that day,
not a soul can convince me that it might have been better if I had
never been born, or your mother, or you, my missing grandchild,
for whom these words are intended.

3

LOOK AT THE WORLD.

If — like rivers, oceans, deserts, plains, those shadowy scars we know to read as mountains — the paths of people forced to flee their homes were also mapped, if the trails such travellers mark with tears and blood glowed red on the cartographer's page, then red would ring each schoolroom globe a thousand times a thousand, those brave expeditions no queen has ever commissioned, no general ever armed, those routes no president-for-life has ever named for himself. I want such journeys registered forever, as if a force invincible as weather had etched those migrations across the earth's body and changed its geography forever.

Tears and blood. Add song as well. In Australia, the Aboriginals believe we sing the very world into existence, and a place does not exist except its song survives, all of us wanderers carrying the melodies home, each person's life a singing trek over consecrated land.

To be blamed for a famine, some Jews understood, was worse than being blamed for the death of Christ. A famine was as real as an empty belly, a pot with nothing to put in it, starving cows and children so hungry they no longer had the energy to cry out for food.

Christ had his churches now, his gold-leafed altars, his priests in velvet prayer robes, his rosary beads in millions of hands signing their devotion to his name. But what could a ruined fisherman give his hunger-wearied wife? What prayer could a shepherd utter whose flock lay down and died? Were there enough rosary beads to count the numbers of whole families felled by typhus? What sins could a farmer confess to whose fields were as dry as the Sinai? No, no, it was better to be blamed for the death of Christ than for this punishing drought. Now only soldiers were doing the killing, but who could predict what dimensions the slaughter might assume?

When Ovid told Reba, "It is time to leave," she wept.

"Why? How do you know? Dov said we would be safe in the Delta. 'People make themselves mad with their hatreds,' he used to tell me. 'People —' "

"And where is the great sage Dov Landau to protect you now from the madness all around us?" The gypsy flailed the air with his hands, as if he could feel with his fingers dangers not yet visible, calamities forming now like the clouds Reba had seen the day the messenger had brought the terrible news from Jassy. "Where has the good cobbler gone, may I ask, if not as far away from Tulcea as possible, to another world entirely, well beyond the reach of his wife and child? So much for his —

When Reba raised her arm as if to strike Ovid, he fell to his knees in remorse. "Forgive me," he said, to Dov or to Reba, one could not be sure. His voice was thin, a whisper of a voice, as if the gypsy had shrunken to the size of a child and lost the volume manhood confers. "Forgive me."

The entreaty spoke to Reba's heart directly, instantaneously, without the time for appraisal that reason requires, and, emptied of the rage she could not even remember, she dropped to Ovid's side in order to console him. He lifted his contorted face to hers, and it

was as if, in his image, she discovered someone for whom she had
been searching for years, some lost relation, another disappeared
loved one, this stranger, this gypsy who had been her vanished husband's friend, now as familiar to her as if he were cherished kin
from whom she had been long separated and with whom, at this
very moment, she was being reunited. She sensed some miracle taking place, though she would not have had the language to describe
it and could not locate through her senses the phenomena which
created for her, there on her knees beside the kneeling gypsy, this
numinous encounter.

"Ovid," she said, and had to restrain herself from touching in
tenderness the cheek she had wanted to slap, "Ovid, why are you
growing a beard? Gypsies don't have — "

"And how many gypsies do you know who must get a Jewess,
her child and himself all the way — " — he pointed to the sky —
"to the moon, if need be!"

"You would come with us?"

"Reba." He rose and she rose with him. "I have lived here for
one year now. I eat at your table. I love your daughter as a father
would, I try to teach her the lessons Dov Landau would have given
her — how could I have spoken about him so cruelly? — and she
and I play the very games with which he would have entertained
her himself. My gypsy relatives are sure I have lost my mind just as
he did. One thinks he's a pelican, the other turns himself into a
Jewish cobbler! Two madmen, no?"

He was laughing and weeping at the same time now, tears catching on his sprouting beard, gleaming there like diamonds on his
cheeks, above his mouth, in the cleft of his newly-whiskered chin.

One month later, Sonia was working in the garden; it was the child's chore to thin the carrot seedlings they had managed to grow in the newly-soaked earth. When she heard the singing in the town square, she raced, without permission, to the music's source. She threw down her trowel and ran into the road she was not allowed to cross by herself, overwhelmed by the sudden conviction that no transgression could be as terrible as the one she would commit if she did not follow this melody that sounded to her so much like a song her father might be singing, had he decided to resume human form — she dreamed this often — and return to his family.

At that moment, racing toward the square, the child Sonia left forever the tranquility of obedience that had characterized her early years and entered that turbulent world into which each one of us passes, where every choice carries its cost, every loyalty its possible betrayal, every decision the seeds of its undoing. Many years later, in circumstances so terrible not even the most prescient soul could have foreseen them, Sonia would wonder how different life might have been had she simply remained in the garden that day, tended to the seedlings as she had been instructed, gone deaf to the music that had so utterly entranced her? Would she and Reba and Ovid have stayed in Tulcea, her mother caring for the house and Ovid running Dov's business until the gypsy's fingers grew too stiff with age to cut the leather for a new pair of boots or stitch the seam in a worn valise? By then Sonia would have been married, living in her childhood house with husband and children of her own, Reba and Ovid settling into peaceful old age under Sonia's care. Could it be, she would ask herself in horror, that all of history would have been different if she had not disobeyed her mother's injunction, a small child's impulse setting into motion a madness that would vanquish millions — millions! — in the terrible years to come?

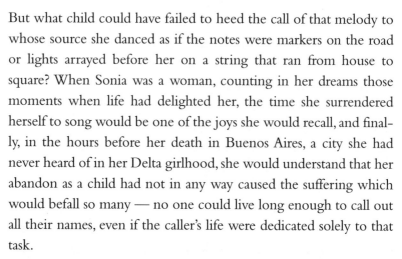

But what child could have failed to heed the call of that melody to whose source she danced as if the notes were markers on the road or lights arrayed before her on a string that ran from house to square? When Sonia was a woman, counting in her dreams those moments when life had delighted her, the time she surrendered herself to song would be one of the joys she would recall, and finally, in the hours before her death in Buenos Aires, a city she had never heard of in her Delta girlhood, she would understand that her abandon as a child had not in any way caused the suffering which would befall so many — no one could live long enough to call out all their names, even if the caller's life were dedicated solely to that task.

Millions!

A fate that enormous could hardly have been triggered by one child's infraction.

When they heard the latch on the front gate snap, Ovid and Reba assumed a customer had entered the yard, though who in town did not know that the cobbler's shop was in back of the house, beyond the chicken coop and vegetable garden and the apple tree whose fruit Reba cooked into sauce they ate all year? As soon as Ovid stepped outside and discovered that Sonia was gone, her trowel discarded by the swinging gate, he guessed immediately that he would find her where the music was — he had heard the singers as soon as he'd opened the door — and he set off for the square without telling Reba where he was going, or why. Let her believe he was fixing somebody's shoe. Later he would tell her the truth and she could punish Sonia as she saw fit; but in fact he would never inform

Reba of her daughter's adventure, so caught up would he become in the singers' explanation of their journey which they invited the whole "family" to join, Ovid's beard and earlocks thick enough now that the group assumed him a Jew like themselves, "and how fortunate it would be for a band of *fusgeyer* to have their own cobbler along!"

With that, the spokesman lifted up his foot and set it on the table Reba had covered with her one good linen cloth. Ovid had invited all twelve of them — seven young men and five young women all dressed in khaki uniforms and brown leather hiking boots laced to the knee, so that they looked like scouts on expedition, or conscripts in training — for fresh-baked bread and jam Dov had made from the berries he had picked on one of his last Delta voyages.

"Do you think in America you won't need manners?" Reba said to the one whose sole nearly knocked over the pitcher of milk. "Who do you think you are, putting feet on a table from which people eat?"

Fusgeyer, they called themselves. Wayfarers. All over Rumania, and deep into the Delta, such bands were assembling. If flight was required, possessions and families left behind, the native ground beneath their feet also left behind, still they would not flee in fear, as if they were criminals whose expulsion was somehow warranted. No. These Jews would go like pilgrims on a holy trek, their songs announcing their presence to anyone in earshot. If their brashness offended her, still Reba was touched by their courage. They reminded her of Dov and herself when they set out from Jassy, hope the place toward which they travelled as surely as if it were marked on the map Dov had drawn himself from directions a peddler had given in a tone so reverent, one might have thought he were describing the route to heaven itself.

The one whose foot was on the table reddened when Reba delivered her rebuke. With his hands he picked up the boot-shod limb and and set it on the floor as if it were not his own leg, as if it were an object someone else had forgotten to remove. He was a slight man with a scholar's pallor, his eyes rheumy from years of reading. The rest of his band looked stronger, artisans and workers used to physical exertion, so that the miles they walked each day from dawn until dusk did not overtax them. Yet Moses Silver was clearly their leader and spokesman. Perhaps he derived his authority from the patriarch for whom he was named, or it may be that in times of adversity, when dangers deemed intolerable turn into daily fare and only that idealist who is shrewd enough can survive with his soul intact — perhaps in such a time a scholar like Moses lifts his head from his books and understands that now History requires that he put his books aside, that he transform into action the words he has been absorbing with a passion so fierce, it could have felled a forest or steered a ship through treacherous storms or slaughtered enough cows to feed an entire hungry town. Who knows what alchemy accounts for such a metamorphosis? The quiet pupil turned orator overnight. The shy youth now the one for whose directives others wait. The distracted child who used to get lost in his own village, winding up in the blacksmith's stall when his mother had sent him to the well for a bucket of water, this same Moses-with-his-head-in-the-clouds now the leader of a dozen *fusgeyer* singing their way out of Rumania, the poor Christian peasants on whom the King had counted to harass the song-borne wayfarers cheering them on instead, greeting them along the dusty roads with gifts of water and milk and bread.

"Your manners may be poor, Moses Silver," Reba said, "but your joke is a good one."

"Joke?" They all spoke the word in unison, the sound rising like steam from each one' plate. "What joke?"

"No joke," Ovid said, watching Reba's face. "I haven't told her yet of your invitation — "

"Invitation?" she said. She was holding on to the hem of the tablecloth, as if someone was about to snatch it off the table, taking dishes with it, turning over the jam pot an scattering bread across the floor.

"We will all go," Ovid said. "You and me and Sonia. All the way to Hamburg and then the boat to — "

Reba said nothing, and although everyone read her silence as assent, a clamor commenced in her mind which would plague her for the rest of her years, a cacophony of voices speaking to her in a hundred different tongues at once, and not one of them a language she understood. *We will be foreigners forever*, she thought, her own words nearly lost in the din.

But she knew she had no choice. Ovid was right: it was time to leave. And here were the *fusgeyer* appearing in town as if they had been sent to receive these newest exiles. Once again she would follow a half-blind gypsy into the wilderness — not the Delta this time, but the world itself.

All the next day Ovid resoled the *fusgeyers'* boots; Reba worked late into the night, sewing for the three of them khaki garments like the others wore; and Sonia packed in her knapsack her favorite rag doll, her father's notebooks (since her father's disappearance, she had not gone to bed a single night without looking at his drawings of Delta birds), and his leather-bound copy of Pascal's *Pensées*, in French.

4

FOR REFUGEES EVERYWHERE, the best route is always the one along which friends might be found. Here is a barn to sleep in tonight. There is an orchard with apples free for the taking. A stream in which to bathe. In that town, you will find a doctor who will not charge you for his services. A ferryboat captain who takes you across the river at night, and knows the currents well enough to navigate in the dark, his lights off, the vessel quiet as a huge fish skimming through the water, the distance to shore an instinctual calculation for which no instruments are needed. Even *fusgeyer*, those brash singers, needed to travel secretly at times, their songs suspended until a danger passed, a warning lifted, a premonition departed.

For such reasons, Moses Silver determined that upon leaving Tulcea, the group — whose ultimate destination was Hamburg, hundreds of miles northwest — would, nevertheless, take a southerly route out of the Delta, through Rumania, across Transylvania, into Yugoslavia, then north to Hungary and on at last to the German port, their journey following the Danube as closely as possible, as if they were amphibians who might, at any moment, choose to slip from land to water in metamorphoses so accomplished, so instantaneous, no one on shore would notice the fins that grew suddenly at these *fusgeyers'* ankles, or the gills that materialized like second chins, or the golden scales their skin now wore.

"Why can't we go by boat?" Reba wanted to know.

"And do you have a vessel that will hold us all?" Moses asked her. "I didn't know you were such a wealthy woman, with a yacht of her own. And what would happen if we capsized? And then of course, there is seasickness. On land a *fusgeyer* can always lie down until a dizzy spell passes, or a cramp. Where can you rest on water from the water's motion? When our people fled out of Egypt, did God provide a boat in which his children could cross the Red Sea? Not at all. The sea parted and they walked across a road, an ordinary road, where only water had been before."

And that was not the extent of Moses Silver's response. For over an hour, he offered an oral commentary on journey after Biblical journey, a kind of Old Testament atlas in which he traced for Reba the multitude of treks that were the sacred precedents of this particular sojourn. By the time he finished talking, she was as exhausted as if she, personally, had walked all those miles with her predecessors. The history that exalted this exodus for the other *fusgeyer* simply added to Reba's fatigue. The group took fifteen days to travel out of the Delta to the Bulgarian border the Danube marks, then through a dozen Transylvanian riverside towns to Orsova, where they would have a day of rest. It was Reba who demanded the respite.

"You did not warn us how difficult the way would be once we came to Turnu Severin."

This was a town some thirty miles south of Orsova, and it was in Turnu Severin — site of the ruins of the Tower of Severin, an ancient medieval fortification — where the party had its first encounter with the startling passage the Danube cuts through the Carpathians, the great gorges in which the water churned, the steep and narrow roads winding up those beautiful wounds the river had carved into the earth. Seventy years later the Rumanian government would build the Iron Gates, a hydro-electric plant that harnesses the river's violence at just that spot where it terrified Reba.

Was it only the water she feared, or did she see the future in its fury, those factories of madness into which millions would disappear? And if time collapsed again at Turnu Severin, as it had in the Delta, she might have shuddered at the knowledge that an Argentinian ruler-to-be named Juan Peron and his beloved wife, Evita, would eventually lie buried outside Madrid, in a suburb known as the Iron Gate — an uncanny correspondence signalling the destiny of Reba Landau's family for generations to come.

"We are not goats," Reba told Moses. "Even God had a day of rest."

"God could afford one," Moses said, but when Orsova was in sight, its harbor a half-moon of boats on a blue bay at the foot of the mountains, a vista so serene even the *fusgeyer* leader felt his own need to be replenished there, he announced, as if it had been his own idea, "To gather strength for the demanding journey we have ahead of us, we will stay in Orsova until tomorrow morning. I have the name of an innkeeper here who is a supporter. Who knows? Perhaps we will even sleep in beds tonight!"

Sonia rode the treacherous miles from Turnu Severin to Orsova on Ovid's shoulders. Unlike her mother, the gypsy had grown more and more buoyant as the trip had progressed from Tulcea, and this stretch of difficult terrain was for him, the highpoint of their odyssey. "Once my family had a circus," he told Sonia, "and my brothers and I learned how to carry each other just like this. Four of us, one on top of the other. We called ourselves 'The Human Tower,' and everywhere we went, people cheered our performances."

They entered the town, all of them bellowing out a gypsy song Ovid had taught them days ago.

"I learned it from a gypsy friend who died in the Delta," he had told the group, who still believed it was Dov Landau, the Jewish cobbler, instructing them.

"How well you have mastered the Romany tongue," Moses had said.

And Ovid had replied, "And you should have heard that gypsy's Yiddish; it could have fooled anyone."

Now even Reba sang, in celebration of the hours of rest she had negotiated. It was the first time she had joined the chorus these last exhausting fifteen days. Fifteen days! She was not even sure this journey was real. It could easily be a dream — a band of *fusgeyer* singing their way across Europe, their leader a frail-looking student, one of their members a gypsy masquerading as a Jew, and the rest of them Jews turned into wandering gypsies. What did she care about Biblical ancestors for whom this had been a way of life? She had never even imagined she would leave Jassy, the move to Tulcea as much dislocation as she would ever have needed. And her new companions — hadn't they, too, forsaken homes and jobs and whole lives rooted in villages to which they would never return? Without doubt, they were all gypsies now. What would become of her house? Who would water her garden and feed the chickens and remember to check in the morning for eggs? What about her furniture? Dov had made it all himself, simple pieces, assembled from pine he harvested in the Delta and transported in the handhewn Silver Queen rowboat he'd abandoned more than a year ago now on that final solitary voyage. Perhaps Dov's disappearance, too, was part of this phantasmagoria from which she would surely awaken, her old life restored to her, her family intact, all of them sleeping in their own beds in Tulcea and Jassy, Dov's friend Ovid still suspect to her, not she and Sonia here in Orsova repairing for bed in an inn run by a stranger, Ovid sleeping one room away, and Dov's resting place — forget that sham funeral! — a mystery never to be solved. Who could tell anymore the difference between waking life and dream, sorrow and nightmare? The moment Reba's head came to rest on the pillow — when had muslin ever felt so luxurious? —

she was asleep, Sonia nestling against her, the child's breathing syn-
chronized to her mother's until the girl, too, slept, lulled by that
symbiotic rhythm as she must have been in Reba's womb. If you
had come to the doorway and seen the way the quilt under which
child and mother lay hidden rose and fell, rose and fell, you would
have thought a single person, not two, lay in that bed, dreaming a
single dream, or passing that night in a slumber so profound, no
dream could possibly intrude.

All that night, Ovid paced. So as not to wake the others, he made
his way to the porch that wrapped around the inn, a dozen rush-
seated rockers creaking in the night's breeze as if invisible ghosts
occupied each chair. And the moon, too, looked like a ghost of
itself, its light a milky blur, a shadow-moon in the densely clouded
sky. Back and forth, back and forth the gypsy walked across the
painted boards, and if you had been there, you would have thought
Ovid, too, a spirit, his pacing a process your ear could follow, though
his presence on that starless night would have been lost to your
sight.

What kept him sleepless? He hardly knew himself, and perhaps
it was not clarity he sought, but the opposite: refuge from the
dreams that might have read his heart to him. For a gypsy, the truths
one can flee in waking hours assert themselves in sleep, and the
dream is a text to study as reverently as a Jew studies the Torah, a
Moslem the Koran, a Catholic the gospel.

"Dov," he said aloud — on such a night, a man so close to his
own soul knows that death could never circumscribe another's —
"I find that I — that is, I think it may be possible — which is to
say, I need to tell you that — but then again, perhaps I don't — how

is it that I find myself — 'to the moon!' I told her — she is so — I
find that I —"

And in the swirl of his own ambivalence, the bearded gypsy
swooned, the porch floor seemed to billow underneath his feet, and
just at the moment he would have gone under, at precisely the
moment he felt himself at the edge of his own endurance, Ovid-
with-earlocks heard Dov Landau's voice as clearly as Sonia had
heard it in the Delta or Reba the night her husband's ghost had visited her in their Tulcea bedroom.

"Love her," Dov said. "You find that you love her."

"Yes," Ovid said, gripping the railing for support. "I am afraid I
do."

"Why afraid?" The cobbler rose from one of the rocking chairs
and came to stand beside his gypsy friend. In the dark, who could
tell where one man stopped and the other began? "I have been
gone for more than a year now. Do you think I wanted Reba to be
alone forever? Who would I rather have at her side, if not you? You
need to court her some, of course. Perhaps you could write her a
poem. Do you think you were named Ovid for nothing?"

In fact, it was Dov Landau himself who, years ago, had told the
gypsy about his namesake, the Roman famous for his verses of love
and transformation, banished to the Delta port of Constanta where
the exiled poet pined for home until he died.

Ovid sat down in the rocker Dov had relinquished. The inn
looked out over the bay, and though the shoreline had not been visible in the darkness, only the soft lapping of water a reminder that
the water was near, it was as if Ovid could suddenly see what his
single good eye had been blind to, what the night had obscured,
what the moon, still hidden by clouds, could not illumine: a pelican lifting from the water's edge, rising steadily higher — past the
tops of trees, the crests of distant cliffs, the shadow moon, the cloud-

dimmed sky — entering finally that unbound region of the heavens in which there is no end to flight, no end to hope, no end to any life that finds its way, however arduous the journey, to eternity.

"Wake up!" Sonia said into Ovid's ear.

The child had woken earlier than the others and discovered Ovid sleeping in the chair her own father's spirit had occupied just a few hours earlier.

The gypsy groaned. "A little more rest, child," he said, his eyes still closed to the morning sun he felt already on his cheek, his arm.

On his lap, Sonia set the two of them rocking. "Wake up, wake up!" she sang to the rhythm of the chair's motion.

How could he tell her he had just fallen asleep? How could he explain the hours on the porch, Dov's visit, the gypsy's confession of love for the vanished cobbler's wife? How could he say, "Sonia, I have decided to marry your mother," but say it he did — "Sonia, I have decided to marry your mother." — and the child grew very still in the manner of someone whose entire attention is concentrated on the not-yet manifest. Think of a diviner searching with a stick for water buried deep in the earth, or a seer in whose crystal ball the unlived future forms like an embryo, feature by feature.

When finally she spoke, Sonia's words took on the quality of the oracular, that grave tone Ovid himself assumed when he was reading her palm to her, deciphering her destiny. "Good," she said. "Because my mother has decided to marry you."

That was the first time Sonia realized that she had the power to penetrate another person's mind. She had no doubt whatsoever that she had entered her mother's most private thoughts, thoughts perhaps unknown to Reba herself, not yet worded, existing as they do in all of us in that interior wilderness, that landscape of dreams and nightmare, that territory of fearful beauty not unlike the Danube Delta whose watery labyrinth Dov Landau had come to know as well as he knew the streets of Tulcea, and into whose depths he had disappeared. She would have to be careful, this child of his, not to vanish like him into uncharted regions, not to venture so deeply into another's mental world that she, Sonia, would not remember how to return to her own.

It was when he had said, "To the moon, if need be!" and those tears had glistened in the first stubbly traces of his beard, that Reba Landau had realized for the first time in the fourteen months since Dov's disappearance the true nature of the tenderness she felt toward the gypsy. She had had such feelings once before, during the first weeks of her engagement to the cobbler, Dov the shy suitor sent by the matchmaker for whose services Reba's father had paid. That Ovid aroused these same stirrings in her now terrified Reba. She did not even have proof, real proof, that her husband was dead, yet here she was, in the midst of convincing herself that she was, in fact, a widow, here she was touched several times a day by images of Ovid fleeting as an airborne feather brushing her cheek or a cinder lifting from a bank of burning logs and glowing for an instant like a tiny meteor whose flight is over before one even knows exactly what it is that one has witnessed. She felt ashamed of her attraction, and frightened by it, but she also believed that if she could summon Dov's spirit to her side one more time, and if she could confess to him her terrible guilt, he would shake his head in good-hearted exasperation, telling her, "Why would I want you to be lonely?" or "Did you think I meant for him to spend his life sleeping in the cobbler's shed?" or "Reba, if people were only as shamed by their hatreds as they are by their loves, we would never have another war, we would all live in peace forever, we would all die smiling, don't you agree?"

And so it was that Reba Landau decided to propose to the gypsy named Ovid — wasn't he already pretending to be her husband? didn't the *fusgeyer* believe the ruse? wasn't Sonia, a mere child, already part of this deception? Better to end a lie by turning it into the truth. If Ovid could not, in fact, become Dov Landau, at least the gypsy could become Reba's spouse. It would be one less madness with which they would have to contend, this subterfuge they were forced to maintain in the midst of their flight from home. As bizarre as it was that she should be imagining a wedding with a Delta gypsy, she a simple Jewish woman from Jassy who used to warn her husband about this very stranger to whom she was about to link her fate and her child's — "Gypsies put spells on children," she remembered herself saying. "They take them away in their wagons." — still it was a plan that returned to their ruptured lives — hers and Sonia's and Ovid's as well — a form in which the future might create itself, marriage a map she could draw quite well, family a country whose language she could understand.

And that was when she made her second decision, one her daughter had not intuited. That was when Reba Landau understood the only condition that would accompany her proposal to Ovid. "I cannot continue," she knew she would tell him, now that they were close to the border. "This is as far from home as I am able to run."

5

JUST A FEW MILES NORTH of Orsova, on the spot where Hercules slew the Hydra and after the battle healed himself in the mineral springs still famous for their therapeutic magic, the gypsy and the widow and the widow's child lived in one of the tin-roofed cabins — workers' quarters — in the woods behind the Hotel Roman, where Reba was a laundress. From one side of the cabin, they had a view of the Danube — many consider that stretch of the river to be its most beautiful — and from the other side, they saw through the trees the emperor Franz Joseph's Villa Elisabeth where he and his wife resided the times they came to the Baille Herculanae spa to take the waters and breathe for a while the beneficent air of the Cerna Valley.

From the cabin, whose front room became the cobbler's shop, it was a short walk, up one hill and down another, to the spa itself where Reba washed dozens and dozens of towels a day, hanging them to dry on a part of the grounds fenced off and hidden from the formal gardens and manicured lawns; there, in the spring and summer, violin students from the conservatory in Bucharest serenaded the patrons who sprawled on wooden chaises or sat at wrought-iron tables at which they took snacks of herbal tea and pastries, or a bowl of cold cabbage soup, or a piece of pickled herring with bread. The guests would be dressed in their own clothes, or if they were between treatments, wrapped in full length turkish-towel robes.

Once, when Reba peered at them through a gap in the fence, they all looked naked to her, every single person, as if, instead of relaxing in the cafe, they were just about to step into one of the hot springs or steam cabinets in which, it was claimed, they would be cleansed of their impurities. She closed her eyes and opened them again, but that did no good: the apparition remained. How terribly fragile these rich and proper people looked, stripped naked, not even a pair of spectacles or a pendant or a pocket-watch left to its owner. Tears welled in Reba's eyes; she turned away. Beyond the fastidious grounds, a wall of vapor rose from the baths, and a stranger might have confused this impermeable mist with fog that never lifted, or smoke from a fire that burned and burned and burned.

On the same day that Reba had this vision, she received the only piece of mail that would come to her for the rest of her life. Who was left in the world to write her? Her whole family had been murdered and her neighbors in Tulcea believed she had gone to America. On the front of this envelope with the strange-looking stamp — a man galloping on horseback over a flat field, one arm swinging a loop of rope over the head of a fleeing calf — someone had printed her name in care of the inn at Orsova where she and Ovid and Sonia had bade farewell to the dozen *fusgeyer* three months ago. The innkeeper had forwarded the letter to the Hotel Roman, where he knew Reba was employed. She held the envelope up to the laundry's window, trying to see the signature inside, but the light revealed nothing she could decipher. For the rest of the morning, she kept the letter in her pocket, and by lunchtime, the still-unopened correspondence seemed heavier, as if the paper had turned to stone in the dark folds of fabric where she had hidden it away. In Reba Landau's mind, there was no doubt that this message was a dire one — since Dov's disappearance, what news had been good? Perhaps someone in Ovid's family had learned he had taken the cobbler's name and pretended to be married to the

widow, and now this gypsy relative was sending Reba a copy of the
curse meant to punish them both. What good would it do her to
read such scathing words? Or she could be holding a blackmail
threat — someone who'd learned about the couple's deception,
asking for money, an impossible sum, lest he report the truth to the
hotel management, who surely would fire the scandalous pair and
evict them immediately from their humble house. Shouldn't she rip
this letter to shreds. pretend it had never arrived, scatter the scraps
in the compost heap behind the hotel kitchen and never mention
it to a soul?

She might have done exactly that, and changed our family's
destiny by her action, and I wonder if the dread she felt had less to
do with the bad news she feared had arrived than with some pre-
sentiment she could not name about the way this message, whatever it was, would shape the future of her descendants — Sonia and
Sonia's offspring, and the next generation, and the next. What might
have seemed an irrational gesture — destroying the unopened letter — might have been, in truth, as wise as the most considered
decision Reba Landau would ever make.

But before she could follow through on her impulse, Ovid
arrived in the laundry room; he had just delivered some newly-
soled shoes to the hotel manager, and the errand gave him a reason
to visit Reba in the steamy chamber where she worked. He wished
she did not have to labor as she did, but how he loved the way the
humid air flushed her cheeks and curled her hair in girlish tendrils
at the edges of the scarf she tied like a helmet around her head.

From the doorway, he saw her holding the letter.

"My mother?" he said, because every day he hoped a message
would come from Tulcea, ending the silence his family had imposed
since the day he'd announced he was moving into Dov Landau's
shed.

Reba studied the envelope. "I don't think so," she said, fixing on

the blurred postmark whose script she knew was a foreign one —
characters from a language she did not even recognize. Now she
was more confused than before; her life existed between Baille
Herculane and the Delta town from which they had come, and the
rest of the world could just as well have broken off from the earth,
become a new planet in the far reaches of space, for all the relation
it had to her.

Ovid peered at the markings. "Bu-e-nos Ai-res," he read. "I
have heard of it. In America, I think. Near New York."

"Moses Silver," Reba said, remembering now her last conversation with the *fusgeyer* leader, how the tears had welled in his eyes
when she had told him, "I can go no further," and composing himself, he had replied, "You are a brave woman to have come this far.
Someday I will write you from America. If you were not already
married — "

Who would have thought, she had asked herself then, that he
was feeling affection for her, when they had been sparring for fifteen days? Well, it was no more strange than the love that had
bloomed in her own heart for Ovid, a man she had always feared.

"I'm sure you mean you will write to us both," she had said to
Moses. "To my husband and me."

"Of course," he had said, but she had heard the catch in his
voice and understood his true intention. What if he had discovered
that the real Dov Landau had disappeared and the cobbler with
whom she travelled was a gypsy named Ovid to whom she was not
married at all?

Now she handed Ovid the envelope. "You read better than
me," she said. "And I have no secrets from you."

He withdrew a single sheet from its container. "He wants you
to divorce me," Ovid said, once he had scanned Moses' note. "He
wants you to come with Sonia to this Bu-e-nos Air-es, where he
works in a meat-packing plant and is learning the Spanish language.

He says his manners have improved and he is sure you will love Ar-gen-ti-na. And then he gives his address." The gypsy stood very still, remembering when he and his brother had toured the Delta with a knife-throwing act, how important it was not to move when you were the one at whom the volley of blades was aimed. "And what do you think you will do?" he said finally, letting himself breathe.

"I think his letter will make good compost," is what Reba said, taking the page from Ovid's hand and crumpling it in her own. But instead of throwing the page away, she stuffed it into the pocket of her smock. That evening she smoothed out the wrinkled note and hid it between her nightgowns in the small wooden chest where she kept her clothes. Of course she had no intention of leaving the gypsy for Moses Silver. But she had never imagined Dov would vanish, and who knew that Ovid would always be there? Everything Reba had taken for granted, Dov's disappearance had caused her to doubt. Keeping the letter was not in the least a romantic impulse; it was a practical act on the part of a woman who had learned that the only thing to be trusted was loss. Ovid could leave one morning and never return; soldiers could pillage the spa, searching for Jews; in spite if her vow to stay here forever, Reba and Sonia might have to flee again, this time beyond the Rumanian border, even perhaps across the sea, and when the officials asked her her destination, she would know what to do, she would be ready, she would show them her letter from Moses Silver: "Buenos Aires," she would say. "In Argentina. I understand it is near New York."

Three months after their arrival at Baille Herculanae, Reba and Ovid asked the head masseur to marry them.

He had once studied to be a rabbi, he claimed, though how he had wound up here, giving massages to aristocrats who tipped him with imported cigars or an occasional bottle of cognac, he never explained. Reba suspected he was a deserter — young Jewish men were virtually kidnapped into the army, treated as serfs, their indenture lasting as long as their health held out. He lived alone, this underground Jew, in a room behind the kitchen of the Hotel Roman, one of the many inns that circled the springs. Early one morning, even before the cooks had arrived to begin preparing breakfast for overnight guests, this exile who in five years had not told another soul of his background or dared to practice his faith or use his true name (at the spa, he was known as Tomas, although his given name was Jacob), this man summoned Ovid and Reba and Reba's child Sonia to his quarters, where he had improvised the ritual wedding canopy from a bedsheet he'd tacked at each corner to the ceiling. The fabric billowed above them, the breeze from an open window filling the folds of the suspended sheet. It was still dark outside, and the kerosene lantern Jacob Pransky, now known as Tomas, had placed on the table beside his cot threw a sphere of trembling light, a radiant circle, onto the canopy beneath which they now assembled.

On the wooden bureau, his only other piece of furniture, he'd placed a bottle of wine, four shot glasses "borrowed" from the hotel kitchen, and Reba's wedding band which she had entrusted to him the night before the ceremony, "so that God can bless it again," he'd explained to the widow and she had consented. Sonia stood between the couple, holding her mother's hand and the gypsy's, happy to have her prognostication verified, and certain her father approved.

Will it surprise you to learn that just at the moment Reba was going to take her vow, she collapsed in a fit of coughing so severe, Jacob Pransky had to halt the ceremony, help her to his bed, steal into the dark hotel kitchen for a jar of honey which Sonia fed her mother with a spoon until the spasms quieted? Or that, once the vows had been exchanged and Ovid had smashed the ritual wine glass with his foot and all that was left to unite them was the placing of the ring on the finger of the bride — at that very point in the service, Reba's ring-finger swelled, as if a bee had just stung it or a door slammed on the tender flesh beneath the knuckle? Once more, the officiant travelled to the kitchen and back, this time for ice he chipped from the block in the ice-box, and Reba wrapped the slivers in a handkerchief she pressed to the afflicted finger.

Finally they were married, though it is doubtful that the union was a valid one. Ovid was not a convert, Reba had no proof of Dov's death, Jacob-who-called-himself-Tomas has not quite finished his rabbinical studies in Bucharest. And who had witnessed the ceremony? Only a child. And where was the marriage certificate? None existed. And when was the marriage consummated? Nights, Sonia would lie awake on her side of the bedroom Reba had partitioned down the middle with a drape she'd made from burlap sacks the hotel cooks had saved for her after they'd emptied the bags of potatoes, onions, beets and turnips. From her cot, Sonia listened for the sounds her parents used to make in their bed in Tulcea, before Dov had disappeared. She did not know what the sounds meant — those moans and sighs and shouts and the bouncing bedsprings' rhythmic creaking — and once Sonia had asked her mother what she and Dov did when they were alone together in the dark, hours after their child was supposedly asleep.

"This is not for children to know," Reba had said. "It is something only married people do. When you are about to marry yourself, I will tell you. Not until then."

Well, weren't her mother and the gypsy "married people" now? Sonia had been there herself, in Jacob's room, the breeze-filled tablecloth stirring over their heads like the wings of a giant bird.

Hadn't Sonia seen Ovid place on her mother's hand the very ring
Reba had received from Dov many years before? Didn't Sonia
remember every word Reba and Ovid had uttered in the ceremony Jacob had conducted? Then why was there nothing but silence
each night from the newly-weds' quarters? Where were the strange
cries and the dancing bedsprings? Where were the whispered
endearments Sonia had been able to overhear in Tulcea, if she
cupped her ears and strained to catch the muted voices of her parents? And why did her mother leave so often the bed she shared
with her gypsy-husband here in Baille Herculane, to sleep instead
on the hard floor beside Sonia's cot? She tried to read her mother's
mind again, as she had done in Orsova, but no matter how deeply
she concentrated, all the child received was the single word "No!"
which Reba repeated over and over again, never a clue about what
it was that she was refusing, only that chant of negation — no, no,
no — and nothing more.

On the third anniversary of Dov Landau's disappearance, Reba
dreamed them naked together in the bed she had left behind in
Tulcea. It was not a dream of the past, however, because the bed was
here in Baille Herculane, flying the route of her exile to the spa
beyond Orsova, a mysterious luminous object passing though the
sky along the Danube's bank and bringing thousands of people outside in their nightclothes, the populations of each riverside town
gathering in the darkness to witness — what? A meteor about to
crash in their midst? A vision sent by God, although not a single
theologian of any faith could interpret the meaning of this glowing
rectangular object whose edges were, many concurred, fringed,
although, for a vision, that seemed an oddly domestic touch for
anyone's God to have included in a celestial apparition. "A flying

carpet!" children shrieked, familiar with tales of genies travelling the world on air-borne blankets, but none of the adults gave that interpretation any heed, close though it was to the truth. A student of the stars believed it a new constellation and named it, after himself, Vatra's Bed. But you will not find the record of his claim in any astronomy book of the time.

In her dream, in spite of the masses that had assembled each night to watch the strange object's progression across the heavens, Reba Landau was the only person in the Cerna Valley summoned from sleep when her beloved bed reached its destination. It hovered outside the cottage and when she opened the door, it came inside and landed so lightly, not a floorboard in the front room squeaked, not a curtain stirred in the wake of the bed's arrival.

She lit a lamp. In the quivering orange light, she knew immediately that the bed was hers and Dov's — there was the fringed white coverlet she had crocheted herself, hundreds of delicate flowers laced together by nearly-invisible stitches, the coarse wool blanket beneath transformed by her handiwork into a bower of blossoms. She folded back the coverlet, and the blanket, and the topsheet, and lay down on the muslin. She closed her eyes. Through the mattress-ticking, she could smell the corn husks Dov had shredded himself and in that confluence of odor and texture, she could feel her own form impressed over the years into the mattress beneath her, the bed having become a mold, as a sculptor might make, of Reba Landau's body. She let herself sink into the contours her own presence had carved, night after night night. She was becoming again the woman this bed had created and when she reached across the space beside her, she felt the heat of her missing husband's flesh. In her dream, she opened her eyes and turned toward that warmth; in the oil-lamp's radiance, Dov's sleeping face shone. Like specters, counter-evidence filled the room: the abandoned rowboat, the shattered nest, the neatly-folded clothes, the coffin they had buried and the headstone that bore his name — "Dov Landau, 1861-1898." But how could such trivia compete with the truth her dreaming senses knew: his tongue in her mouth, a hand on her breast, his fingers stroking open and wet that place the gypsy's touch had never softened once? Soon they were not two bodies at all, Reba and Dov, but a twined being whose single cry rose like the voice of a new animal born in the world.

It was that cry that woke her from the dream, and with the throb of it still in her throat, she searched out Ovid in the dark, Dov's heat still on her hands with which she guided the gypsy into that deeper dark, her own body's Delta, in which he travelled like a man who had made this journey a thousand times before, and knew the way well enough to lose it in that steamy wilderness where he would have gladly disappeared forever.

"Aiiiii!"

Now they're married, Sonia thought, the strange music of this second ceremony calling the child from her own dreams, who watched on the curtain between her and the adults the shadows of Reba and Ovid joined at last, in conjugal embrace.

Were he still alive, and I could read him this much, my psychiatrist-husband would approve of a story in which a dream's wisdom frees a woman from grief, restores to her life the very joy she feared had vanished for good. But what would he make of the next scene in this narrative, the one in which Sonia discovers, the following morning, the fringed coverlet heaped by the front door, as if someone had left it there as a wedding gift, this bouquet of crocheted flowers, this hand-woven relic from their lost life in Tulcea?

Oh, he would scorn what he liked to call, in the language of his profession, my "propensity for magical thinking," which was his way of telling me to give up the hope that your mother might still be alive, or that we would ever find you, our own grandchild lost to us in our very country, perhaps in Buenos Aires itself, in the next neighborhood or — who can deny the mad possibility? — even on the same street where I now sit writing, beneath the tree your real mother climbed as a girl.

"Enough," he would tell me, seeing the turn my project had taken. "You must get on with your life as it is. To spend your days making up a fairy tale — "

Do not think you are reading a fairy tale. Do not think I wrote these stories to mesmerize the child you were when I was searching for you. Do not think — late in your life, I imagine, long after my death, moved, perhaps, by a dream of your own to learn the truth of your stolen past — do not think that now these words you read on this page have nothing to tell you about the family from which you came and from which you were kidnapped that terrible night two months before your birth in the prison where your mother died without even being allowed to hold her infant once — just one embrace she could have taken with her into her death! just one embrace whose warmth your body would remember, no matter how completely they believed they had eradicated her existence! — no, no, no, not even once.

Granddaughter, darling, heart whose heart I listened to once with my own ear pressed against your mother's womb, what story could be more unbelievable than the one of your own abduction and the miraculous events that have brought you here, in a future I can barely foresee, to a bank vault in Buenos Aires, to a safety deposit box in your mother's name, to these tales about your great-great-grandmother Reba and all the tales that follow, the last one being about that day you discover this book I am writing for you, the one you are are holding this very moment in your trembling hands?

Who survives in this world without some magic she can never explain?

Who?

6

I HAVE TRIED TO IMAGINE what it was like for my mother Sonia to grow up at Baille Herculane, and the stories I fashioned seemed for a time plausible versions of those years at the spa, but when I re-read the tales I had constructed, each one fell apart like a poorly-made garment or an ill-designed chair that collapses under the weight of its maker. I wanted Sonia to have a girlhood quintessentially normal, almost idyllic, years of respite from the traumas of Dov's disappearance and the flight from Tulcea. I invented play-mates for her, and a school she travelled to in Orsova, and an accord with Reba so profound, mother and daughter never argued, or felt estranged from each other, or blamed one another for the hardships life had conferred on them, or begged each other for forgiveness after particularly wounding battles in which each said things they later regretted and wanted to retract. (Unlike written texts, spoken words are never revisable; every utterance enters the record, lies and curses and angry epithets preserved in the memory like glass-cased original manuscripts, under lock and key).

Here is the history I did not want to write: my mother Sonia never had a single friend her age (the other children of hotel staff found her strange, this child rumored to be a Gypsy orphan adopt-ed by the Jewish cobbler and his laundress-wife, this girl who claimed she could read their minds, which they denied, but who fixed on them a gaze so deep, they felt it a fish-hook on which their thoughts were, one by one, impaled); she only went to school in Orsova for two terms (each morning she would vomit up the breakfast Reba made her eat, and such a spate of ailments overcame Sonia she stayed home sick a third of that terrible school year), and mother and daughter were often at odds — minor disagreements that gathered between them like dustballs under a bed, and full-fledged fights in which one of them would bring the screaming to an end by some act of physical destruction which would silence them both: once Sonia ripped open the seam of her down-filled pillow and Ovid walked into a storm of feathers they would find on a chair or in a bowl of soup or floating singly through the house for months to come; once Reba yanked down the curtains she had made for the kitchen window, pitching the panels into the snow. It was as if by ruining some object, they could make concrete the damage their rages were doing to themselves, and soon one of them would weep and the other would offer consolation and they both would vow to never lose their tempers again, though they knew that they would.

Perhaps if Dov had never disappeared, Reba and Sonia would still have battled. By temperament, the mother was a practical woman and her daughter a dreamer much like her father had been. Why should Sonia spend an hour doing her mending chores, when she could be sketching the chickens the hotel kept for eggs? Why join her mother in the laundry after finishing her lessons with Ovid (it was the gypsy, finally, who taught her to read and do her sums) when she could wander in the woods for hours, learning the names of plants and roots, mastering birdsong, collecting stones she kept in labelled mason jars — granite, quartz, obsidian — on a shelf beside her bed?

And surely it is true that mothers and daughters feud, even in cases when their natures are similar, even in families living out intact the stages of domestic existence, all the members passing through the decades together, under a common roof, comforted by one another's reliable presences: soon they, too, will chafe against those very bonds which, for a time, had pleased them. Even if Dov had returned from the Delta, or their relatives been spared in the Jassy pogrom, or the flight from Tulcea cancelled at the last minute, still Reba and Sonia may have battled for years, Dov instead of Ovid trying for awhile to bring about peace, then resigning himself to the discord which if anything, was heightened by his failed attempts to mediate.

But sometimes, in the midst of an argument — just as Reba's voice rose into a screech that left her throat sore for hours, just as Sonia slammed the door with such force the windows rattled in their frames and the cake in the oven fell — at those moments when it seemed that neither of them could see anything beyond their anger, all their losses would flood the room exactly as the waters of a swollen river will break without warning from the banks that have contained them and pour through windows, doors, crevices not even a mouse could enter on a dry day. And just as such an emergency jolts us out of our lesser trials, so Reba and Sonia would rush to each other in a mutual rescue from the sudden shared memory of all they had suffered, the reason for their current dispute lost to them, unimportant, silly in the light of their true condition.

On the eve of Sonia's sixteenth birthday, Reba (dictating to Ovid, who acted as her scribe) wrote her daughter a letter on hotel stationery, "like a fancy lady on holiday," she noted of the paper she had chosen. "What guest is richer than me, who has you for a daughter, even if sometimes I lose my temper and yell that you are giving me heart pain? If you could see inside my heart, you would see a thousand pictures from the day of your birth until now, every one of them beautiful, so many moments I treasure, how to pick out a few for you now? But I am doing this exactly. I am giving to you my most precious memories, like a rich woman gives her daughter jewels, or fine crystal goblets for her dowry chest.

"I will never forget when the mid-wife put you at my breast for the very first time. How does the baby know what to do? How does the mother? Wasn't it a miracle, the way your little mouth searched for my nipple from which you had never taken a drop before? I don't think your eyes even were opened yet, not one look yet in this world you had just come to like a total stranger, which we all are in the beginning, isn't that true? Probably I smelled the same to you outside as when you were in me; probably that was one thing you could feel safe about, everything else so different, so bright, such a shock how the mid-wife slapped your behind — I screamed out myself then, "Stop!" even if I knew it was to get you to breathe. Truly, Sonia, when she put you at my breast, you were shaking as if you were freezing cold, but it was July, a hot afternoon, even the birds were quieted by the heat. As soon as you smelled me, you grew calm. I felt peace from your head to your feet. I knew how to help you get the milk in your mouth, and I knew how to press down on my breast so you could have air, and I knew to switch you in awhile to the other side, fast enough so you wouldn't cry, because you were still hungry and without patience for all this moving around. That I could feed you like this from my own body! That your sucking was perfect! If you had been born already with words, saying whole sentences like a grown-up that day, do you think your mother would have been more excited than she was by the way you nursed that first time?

"And, Sonia, once, in Tulcea, when your papa was off for the day in the Delta — how many times he took those trips and who would ever think once he would never come back? — he left

unlatched the lock to his shed. All his tools, so many shelves of
boots and shoes you wondered sometimes, were there so many feet
in one town? I've made your lunch, a platter of cold fish and tomatoes, and call for you though the back door, because you've been
playing all morning in the yard. You had a sand-box there, with a
pitcher of water you liked to mix in, and a swing, and a doll I made
for you from socks — remember her eyes were two green buttons
and she had a smiling mouth I embroidered, and a calico dress? I
call you and call you, and then I walk out into the yard: no child in
sight, and the doll I see sleeping in the bed we built from a wood-
en crate. Then I look down the gravel path to the shed, and the
door is swinging back and forth like a stiff flag. All those sharp
tools? Did I ever run so fast in my life? Never! And already in my
mind I'm grabbing the cutters out of your hand, or the hammer
you could bring down on your fingers, and I'm hearing myself
scream, 'You could have hurt yourself badly! You know you are
never allowed — ' But what are you doing? Sitting on your papa's
stool, his cap with the visor practically covering your eyes, his apron
hanging from your neck to the floor, and polishing somebody's
boots with a chamois cloth black with paste you're rubbing into the
leather. Four years old and doing a very good job! Could I be angry
at such an adorable child? A rich lady would have taken a picture,
which I suppose I did with my heart, and who needs a better cam-
era than that? Not Reba Landau.

"One more. One more for your birthday. This one will surprise
you because it isn't from when you were little, no, it is from just last
year. Just because now and then I blow up, or you, or please help
the neighbors, sometimes both of us together and we are not whispering when that happens, do you think that means I don't get tears
in my eyes at the sight of you still, such a beautiful girl you've
become, and the image of your father? If he could have seen you

that night last summer. We had all gone to bed hours ago, but as usual I couldn't sleep and I decided some hot milk would help, even though the weather was so warm you didn't need a sweater at midnight. In the kitchen, the full moon was so bright, it was like morning in the room. To see the stars, I took my cup outside. You were sitting there, alone, under the weeping cherry tree whose white blossoms in spring always remind me of the day I married your father, Dov. His seven notebooks were stacked up beside you on the grass, and you were studying them, page after page, as if you had never seen them before. I could see your face so clearly! Such an absorption! If someone had told me, 'She has found the notebooks of Leonardo DaVinci,' or some other genius whose name I never heard. I would have believed them. I will always remember the expression you wore, like a person praying, it was that serious and learned and wise. Wise is the word I am looking for most. Like a rabbi, is what I felt, those notebooks holy in your hands, holy. Seeing you there, under the tree in your nightdress, I reminded myself of everything important. And I knew our quarreling would pass away like a fog we wouldn't even remember when it was gone. I slept better that night than for years before, which you know has been hard for me — sleeping — since the day your father disappeared."

She signed the letter herself and sealed the envelope with wax and printed Sonia's name with great formality and care. Like a rabbi, is how Reba Landau felt, those words she had composed holy in her hands, holy.

Think of that letter given by Reba to Sonia on her sixteenth birthday, who would give it to me on mine, who would pass it on to your mother on hers, who would transfer the heirloom to you on yours. Don't you have it before you now, your great-great grandmother's gift, as surely as if it had been passed down our line of women, one generation to the next, a family spared catastrophic pogroms and exiles and Final Solutions and Dirty Wars? Doesn't this tale restore to you one more piece of your legacy, a story you were meant to inherit, your ancestral bequest?

7

THE SUMMER SONIA TURNED EIGHTEEN, she apprenticed herself
to Mititei, the head masseuse at Baille Herculane. She was called
Mititei because her muscled fingers and forearms had taken on the
appearance of the hard little sausages from which the name derived;
at the spa, she was famous for the force of her massages and later, in
the baths, her patrons would show off, like jewels, the bruises their
sessions with Mititei had engendered.

"Bird hands," Mititei announced when Sonia first asked to be
trained. The masseuse examined the girl's delicate fingers and poked
at her palms' translucent skin — did Mititei see what Ovid did in
those living maps? She tapped each tiny knuckle with a spoon.
"Study embroidery, not massage."

Sonia persisted. "If you let me work with you for a few days,
you'll change your mind."

The woman slid the spoon under one of Sonia's wrists and lifted up: the hand rose in the air like the bird Mititei had called it, the
thumb a fluttering wing. Then she slid the spoon away and gravity
pulled the bird-hand down, as if it were a fledgling not yet ready for
long-distance flight.

"You must know something I don't know," Mititei said. She
shrugged. She was a practical woman, but she was not an unrea-
sonable one. In spite of her doubt, she yielded. "We'll begin at eight
in the morning."

What Sonia knew was that her hands could heal. Reba had come to depend on their powers for curing the searing headaches that had started on the day the search party had returned from the Delta without Dov, and continued to afflict her all these years later in Orsova. One night, several summers past, an attack had woken Reba from her sleep; Sonia had found her mother weeping in the dark at the kitchen table, her stricken brow pressed to the table's surface as if the oak might absorb the pain. In the rush of tenderness, the daughter placed her palms on her mother's crown, then moved her hands slowly over temples, ears, ending at the base of the skull where she cradled in her hands her mother's head as if it were an infant she were comforting from a bout of colic. "Is it better, Mama?" Sonia had asked.

"Completely," Reba had said, sitting upright. "The pain is completely gone. My daughter Sonia has magic hands."

Magic hands. Ovid smashed his thumb with a mallet and Sonia lay two fingers on the bruise; she could feel the swelling recede and heat of the injury vanish. Reba turned her ankle in the yard and Sonia lifted her mother's foot to her lap, stroking the joint until the redness faded and the throbbing stilled; a few minutes later, Reba walked back to the house without a trace of limp in her step. And what about the morning Sonia woke with fever and chills and pain in her stomach so severe she had to crawl to the outhouse, her nightdress dew-soaked and streaked with grass stains that never would wash out? Back in her bed, she tried the remedy of touch on herself, her hands flattened on her abdomen, her mind become the lake of light she'd witnessed in the Delta, that shimmering pool from which Dov had risen as a pelican, that radiance which now flowed down her arms through her fingers into her belly hard as an iron pot in which some poison stewed. First her stomach softened, then her fever broke, and then her cramps eased until the illness was a memory which faded, too, in that luminous bath in which she floated, her hands the source through which the light-spring flowed.

If Mititei was sought out for her vigor, Sonia soon was known at the spa for massages so gentle, she barely touched the skin of the person she was treating. Her hands, it seemed, hovered in the air just above the body, and the one in her care felt a stirring like faint wind, and often a warmth in the muscles over which the hands were raised. When Sonia's palms made contact, they landed so lightly on shoulder or back or thigh, it was as if butterflies had settled there, briefly, before lifting off again. Yet everyone talked about how in an hour they were not only relieved of the ailments of which they had complained, but felt themselves healed of illnesses whose symptoms had not yet sprouted, of injuries not yet suffered. A sense of deep well-being, stretching into the future, stayed with them for days. "Magic hands," her clients murmured to each other. "Magic hands."

When the famous violinist, Eliezar Pearl, arrived in Baille Herculane to take the waters for his asthma, he had already heard of the young woman born in the Danube Delta whose simple touch had the power to heal. From friends who had visited the spa, he learned of the rumor that she was the child of a gypsy who had schooled her in the mantic arts — supposedly she could read minds, too, and predict a person's fate from the lines on one's palm — and only in Orsova had she been adopted by the Jewish cobbler and his laundress wife who had brought her there from her Delta birthplace. What had become of her gypsy father was a mystery, and a tragic one — "You will see it in her eyes," the friends said. "You will see the pain." They told Eliezar that during their treatments with Sonia, she'd hummed gypsy songs, one quite like a rhapsody he'd played at his last recital in Vienna, right before the asthma had forced him to cancel the rest of his concert tour.

And so it was that the wheezing violinist, thinner than usual from his illness, and so pale that his skin looked like the resin with which he treated his bow, came to see Sonia Landau his second day at Baille Herculane. Wrapped in a towel which exposed his bony shoulders and knees, his bare feet splayed like a duck's on the tile floor, his usually-lacquered hair turned by the massage room's humidity into an unruly frizzed mop, the famed musician Eliezar Pearl blushed before the healer, made a stuttered appeal — "D-d-d-do y-you th-think y-y-you c-can hel-help m-m-me?" — and began a fit of coughing so severe, his towel fell off, his face turned blue, and Sonia, fearing he might suffocate before her, placed her mouth on Eliezar's and sent her own breath streaming into him. His coughing ceased; his color returned. She led the naked Viennese prodigy to the table, where he lay face down, and she moved her hands like wings over his back; then she bade him turn over and repeated the process, the hands swirling across his hair-tufted chest as if she were tracking the spasms that had stolen his breath from him. He could feel his lungs relax and fluid drain from them as if Sonia were a surgeon who had lanced them dry. He could feel the soreness fade from his cough-wracked breastbone, from the muscles around his heart, from the heart itself, from his rib-cage. His breath came evenly now, without a trace of rasp or whistle. His breath sounded now like feathers, lifting and falling on a mild breeze. When in his forty-six years had Eliezar Pearl ever felt so well?

"Well," said Sonia, "I think we've come to the end of the hour."

Not a word about saving his life! Such modesty. And her discretion: as if he had dropped it accidentally and not in the midst of a strangling attack, she handed him his towel. As if he were not naked, and in full erection, and grinning at her like a gawky boy who has fallen in love, which he surely had, for the first time in his forty-six years.

Instead of the week he had planned, Eliezar stayed at the spa for more than a month. What did the violinist tell his wife, a successful attorney retained by the wealthy to write their elaborate wills? That she should remain at home. That he would spend his convalescence composing a new piece, work which required as much privacy as possible. That she should consider this absence simply a leg of his scheduled tour, and that they would go on a nice vacation when he returned. He knew she would not contest him, except perhaps on the matter of the vacation, which she would suggest they take the following year, perhaps, when her work-load was lighter, or he felt stronger, or her brother and his wife could join them, having returned by then from his medical studies in London (for what would she and Eliezar manage to talk about for a fortnight alone in some Tuscany village, or Riviera hotel, day after day the distance between them wide as the Mediterranean to which they would have come for this interminable holiday?).

And so, as if he did not have a wife in Vienna, Eliezar Pearl courted Sonia Landau with the same intensity, the same single-mindedness, the same devotion he had given since childhood to his music. Each dawn he awoke in his elegant suite on the hotel's top floor, took his breakfast on the balcony overlooking the spa's gardens, the mountains, the verdant Cerna Valley, the Orsova Harbor and the gorges beyond it through which the Danube churned, that violent whitewater reduced to a delicate froth from where the prodigy gazed. Here the world lay before him like a beautiful composition in which all elements were in balance, and in that spell of harmony, he worked until lunch on the piece for violin he was composing himself and which he had already named "Sonia's Concerto," he for whom the word "romantic" had only referred to a particular musical school with which he was identified. Here at Baille Herculanae, more than his health had been transformed. Sometimes he felt like Hercules himself, frailty slain like that ancient hydra, the man Eliezar Pearl now saw in the mirror handsome and robust, not that sickly image he'd camouflaged with hair pomade and rouge before performances, and custom-made tuxedos meant to hide his scrawny frame. Already he'd gained ten pounds! And the hikes he took on the miles of trails in the surrounding forest had given him color and muscles in his legs and a growing knowledge of birdcalls, berries and the medicinal properties of certain plants: he could live in the wild if need be, he could forage for food, he could fight off unfriendly animals — oh, his adventuresomeness was boundless, his courage infinite, he who had never played a game of croquet for fear of injuring his valuable hands or setting off, with even the mildest exertion, a bout of wheezing for which he would need a week in bed to recover. That self lifted off like the haze he watched rise from the Carpathian hills, the vapor disappearing into the clouds, leaving behind the unwavering mountains and the valley's green cleft and the beautiful Danube beside which he had kissed Sonia Landau three times now during the strolls they took in the evenings through the gardens of Baille Herculanae and deeper, deeper, deeper into the moonlit woods.

And besides the concerto, and the evening walks, with what would he woo her?

Serenades, in which the pieces most precious to him in his repertoire suddenly revealed to him their true significance: love songs for Sonia, written by Schubert and Brahms and Tchaikovsky and Mendelssohn long before she had been born, but meant for her nonetheless, Eliezar was sure.

Gifts by the dozen: roses, of course, and chocolates he ordered by the pound from a confectionary in Orsova, and the garnet brooch that had been his mother's which he'd carried for luck since the day of her death. Poems he wrote on the same expensive parchment he used for his musical compositions, and drawings he made with India ink of Sonia's face in every imaginable mood. A book of Shakespeare's sonnets. A silver bowl. A pair of silk stockings. A lapis stone.

"And if I could take you anywhere in the world," he said, "where would you like to go?"

"The Danube Delta," Sonia said, without hesitation. "I know a lake there — "

"Ah," he said. "A resort of some kind? A spa like this?"

"Oh no," she told him, her voice falling to a whisper. "Nothing like this."

He saw in her eyes the pain his friends had told him he would find there, but then that sorrow vanished like dew burned off by a morning sun so intense, everything in the path of its radiance loses its form, gives itself up to that subsuming light. In the thrall of music, he had experienced transport, and witnessed it in colleagues overtaken by the beauty of a certain concerto or a particularly powerful overture, but what was the sound Sonia heard that changed her, before his very eyes, from a sad and lovely woman he had been about to comfort into — he could think of no other word, though he did not consider himself in any sense religious — an angel, diaphanous, beyond his reach?

He was a great reader, Eliezar Pearl, and one night when he could not sleep, he opened a collection of stories by Anton Chekov that a friend in Moscow had sent him on his birthday. Lines from "The Lady with the Pet Dog" seemed to him as personal and pointed as if the Russian writer had scribed the tale specifically for him, had intended it as a letter which Eliezar was now receiving. "In the past," Chekov wrote of the aging, married Gurov, "he had met women, come together with them, parted from them, but he had never once loved; it was anything you please, but not love. And only now when his head was gray he had fallen in love, really, truly — for the first time in his life." And further down the page, Chekov said of Gurov and Anna — couldn't the names be changed to Pearl and Sonia, and the story barely altered? — "They forgave each other what they were ashamed of in their past, they forgave everything in the present, and felt that this love of theirs had altered them both."

At those lines, Eliezar wept. He had not yet told Sonia about his wife, and she had not shared with him the secrets of her girlhood. What would happen to their beautiful romance when she learned he was a married man? And what had happened to her in the Delta that she refused, so far, to share with him? The book fell from his hands. There was nothing he could not accept about her, but surely when Sonia learned of his subterfuge, and the true facts of his life, she would faint or spit in his face, and surely she would never speak to him again. He cried and cried, and when his tears were spent, his sobs turned to heavings in his chest, and soon his rasping turned to wheeze, that faint whistle like a train trapped in a collapsed tunnel, signalling for help beyond the airless passageway in which it was trapped.

What brought Sonia, that night at that hour, to her suitor's suite? She had never come to his room before, although he had asked her many times on their woodland walks to return with him to his chamber. When he heard her knock, and her whispered, "Eliezar, it's me, Sonia!" through the keyhole, the stricken violinist crawled to the door and raised up on his knees for the moment he needed to undo the lock. When Sonia turned the knob, Eliezar Pearl was sprawled at her feet, and for the second time in the month he had known her, she added her own breath to his and lay her magic hands just over his heart. In five minutes the attack was over and she had helped him back to the bed where, just hours earlier, he had been dreaming of her beside him on the satin sheets. He was certain now of what he had not yet been willing to word before: he could not live without Sonia Landau.

"There is something I have to tell you," he said. She was sitting on the bed's edge, holding his hand between her own as if she were cradling a fledgling fallen from its nest.

"If it's about your wife," she said, "I've known that for weeks."

Clairvoyance, or intuition, or knowledge brought to her by a hotel guest, or the manager himself, or an anonymous note she found in the pocket of her white smock: does it matter how Sonia learned the truth? What Eliezar read on her face was forgiveness — for being married and keeping it from her, from pursuing her when he was not free, for allowing this love between them to grow when he knew the pain it would bring to so many. She forgave it all, he could see, as Chekhov's Anna forgave Gurov everything.

"Sonia Landau," Eliezar said. "It is true I am married, but I have to tell you that until meeting you, I have never been a husband and I have never had a wife."

"Yes," she said, kissing him lightly on his brow. "I have known that, too."

"Your parents will hate me."

"I have talked with my father," Sonia said, because she had, in fact, consulted Dov Landau in one of her reveries, summoning his spirit and waiting until the room filled with his silent presence. Although it would have looked to you as if Sonia were talking to herself during those encounters, she knew her father heard every word she confessed and confided, and led her to the answers she needed for her most pressing questions. "He understands."

"What is it that he understands, Sonia?"

"Miracles," she said, and lay down beside the famous violinist whom she would legally marry in a year and a month, though this would be the night — on the satin sheets of the Hotel Roman, where her mother worked as a laundress and her step-father fixed the shoes of the wealthy guests who vacationed here — this would be the night that Sonia Landau and Eliezar Pearl vowed to be husband and wife, "until death do us part," they murmured together, "for as long as we both shall live."

What Reba said:

"I absolutely forbid it."

"He will leave you a widow with children to raise."

"He is old enough to be your father."

"A man who deserts one wife will desert another."

"You are throwing away your youth on him."

"What makes you so sure he is getting a divorce?"

"What makes you so sure he will marry you?"

"I will not come to this wedding."

"I never could reason with your father, and I see I can't reason with you."

"Just don't expect my blessing."

"Don't confuse this blessing with my approval."

"When Dov and I decided to leave Jassy, my mother said she would never forgive me, but still I went."

"She did forgive me."
"As long as you love him."
"As long as he loves you."

What Ovid said:
"In this world, love is always a miracle."

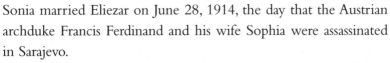

Sonia married Eliezar on June 28, 1914, the day that the Austrian archduke Francis Ferdinand and his wife Sophia were assassinated in Sarajevo.

Imagine: at perhaps the very moment that my famous father smashed the wine glass with his foot in the ballroom of the Hotel Roman, a Serbian student fired the shots that started World War I. The cheers of the wedding guests when my father broke the glass entered the world's ear at the same time as the screams of the crowd who had just witnessed the murder of that other couple. struck down together in their royal touring car.

Well, when Reba and Dov married in Jassy, weren't whole villages burning nearby, conflagrations just beyond the tiny wooden synagogue in which a few candles flamed as if to remind the celebrants of the soldiers' lethal torches?

And who danced at the wedding of Reba and Ovid, at that makeshift ceremony outside the hotel kitchen, if not the ghosts of all the murdered Jews of Jassy, our own ancestors come back from restful death to the world from which, in one brutal night, they had all disappeared?

Soon, sweetheart, I will tell you the story of my own wedding in a DP camp just after the Second World War, how I made a dress from burlap sacks that covered the rat-bite scars on my arms; how your grandfather still reeked, months after liberation, from the disinfectant with which he had been doused, three times a day, a Dachau survivor's acrid cologne; how the rabbi mistakenly chanted *kaddish*, the prayer for the dead, instead of the marriage blessing over the wine, so used was he to the rituals of grief, to the lamentations for the lost millions who vanished into the ovens, nothing left to bury, every trace turned to smoke.

Thirty years later your parents would marry in this very garden whose roses right now bathe me in their perennial perfume. Even as the orchestra leader raised his baton under the striped tent that billowed in the threatening wind, and the bride and groom grasped each other in that doomed embrace the tango demands, and the few dozen relatives and friends wailed like mourners a tango song while your parents danced, which of us there — a late summer in 1974, Peron alive for another six months, still waving from balconies with his showgirl-wife to the worshipful crowds below — which of us there on that particular wedding day could have imagined the next round of pain for which it seems we were all rehearsing? A tango without any orchestra, that slow march on Thursday afternoons we mothers made in the Plaza de Mayo, our white kerchiefs like bridal veils on our graying heads, and the names of our missing children bitter vows we repeated over and over and over again.

8

ALTHOUGH MY PARENTS MARRIED on the eve of World War I, my father Eliezar was spared conscription because of his age and his health and his musical fame. When word of the first hostilities reached the spa, he cancelled his upcoming concert tour, established residency at the Hotel Roman and gave private lessons for the next three years to musical prodigies from all over Europe. Baille Herculanae would surely be safe from the battles and bombs, the mineral baths far from the fighting zones and blessed by the ancient gods. Hadn't Eliezar Pearl married a healer whose powers came straight from those sanctified waters? So what if the Romans had been pagans? This place was the site of Hercules' miracle, awesome as any Biblical deed.

Who quarrels with magic when they need it?

Who turns skeptic when the guns are raised?

Although it took her some time to convince them, at last Sonia was able to persuade her mother and Ovid to move from their cabin to a hotel suite on the same floor as the one in which she and Eliezar now lived.

"And you both can retire," Eliezar insisted. "I happen to be a wealthy man, and Sonia has told me how hard you both work."

"I would not want to be idle," Ovid said, though he had to concur that being a cobbler was crippling his hands; after a twelve-hour day in his shop, his fingers were swollen and stiff, and lately the pain in his left wrist was so bad that Sonia was giving him treatments every morning and every afternoon. At night he would soak his hands for an hour in hot water mixed with mineral salts, but whatever healing took place overnight would be undone by the next day's exertions. He had come to this labor late, inheriting Dov Landau's skills, but not the agility the work required. "My father could not even pick me up," the gypsy recalled. "Thirty years old and his joints so red, I used to think his hands might burst into flame right in front of us. We would have to cut his food for him on his worst days."

"You see?" said Eliezar. "It's a family disease. If you're not careful, Reba will be feeding you like a baby before we give her a grandchild of her own. I understand your wish to be occupied, of course. But something less taxing. Some hobby, perhaps, you could — "

"I read palms," Ovid confided.

His son-in-law gazed at the man he believed was Dov Landau. "A gypsy talent in a Jew?"

Ovid was about to offer his usual disclaimer: how he had befriended gypsies in the Delta and mastered their ways — palm-reading, intricate dances, songs he sang in so perfect a Romany tongue, he had been made an honorary member of a local gypsy family to whose eldest son he had had grown as close as a twin.

"In the Delta — " he began.

"In the Delta, what?" said Eliezar, Sonia's origins there still a mystery to him, though he tried to assure her that nothing she might confide could alter his love. Once he started to tell her he'd heard she'd been a gypsy orphan whose parents had died in some calamitous accident — a fire, it was rumored, and someone else believed they'd drowned — but he held back: she had a way of disappearing so completely into her memories, he felt bereft even as she walked beside him, or sat across the table from him, or lay beside him in their four-poster, satin-sheeted bed. Better to leave the past unworded. Better to let the secret alone that could claim her so deeply, he feared sometimes he'd wake to find her gone, literally transported to the Danube Delta of her mysterious girlhood.

Now the cobbler was behaving as strangely as his daughter, invoking the past and silencing himself, beginning a story he could not tell, a tale that started, "In the Delta," and ended there, as if the rest of it had vanished, the words he would need for his narrative like a flock of seabirds leaving on migration the moment he came upon them.

"I will speak to the hotel manager in the morning," Eliezar told his father-in-law, bringing the two men back to the present, to the brocade sofa in the sitting room of the newly-weds' suite. On the table before them, a silver tray on which rested a plate of sweet pastries and demitasse cups of the finest German china. "I am sure he'll have you reading the palms of his guests before the week is out."

"Would you like me to read yours now?" the gypsy asked the famous violinist. "I would be happy to do it for you."

Eliezar Pearl looked at his elegant hands — the long fingers, the manicured nails, the skin he bathed each day in rosewater and rubbed with eucalyptus oil. He turned them over in his lap and studied the finely-creased palms as if he, himself, could decipher his fate in the mapped flesh.

"I hope you will not be offended," he said, "if I confide that I, myself, am not a believer," though when Eliezar extended one of his hands toward Ovid in a gesture of good-will, he was surprised to find it shaking so badly, he had to steady it with his other.

The gypsy pretended not to have noticed, but he knew from experience that when a person, believer or not, scans his own palm and trembles as Eliezar had done, the actual reading confirms the fear: tragedy under the second finger, loss under the third, the life-line broken in half.

Late in 1917, the war that turned the cities of Europe into overnight ruins, as if time itself had been exploded in a single bomb blast, crossed the Danube into Transylvania and ended in an hour the tranquillity of Baille Herculanae.

In a story, as in life, when sirens sunder the quiet of daily routines, the writer rushes to locate those in her chronicle to whom she is closest, as if she still had power over the safety of loved ones.

Dusk, then.

In her sitting room, Reba relaxes on the velvet chaise and works on the sweater she is crocheting for the child Sonia carries, two months more until the baby's birth (a boy, Reba wrongly believes, because Sonia is carrying low). Sonia has gone to soak in the baths, this time of day her favorite for an hour alone in the medicinal waters, the sky a deepening violet now and the half-moon like the body of a pregnant sister come for a visit this summer evening. In the hotel lobby, Ovid sits on one side of the gilt-edged writing desk at which he is reading the palm of a ballerina from Bucharest, visiting the spa for treatment of a knee sprain, and Eliezar has greeted them both, his father-in-law and the ballerina, on his way outside for his nightly walk in the moon-washed woods.

From this distance of time and dream, it is as if I am perched on the hotel roof, or higher, my panoramic vision able see them all — Reba, Ovid, Eliezar, and my mother Sonia still carrying me in her womb — to embrace them all in a single love-driven gaze that watches on in horror as the tableau shifts from idyll to doom, the story-teller forbidden to rescue those for whom life has other intentions.

To be so helpless in the face of such peril.

To be the reporter, and nothing more.

For when the sirens began to wail throughout the Cerna Valley, as if that crevice in the earth were protesting its own violation, peasants and patricians alike raced for shelter from what they knew was about to befall them: like a many-headed hydra, the war had finally tracked them down and they would need a Hercules to save them from this beast at their backs.

The bombs rained down and the artillery battered the countryside, and hundreds of fires raged through towns and forests, so that from a high-enough position, the Cerna Valley would have looked like an erupting volcano whose citizens fled from one explosion to another, houses burning and churches collapsing and the windows of the Hotel Roman turned into a thousand knives of glass flung through every elegant room. In that barrage, Ovid and Reba would perish, their shelter turned into a crypt sealed on its victims when the hotel roof caved in like a rockslide. And in his beloved woods, Eliezar would fall dead of crossfire that must have sounded to him like some dissonant symphony of cymbals and drums rending the suddenly-acrid air. My tale has turned so terrible, I cannot fashion a narrative more embellished than the one I have just managed to write. Once the weeping begins, who has the heart for words?

But I can summon the spirit to record my mother's survival in the legendary waters of Baille Herculanae.

When she heard the sirens, and after that brief overture, the artillery volleys and bomb blasts and rifle rounds, she filled her lungs and descended, her body flattened like a fish against the pool's concrete wall. When my mother remembered those hours she lived underwater, swearing she came up for air only three times, she insisted that her womb retracted, the baby she carried within her reduced to a fraction of its size during the siege, expanding again to its proper proportions only when the danger had passed and Sonia Landau was able to surface. During the battle, she would recall, not a single explosion disturbed the waters in which she hid. When she huddled together in the dark with other survivors of the "minor skirmish" military historians would claim had occurred in Baille Herculanae, what kept my mother from going insane, or flinging herself into the fire that blazed now in the surrounding woods, or drowning herself in the very pool in which she had so miraculously survived?

"It is true," she would tell me many years later, "when I realized they were all dead, my mother and Ovid and Eliezar, I started screaming 'Let me die, too! Let me die, let me die, let me die!' And perhaps I would have — I was in shock, blue as a corpse, I later heard — but in the ambulance that took me to the hospital in Orsova, I felt you kicking, over and over, your tiny feet pounding against my body, and then I heard your voice — of course you will not believe this, but I swear it happened exactly as I say — your voice calling, 'Let me live, Mama, let me live, let me live!' Tell me, what mother could fail to be moved by her unborn child's plea?"

Granddaughter, sometimes I wonder if your mother, too, didn't survive the insults and the beatings and the endless hours of interrogation those months between her abduction and your birth only because you called from her womb, in a secret voice not even the guards could hear, "Let me live, Mama, let me live, let me live!"

In your dreams, do you remember that chant?

When the day arrives that you begin the search for your true identity, claim those words as evidence sure as fingerprints or genetic markers that you are the descendent of Reba Landau, and her daughter Sonia, and her daughter Rachael who is writing this family chronicle for you, and Rachael's daughter Miriam, who was your mother and intended to name you Marcella, "because it sounds like music," she said to me at breakfast, the day before she disappeared.

9

DEAR MARCELLA, like you I was born in the midst of unspeakable violence, death the midwife attending my arrival. Actually it is like this for every human being in this world — each infant's first cry counterpointed somewhere by someone's final word or wail, and a recording of any moment's births and expirations would allow us to hear, over and over and over, the harmonics of that mortal music sung by the new-born and the dying, a great choir whose voices resonate in eternally perfect pitch. Shamans, yogis, prophets and saints listen all their lives to that chorus. The rest of us hear it for an instant, if we are blessed. Did you hear it at the moment of your birth in a secret La Plata prison, Marcella, or I during mine in Orsova Hospital, the pain-wracked victims of the prior night's raid filling the ward where my mother suckled her just-delivered daughter?

Sing with me, Marcella, whose name sounds like music. Sing with your *abuela*.

An orphan and a widow overnight, my mother Sonia became a mother the following day. In forty-eight hours, her identity in the world had been completely revised, family relationships shattered and created in the blink of an eye. When the grief came to claim her, the nurse would bring Sonia her infant, and as soon as my suckling began, my mother's sorrow would yield to joy.

That we had lived!

That her daughter was healthy!

It was not Hercules who had interceded and blessed the waters in which the pregnant woman had hidden without drowning, or going into labor, without a single shell dispelling the placid surface of that sanctified pool. No, not Hercules, she knew, but her father Dov Landau, his pelican-spirit still here with her in the hospital, his wings like gentle fans keeping her and her new-born cool in the sweltering ward.

But then, in the midst of her gratitude, the deaths of Reba and Ovid and beloved Eliezar would detonate yet again in her memory, exploding her fragile well-being. Dov's presence would vanish, and still holding me to her breast, my mother's tears would begin anew, the names of my lost family a mournful lullaby with which she sang me to sleep.

When I was one week old, Mititei, the masseuse with whom my mother had apprenticed, arrived at Orsova Hospital.

She had looked for my pregnant mother for hours after the raid, missed her in the melee, given her up for dead, and was still mourning the demise of our entire family the day she discovered that Sonia Pearl had been rushed to Orsova in a military ambulance, the young woman's water broken and her contractions coming less than five minutes apart.

"She hid in the baths," someone told Mititei. "She came out of the waters like a new-born herself, blue and wrinkled and no idea where she was at first. Only God can tell us how she survived."

Still recovering from her injuries — Mititei had bruises vivid as tattoos all over her body — and numbed by the devastation at the spa, the news of Sonia's survival came like a miracle for which she had been praying.

"Thank you, God," Mititei wept. "Thank you for still existing."

With the sudden strength of rediscovered faith, she went to the barn converted to a warehouse now for unclaimed goods the rescue teams unearthed each hour in their grim excavations, and there she loaded a wheelbarrow with my mother's inheritance: Eliezar's violin case, a cake of resin shattered like stars against the green velvet interior; Ovid's opal ring; Dov Landau's leather-bound notebooks; and from Reba's bureau, a white crocheted coverlet exactly like the one she'd hooked herself in Tulcea, two cotton nightgowns, and a letter bearing the stamp of a man galloping on horseback over a flat field, one arm swinging a loop of rope over the head of a fleeing calf.

Why did these particular artifacts escape destruction when the hotel caved in on itself?

When has fate ever cared about plausibility?

Sonia Landau was sitting on the roof-level sundeck when Mititei entered the hospital grounds with the wheelbarrow she had pushed all the way from Baille Herculanae. Even from this distance, my mother recognized the head masseuse and might have thrown herself from the roof four stories down to the ground below, had not the fence through which she peered restrained her. "Mititei!" she screamed, though the injured woman had already vanished into the building. "Mititei, it's me!"

In wartime, a hospital loses its hush: doors crash open and shut;

alarms summoning emergency teams go off so frequently, they begin to sound like an ensemble of strange church instruments; doctors and nurses yell orders at each other down corridors crowded with the wounded, whose cries — "Water!" and "Mama, I need you!" and "Dear Mother of God, help me!" — fill the halls day and night, never a lull in that choir of pain. The voice of one small woman wandering the wards, calling out the Rumanian word for sausage — "Mititei? Mititei?" — would surely disappear unnoticed into the din.

But finally, on a floor of bandage-swaddled patients, my mother found her friend from Baille Herculanae, steering her cart between the rows of beds and calling out the healer's name — "Sonia? Sonia?" — like a peddler hawking goods from a wagon, maybe a tonic good for cough or bottles of lineament known to cure the most recalcitrant lumbago.

"Mititei? Mititei?"

"Sonia? Sonia?"

What duet has ever been more beautiful than the one those two women sang before the dozens of wounded who were their audience, and whose own voices rose up, too, in a chorus of cheers celebrating the reunion?

My mother wanted to return to the spa, but Mititei convinced her the devastation was so terrible there, it would be years before tourists would visit Baille Herculanae. How would they live without customers for their treatments?

"I am not even a healer anymore," Sonia said. "I tried with some of the patients here, but nothing."

"You expect too much from yourself. Only nine days ago — "

"Nine days ago I lost everything. Including my gift." She lifted her hands. "Believe me, Mititei, they are as dead as Eliezar's, as my mother Reba's, as Ov — "

"Ovid. You can say it, Sonia. I know the story from your mother. I know about the real Dov Landau."

Sonia Pearl was weeping now. "A family of ghosts. Even me. Not one of us left alive, not one."

On the edge of my mother's bed, Mititei was holding me in her arms. She took one of my mother's hands and placed it on my infant heart. "Here, Sonia, feel. The baby is alive. The baby is alive. The baby is alive."

Like a mantra transmitted from teacher to student, my sorrow-dazed mother repeated Mititei's words herself, at first like the sounds of a tongue foreign as the Spanish she would come to learn years in the future, and slowly the utterance — "The baby is alive, the baby is alive, the baby is alive" — revealed its truth to Sonia Landau Pearl. The pulse of my heart on her palm entered her spirit as deeply as her own touch had penetrated the souls of others in the past.

Marcella, at seven days old I was my mother's healer, just as you were mine, the day I learned of your birth in that prison where your own mother died. "The baby is alive," I told your grandfather, those words as incomprehensible at first as they were for my mother in her own despair, when I was one week old. Sixty years later, in Buenos Aires, I would repeat again and again that same invocation I had heard as an infant in Orsova, now a prayer I wanted my husband to join me in repeating: "The baby is alive, Jacobo! The baby is alive, the baby is alive, the baby is alive!"

10

TWO HUNDRED MILES NORTH of Orsova, beyond the mountains and through the Banat Plains flat as the Argentine pampas, Sonia Landau Pearl and her infant daughter, Rachael, rode the train to Oradea, accompanying Mititei on her return to her girlhood home. A doctor at the hospital where I had been born had given them the fare as a gift.

Why would the masseuse adopt, as it were, my bereft mother and her newborn child, bringing us with her to the Catholic family that had disowned her decades ago for eloping with a Jew who would die just two years later from influenza, Mititei a widow at twenty just as my mother was now?

And why would a doctor to whom we were strangers buy us the tickets for the overnight train ride, that rail one of the few in the region the Germans had not blown up in their drive toward Bucharest, the Rumanian capitol which the Axis armies were headed for, leaving the Cerna Valley and the plains of Banat strewn with the wreckage of their sudden assault?

I have no explanation for the generosity of the masseuse or the doctor; but in a tale motored by violence, that terrible engine of history, it is important to remember the instances of goodness that appear in these pages like the beautiful fleeting tableaus my mother would have glimpsed through the window of the train speeding us to Oradea: white sheep grazing in a pasture; a stand of silver beech trees; hundreds of starlings gliding in orderly migration across an unharmed sky.

In my father's velvet-lined violin case, I lay swaddled in one of my grandmother's nightgowns and the crocheted coverlet that was now my inheritance. Inside the compartment built into the case's lid to hold a cake of resin, my mother had placed Ovid's opal ring, and between the clasps in which Eliezar's horsehair bow had once been secured, she'd wedged her father's notebooks and the letter from Buenos Aires her mother had chosen to save. There, in my first cradle, the artifacts of my vanished family surrounded me like talismen to keep me safe on the journey we had undertaken.

When the train slowed for a moment on the edge of the forest where my father had died, as if he might have survived after all and the conductor was allowing time for the violinist to appear, did his spirit show itself to me as Dov's had come to my mother in the Danube Delta? Did Eliezar Pearl's manicured hand press against the glass beneath which I slept in the case he had carried all over Europe? Did I open my eyes to my father's palm conferring on me a silent benediction before the train sped off again, my mother weeping good-bye to the beloved ghosts of Baille Herculanae? Do I still carry with me the imprinted image of his splayed fingers and the map etched upon his skin: tragedy under the second finger, loss under the third, the life-line broken in half? Or did I sleep from the moment we left Orsova until we arrived the next morning at our destination, this memory of my father's presence invention rather than recall, wish rather than fact?

Suppose that all our lost kin — the massacred relatives from Jassy; Dov vanished in the Delta; Reba and Ovid and my father, Eliezar — suppose all of them waited together on the edge of the woods adjacent to Baille Herculanae as our train slowed on the curve of track that met the forest. Our entire dead family raised

their hands in a greeting and sang in unison my mother's name —
"Sonia! Sonia! Sonia!" — and she answered back in a cry of
acknowledgement others on board, even Mititei, mistook for a
pain-wracked wail, a shriek of grief, a mourner's howl, but no: it
was the scream of a woman in labor, not unlike her cries during my
birth just weeks before. Now it was her own life she delivered, still-
born, memory lost like an infant unable to survive in the world into
which it has been cast. Through the window, Sonia handed her past
to the ghosts of her kin, the train sped off, and my mother lapsed
into a silence about her first twenty years which — even after her
amnesia abated — she would maintain for six more decades, until
she told me the story of Dov Landau's disappearance, reclaiming at
her death the voice that became my inheritance, and which I pass
on to you, Marcella, in these tales you are reading now.

Perhaps, in the Buenos Aires bank vault where you discover the
truth of your life, you will scream as my mother did on the train to
Oradea, sure you have seen your lost relations lifting their hands in
a greeting to you, calling your name — Marcella! Marcella!
Marcella! — from the bank's lobby where we will have assembled
together, all of us waiting so long for this reunion, waiting so long
for you to find us, to bring us back from the zone of the vanished
to which we have been so long consigned.

In Oradea, Mititei learned that her parents were dead, her two
brothers gone to America years ago, and her sister, Flora, become
Mother Superior of the convent behind the Church with the
Moon. The family that was to have taken us in existed only in
Mititei's memory, her ties with them broken for thirty years in
which they had remained, for her, the family of her girlhood, still

gathered in her dreams around the oak table from which she had been banished, still tending the garden and feeding the goats and walking to Mass on Sunday mornings at the very church — Biserica cu Luna, Church with the Moon — where Flora, now Mother Catherine, peered through a grill in the convent door at the refugees from Baile Herculane: a masseuse and a healer and the infant who slept in a violin case converted into a cradle.

"Flora," Mititei said. "It's Marie. Don't you remember your big sister, Marie?"

Behind the grill, the nun's eyes narrowed. "I don't believe — "

But Mititei had started to sing a lullaby the girls' mother had crooned in their childhoods, and as the sound of those notes from their earliest years reached Mother Catherine's skeptical ears, her eyes flooded over, the door swung open, we entered, and in that silent cloister my echoing cry must have sounded like dozens of babies — dozens of Jewish babies — calling for their food in those stone-quiet convent halls.

My mother had forgotten everything, even her own name. For a time, Mititei recited for her the facts of her life as she knew them — a Jewish childhood in the Delta; Dov Landau's disappearance; the terrible famine and ensuing pogroms; the journey across Rumania to Baille Herculane where Reba worked in the laundry and Ovid was a cobbler and Sonia discovered her power to heal; the arrival at the spa of Eliezar Pearl, the asthma-wracked violinist; their courtship and marriage; the bombing raid during which Sonia, nine months pregnant, hid underwater in the mineral baths; the deaths of her parents and husband; my birth in Orsova, where Mititei where would find us, bringing us here on the train to Oradea, to this convent behind the Church with the Moon.

"Why is it called 'Church with the Moon?'" my mother asked once, as if that were the only detail that seemed familiar enough to her to warrant a question.

Mititei took her outside. It was morning, and a half-moon still floated in the sea-gray sky. The women walked across the grass from the nunnery to the church.

"There," said Mititei, pointing to the metal sphere suspended within the church tower. Half-shadowed, half-light, the globe was the moon's twin, the heavenly body's phases mirrored by its earthly double. Even when the real moon was invisible, obscured by clouds or a fog so thick the stars vanished as well, the tower-moon kept a perfect record of each night's lunar progression.

My mother stared at the device, at this simple object in which the moon's ongoing life had been recorded, stored, revealed without pause for more than a hundred years. Her eyes brimmed with tears.

"That is the moon," she said, pointing with her own hand to the sky. "And that" — she moved her hand from sky to tower — "that is the moon's memory." She placed her palms on the crown of her head, as if she were recalling one of her forgotten healing positions. "Who stole mine, Mititei? Who?"

Who stole yours, Marcella?

Who?

One month after our arrival at the convent, Mititei found a job as a masseuse at Baile Felix, five miles from Oradea. For a week or so, she rose at five a.m. in order to catch the train that would take her to the spa by the time the first clients arrived for their massages after their morning constitutionals, and she did not return to Oradea until eight in the evening, far too late for supper with the nuns and their refugees, the amnesiac Jewess and her infant, Rachael.

For a time, Mititei explained to my mother, she would move to the spa alone, her meager earnings just enough for renting a room in a local boarding house where many employees lived. As her clientele grew, so would her income — at the baths, a masseuse made most of her money from tips. "Then I will send for you and the baby," Mititei said, though privately she worried how she ever could manage to support them all herself, Sonia's healing powers lost, her gift a casualty of war as surely as her vanished memory, as Reba and Ovid buried in the rubble of the Hotel Roman or killed, like Eliezar, in the Cerna Valley's fire-wracked woods.

"I would rather stay here," my mother said.

"We are not nuns, Sonia."

My mother closed her eyes. She saw the robed sisters of the Convent of the Church with the Moon gliding in processional to chapel, and she could hear them chanting their prayers in Latin, the language as foreign to her, as moving, as the memories Mititei claimed were Sonia's own. Reba, Dov, Ovid, Danube Delta, Baile Herculane, Eliezar Pearl: wasn't this a novena worthy of a habit and rosary beads and a nun's new name? Hadn't she left the past behind as surely as a novitiate renounces her old life and comes, like a refugee, to the convent's door?

"Sonia," Mititei said, because she sensed the nature of my mother's reverie, "a convent is not a place to raise a child. Is it?"

But how could Sonia answer that question? If she did not have a single recollection of her own childhood, on what should she base her decisions about her baby's upbringing? On the tales Mititei claimed were Sonia's lost history? That was a story of dislocations, violence, deaths. "And love," Mititei insisted. "Remember how much love there was." Was. Was. Was. Who could find consolation in such pervasive loss? Why would she want her daughter to have a life anything like the one Mititei insisted Sonia had lived, in a world so perilous she did not want to return to it herself? Such a chronicle of Jewish grief! Better to baptize the baby, and herself as well, and petition the nuns to let them remain here in the cloister, where everyone shed their pasts so completely, they might as well have forgotten them, they might as well have lapsed into amnesias so profound, even their dreams were purged of their parents' faces.

In Sonia's dreams, no person appeared, no room in which she might have lived, no yard, no tree she might have climbed as a child, no song from those years, no voice so familiar she'd wake in dazed assurance that its speaker was kneeling at her bed in the convent room she shared with her baby. Night after night, the same strange image visited my mother — a pelican rising in swift trajectory from a shining lake to a sky so bright, its radiance subsumed the water, the bird, the dreamer herself. Just before dawn, when the first bells sounded in the sacristy, she would open her eyes slowly, ready to shield them from the strange illumination of her nocturnal world, but in the nunnery, it was still dark and my mother could hardly make out the features of the infant sleeping beside her in the velvet-lined violin case that was my first bed.

Was I baptized? Did I grow up in the Church with the Moon Convent, the only child in the cloister my mother considered, for a time, her first home as well as mine?

No. We left when I was one year old. My only memories of the convent are the ones I am just this moment discovering, this scribe like a sleeping woman whose dreams are visited by images turned to words on a once-blank page. Where does this story come from, Marcella, if not from my own forgotten past? What is a tale, except the form we give our fleeting recollections, a glimpse of a life rescued from that daily amnesia to which we all succumb?

Dearest grandchild, think of that sphere in the church tower recording the phases of a moon whose light is so distant, it reaches us long after it actually glowed in an earlier sky we can only imagine. What are these words if not long-travelled light from a vanished world?

Biserica cu Luna.

Church with the Moon.

"The moon's memory," my mother called it, longing for her own.

One night, in the middle of a pelican dream, Sonia Landau Pearl woke to Mother Catherine's cry: "Fire! Fire! Fire!"

All the sisters were running through the dark halls in their muslin nightgowns, their cropped heads uncovered, their feet bare. Joining them in the rush for the front door, in her arms her baby wailing like a tiny alarm set off by the blaze, my mother wondered for a moment who these women were, huddled with her now on the snow-crusted grass in front of the burning convent. She saw flames shooting from a window, and a dark halo of smoke seemed to circle the roof. The fire brigade was arriving, horse-drawn wagons filled with men from town who charged the cloister now with buckets of water and hoses attached to the pump in the town square. Some of the sisters were screaming, "Mother Catherine's inside! Help Mother Catherine!"

Before my mother's eyes, the convent turned into the Hotel Roman, the nuns her neighbors from the spa, the baby in her arms unborn for hours more and Sonia Pearl, just risen from her underwater bunker to the bombed ruins of Baile Herculane, crying, "Mama! Ovid! Eliezar!" One of the sisters grabbed me from my hysterical mother — "Let me die! Let me die, too!" she was yelling now as she had then — and two others tried to lead her toward the church — "I am so dizzy!" she whispered, her knees buckling beneath her — and she might have passed out on the vestibule floor, the night-shirted priest rubbing snow on her temples to rouse her, had not someone called, "Look, look, Mother's been hurt!", and rather than fainting, Sonia broke from the nuns who were holding her up and raced toward the stretcher four firemen rushed toward an ambulance just now arriving at the smoke-blackened convent of the Church with the Moon.

Biserica cu Luna.

Baile Herculane.

"I'm a healer," she rasped, her throat raw from smoke and from screaming her family's names. Reba, Dov, Ovid, Eliezar. She could feel the vibrations in her palms and her fingertips. "Where are her wounds?"

Mother Catherine's injuries were minor — first-degree burns on the soles of her feet from trying to stomp the flames out herself, and the harm to the convent equally slight: the fire had been confined to the kitchen, and most of the smoke damage repaired with scrub brush, paint, the remedy of cleansing air. And because Sonia Pearl's amnesia was gone, the priest declared the fire an instance of divine intervention, staged by the Lord for the very purpose of restoring to my mother her power to heal.

"Throughout the Bible, one can see how small calamities precipitate miracles. It is as if one must be shocked into alertness in order to receive them."

Even Mititei, never a religious person herself, attended Mass daily for the rest of her life, glad to have been spared God's call to attention (she was in Baile Felix that night), but stunned into faith, nonetheless, by Sonia's recovery at the Church with the Moon.

My mother's memory came back in stages, so that she seemed

to be watching photographs develop: the gradual clarification of details, hazy outlines growing sharp and specific, the almost-unbearable beauty of emerging particulars. When she looked at my face, my father's rose from my infant features and rested beside me on the bed where I slept. So that was what he'd looked like! The dear angles and planes, the precious mole just under his left ear, the sea-green depths of his eyes. And then the texture of his beard would prickle her cheek, and the pressure of his warm hand on hers, and the smell of his imported French cologne. One night she awoke to a Schubert violin concerto, the entire room vibrating with each stroke of her husband's horsehair bow.

On the fourth day of her recovery. she remembered the last conversation she and Eliezar had had. He was worried about his mother, alone in her apartment in Prague, no mail now for several months, rumors about destruction in the city brought by visitors to the spa. In her last letter, she had written: "I was very upset when you divorced. for although I never much liked your wife — a cold woman, I thought from the start — a vow is a vow. But I apologize for refusing to see you when you came to Prague for the proceedings, or since. After all, a mother cannot divorce a son, or vice versa. To even attempt it is a sin. Still: what could you be thinking, marrying a girl half your age, and not from the educated class, and now you say she is having a baby by the end of the year! Eliezar, to be starting a family at your stage of life! In music you may be a genius, but in life you have always lacked the simplest common sense. Still, you are my only child and I will try to help you face the problems that surely lay ahead for you. Now it is too dangerous for either of us to travel, but when this terrible war is over, I want you to bring this Sonia and my new grandchild to visit me here. In spite of my misgivings, I will practice opening my heart. Please say you will come to see your loving mother, once it is safe."

Sonia remembered the letter verbatim, just as her husband had read it to her. "Of course we will," she had said when he'd finished. "Of course we will go." She said it again, aloud, to me — "Of course we will go" — in our room in the convent. Then she retrieved from under the bed the violin case for which I was now too big, checked on the salvaged treasures inside — Dov's notebooks, Ovid's ring and Reba's coverlet and the letter from Buenos Aires. To these things, my mother added the rosary beads Mother Catherine had given her for healing the burns on the soles of the nun's feet, the few pieces of clothing the sisters had donated to the amnesiac refugee and her baby daughter. She shut the case and bound it with twine. She bathed me and dressed me and took me with her to the dark chapel of Biserica cu Luna, where I slept in her arms for hours. The next day we left for Prague.

11

WHEN I GREW TALLER than the sills of my grandmother's drape-swathed windows, I liked to look down on the Old Jewish Cemetery, twelve-thousand ancient graves piled a dozen layers high. Across the street from the cemetery rose the elegant House of Artists where my father had performed to standing ovations that brought him back for encore after encore. I imagined twelve-thousand spirits awakening from their endless sleep to his Mozart and Bach, my father's music transporting them out of their crowded entombment, all those ghosts joining his living audience each time Eliezar Pearl picked up his bow and played.

My mother and I had arrived in Prague to martial music, brassy and rude, an uneasy alliance of Czechs and Slovaks celebrating their independence in Wenceslas Square. From the train station, my mother carried me through the massing crowds, shielding my mouth with a handkerchief from the confetti that fell like ash through the summer air. "Kaprova Street?" she shouted into the din of drums and trumpets and thousands of voices cheering for the marching bands and float-borne dignitaries and uniformed squads goose-stepping down the brick-paved boulevard. "Kaprova Street? Kaprova Street?" Who would hear a single weary woman in the midst of such cacophony? Finally a finger pointed her toward the Jewish Ghetto, two miles north, and by the time we reached my grandmother's building, the noise of Independence Day had faded and I had fallen asleep in my mother's arms.

When my grandmother opened her apartment door to the timid knock, and saw Sonia standing there with the baby who so resembled Eliezar, but Eliezar nowhere in sight, Anna Pearl knew immediately who we were and what her son's absence meant. Perhaps she read her loss on my mother's face, perhaps rumors had already made their way from the Rumanian spa to Prague that the famous violinist had died months before in a bombing raid. Or perhaps a mother does not need any information at all to confirm the nightmares that begin the moment her child is imperiled: Anna Pearl's dreams of her son in danger had ensued that same summer evening the war had come to Baille Herculanae.

Without a word, she ushered us into the parlor whose papered walls were covered with framed pictures of my father performing all over Europe. In the corner of the room, more pictures covered the top of the grand piano on which I would improvise two-fingered melodies before my feet even touched the floor. Nanna's husband, dead now a dozen years, had taught piano to the children of Prague's intelligentsia, the flat on Kaprova Street already a musical salon when my father began his violin lessons, playing from memory Debussy duets with his father before he was nine years old.

Nanna took my mother's elbow and guided her silently down the hall that ran the length of the apartment to the kitchen where she opened all the cupboards in order to display dishes and cups and the staples on hand, stirred the kettle of barley soup simmering on the wood-burning stove, and then retired to her room to wail for the son she would never see again. Although we were in a Prague building in which not even dogs were allowed, her cries like that of an animal snared in the same woods where the violinist had died.

Marcella, I know I am supposed to have been too young — not even a year old — to remember anything about that day, but I can hear Nanna's grief as clearly as I would hear my own, decades later in Buenos Aires, when I learned of your mother's death. Sometimes, here on the veranda or in the nursery that awaited your birth, a choir of women — Reba, Sonia, Nanna, myself and your mother — join voices in a fused lament whose pain and beauty summon each other in aching counterpoint. Dear child, when you learn that you belong to us, and your own sorrow frees itself as sound, remember how grief can turn itself to music, how an unholy shriek can become sublime.

For weeks after our arrival, my mother, Sonia, tended to her mother-in-law much as Ovid had cared for Reba after the news of the Jassy massacre. Sonia lay cool cloths on Anna's fevered brow, she fed her spoonfuls of broth and tea, she brought her more blankets when attacks of chills left Anna shivering in the same sheets where she had burned just moments before. Sometimes my grandmother grasped Sonia's arm as if it were saving her from quicksand or flood waters or quake-sundered earth, as if the older woman's very survival depended on this girl about whom Anna had written Eliezar: "When this terrible war is over, I want you to bring this Sonia and my new grandchild here to visit. In spite of my misgivings, I will practice opening my heart." One morning when Anna was sure she would die from her grief, it was over this very heart that my mother's hands hovered until the pain in my grandmother's chest subsided and she sat up in the bed from which she'd believed she would never arise. With the edge of a blanket, she blotted away her tears, took several deep breaths, smoothed her unkempt hair with her fingers.

"How long have you been here, Sonia?" she said.

"Nearly a month."

"Tell me, my dear, have I held my granddaughter yet?"

"No, not yet."

"I would like to do that now," she said, beginning to weep again. "If she isn't afraid of me."

And so it was that my father's mother took us in — the woman my mother called "Anna" now "Nanna" forever to me — not merely out of obligation, as my mother had imagined would be the case, but because her heart had broken so wholly in grief, her hardness toward us had broken as well. It was as if she had lost entirely the memory of her breach with her son over his divorce and remarriage to "this Sonia," the girl half his age who worked in the baths at Baille Herculanae where he had gone for a brief visit and remained for three years, in whose woods he had died while walking the trails he had come to know as intimately as the musical scores he'd mastered in his youth.

And the infant his mother had chastised my father for siring so late in his life?

"Eliezar's miracle child," she called me now, though she never knew the story of my pregnant mother's underwater survival all those hours the bombs fell on the spa.

"We came here after your father died," is what my mother told me whenever I asked her how we had wound up in Prague, hundreds of miles from my Orsova birthplace.

"By train?" I would say. "Or did we walk?" I knew stories about refugees trekking over Europe, all their possessions bundled on their backs. "Or did someone drive us?" I'd ask, imagining my mother and me chauffeured by an Allied general, probably a Frenchman, who'd loved my father's music and asked for the honor of rescuing Pearl's widow and infant from the ravages of war. "Or did we — ?"

And suddenly she would have fallen asleep, or bounded from the room to stir a stew about to burn, or realized she hadn't picked up foot salts at the chemist's when she'd done the marketing that morning. She never said, "I don't remember." She never said, "I can't talk about the past." She never forbade me the questioning I continued all through my childhood, imagining for myself the answers her silence protected, so that soon my asking was merely a pretext for beginning a story I'd invented myself about our journey to Prague, or my parents' courtship in Baille Herculanae, or my mother's life in the Danube Delta, which I only knew about because I found Dov Landau's notebooks one day in her bottom bureau drawer. I would hardly notice that my mother was gone, so engrossed would I become in my own emerging tale to which, it seemed, someone else was listening in rapt attention — someone else — though I was the only one in the room.

When I was four, my grandmother started losing her sight and by the time of my fifth birthday, the world passed before her in a milky cloud. She would stare at my father's photographs through magnifying glasses that rendered the images ten times larger than they were, but all she saw were amplified blurs, the same haze my face had become, no matter how near her gaze I stood. She navigated the apartment with a cane, and the comfort of familiar territory: this is where the umbrella stand is, here is the love seat, the piano is just beyond my toe. Outside, my mother steered Nanna by the arm, as if the older woman were a kind of motorized toy moved by her daughter-in-law's volition. And every morning Sonia massaged Nanna's temples and lids and fluttered her fingers in the weakening field of energy she felt above my grandmother's failing eyes, but other than relieving Nanna of the panic attacks with which she often woke as the cataracts thickened, my mother's treatments failed. Perhaps Dov Landau had turned himself into a pelican and spoken from the sky to his human child, and perhaps the pregnant Sonia had survived a night of bombing by holding her breath for hours in the spa's magical waters, and perhaps I was truly "the miracle child" Nanna called me, but we were not going to be able to add to this catalogue of wonders the curing of Nanna's blindness through the agency of my mother's "magic hands."

"I have heard of a surgeon," my grandmother said finally, "who has had a few successes with my condition."

"And when he isn't successful?" my mother said.

"Then I will be completely blind," Nanna said, and I watched her scan the room from one end to the other, as if she were imagining the loss of even these vague forms she could still decipher, this play of shadow and light whose dance she could still enjoy.

Like most adults, the women spoke in my presence as if I did not understand their words, or would not grasp the gravity of their exchange. Why do we persist in our belief that our children live outside the range of our trials, spared our traumas and vicissitudes, as if the truth were an illness like measles or smallpox against which they have been inoculated? The daughter we think is sleeping lies awake in her bed, listening to the curses her parents hurl at each other, the slamming of the door, the weeping, then the tender entreaties for forgiveness. The son engrossed in a jigsaw puzzle concentrates as well on his father's whispered endearments to the mistress he has phoned, or his mother's confession to her visiting friend that she has taken a lover herself. The feared eviction, the firing, the overnight looting of the family store: even the baby smells disaster fouling the household air like untended chops burning in the skillet.

Completely blind!

Didn't half the people on Kaprova Street swear my mother's treatments cured them of ailments that doctors claimed were hopeless or altogether non-existent, illnesses pills and tonics could not touch? If Sonia Pearl's powers did nothing for Nanna's sight, why would a mere surgeon be able to help? My hope faltered like a dimming faculty whose failure I was helpless to stop. For me, too, the world was darkening, Nanna's encroaching blindness a cruelty I could not understand, a fate I raged against on her behalf (as if ripping my pillow to shreds or shattering the fruit bowl or scrawling my name in black ink on the bathroom wall were exorcisms meant to scare away the demon who had cursed her eyes), a sorrow weeping only worsened those nights I cried alone in my room for what had befallen her, and me.

On the day of Nanna's appointment with Dr. Roth, I rode the trolley with the women through the city's broad boulevards. Pear trees flowered, and the tiny white petals of the weeping cherry blossoms cascaded like showers of snow through the balmy summer air. Like an excursion guide, my mother named for Nanna the structures we passed — Pinkas Synagogue, Bethlehem Chapel, Charles Bridge, Wallenstein Palace, Hradcany Castle, the towering spires of St. Vitus Cathedral — as if we were on a tour of Prague's architectural wonders instead of enroute to the surgeon to see if Nanna's vision could be saved. And Nanna joined the sham, offering historical anecdotes about the streets through which we travelled: how Mozart's Don Giovanni premiered in the Tyl Theater, how the Hapsburgs robbed the castle of innumerable treasures still hoarded in Vienna, how my father loved to visit the Loretto Shrine to listen to the carillon when he was a boy. The women's chatter confused me. Of the three of us, it seemed I was the only one aware of the gravity of our errand. As if they were strangers, I wanted to scream to my mother and Nanna, "Shut up! Don't you know my grandmother is going completely blind?" But I said nothing and soon we were disembarking, Nanna's recently-acquired cane tracing the steps she slowly descended.

On Karmelitska Street, we passed the beautiful gardens of Vrtba Zahrada, the perfumed air — geraniums, roses, peonies, verbena — too sweet, I thought, for this grim day. I rang the bell that summoned the elevator. First the solid steel door opened, then the grate, and we stepped inside the cubicle, so much like a cage, where a gnomish man in a uniform perched on a stool by the controls. The doors slammed shut. "Floor?" he said, and my mother said, "Three, please," and we ascended in the pulley-driven box. I rode an elevator every day in our apartment building, but this morning my stomach lurched as if I'd never made such a ride before. I was sure I would faint, or vomit, or fall down in a fit like our neighbor Mrs. Levy, whose convulsions I had witnessed just a week before when she had succumbed during afternoon tea with Nanna.

"Is Mrs. Levy always scared?" I'd asked my mother that night, who'd explained that the woman had no control over when a seizure would befall her.

"No, she has no memory of her fits. It's the one good thing about her illness," my mother said, perhaps nostalgic for her own amnesia.

"If Nanna goes blind, will she forget what I look like?"

My mother had drawn me to her. "You never forget the faces of people you love, Rachael. No matter what happens, you never forget their faces."

We entered a room more like a parlor than the waiting room it was: Oriental rugs, velvet wing chairs and brocade-upholstered couches, silk-shaded lamps upon whose porcelain bases hand-painted peacocks fanned their elegant tails. On one wall, a reproduction of Monet's "Water Lilies;" on another, a series of small framed oils, the same stately tree in each of the seasons. Such a visually-opulent room welcoming patients with eye afflictions may seem a paradox, but Nanna appeared to be reassured by the beauty my mother described to her, as if the tour had simply moved indoors. By the time the nurse guided Nanna from the sofa where we three sat, leaving between my mother and me the space of my grandmother's absence, even I had almost forgotten we were in a doctor's office, rather than guests whose host has gone to take a call or see how the cook is coming with dinner. The nurse in her white uniform — "Mrs. Pearl, the doctor will see you now." — reminded us of where we were, and why, and when the nurse spoke Nanna's name, I felt the smallest shock pass through my grandmother's body into mine.

Here is a larger shock: Simon Roth would, in fact, restore Nanna's sight in an operation scheduled for the following week, her recovery so complete he would use her case in lectures all over Europe. And in a book he wrote for other physicians about cataracts, an entire chapter was devoted to the surgery on Nanna's eyes. "For my favorite patient," he declared in his penned inscription to her, "a lovely lady I have been grateful to know and honored to help." The words made Nanna blush, though she would never know the full extent, or nature, of the brilliant doctor's gratitude.

After that first consultation, which lasted an hour, Dr. Roth himself brought Nanna back to us — she held his arm as she would have held my father's had he lived — and perhaps the little gasp I heard my mother make had something to do with the sight of Nanna supported by a man Eliezar's age (later she would learn that they'd gone to the same school as boys), one of those unpredictable reminders of her grief for which my mother could never prepare, from which she struggled to recover even as she suffered through the painful moment. Not until I was older myself, and had my own losses to survive, would I understand the energy such a process demanded of her, the enormous psychic resources upon which she had to draw. If my mother had allowed herself to weep each time her sorrow stirred, she would have spent the better part of her life in tears. When a person has suffered as much as Sonia Pearl — orphaned and widowed and twice a refugee at the age of twenty-four — what we call "strength" in such a woman is the strength to keep the anguish contained, much as the relics of that lost life were locked in my father's violin case: Dov's notebooks, Ovid's ring, Reba's coverlet and the letter Moses Silver had sent her from a place called Buenos Aires, halfway around the world.

So was it grief that made my mother gasp, or grief's cure, coming toward her in the form of Simon Roth, M.D.?

"Sonia Pearl," my mother said, offering her trembling hand to the handsome surgeon who, several months after Nanna's operation, on an outing with my mother to the Franzenbad spa, would murmur into the young widow's ear, "Your mother-in-law is not the only one who feels as if she is seeing everything for the very first time."

Until that moment, my mother had not acknowledged that she and Simon Roth were lovers. They had not yet been physically intimate. They had lunched together several times since their fateful encounter in his office, and he had sent her flowers once, and today — her twenty-fifth birthday — he had arranged this excursion, cancelling his appointments and telling his wife to go ahead and eat with the children, don't hold supper, he would be at the hospital well into the evening, perhaps he would even spend the night in doctors' quarters if his rounds took too long. In fact, he would take my mother to a suite he had reserved in the spa's fanciest hotel — had she returned to Baille Herculanae, my mother would wonder, its destruction a nightmare from which she was only now awakening? And later, in the satin-sheeted bed, Simon turned away from her in sleep so all she saw of him was the curve of his back, how could she tell that body from Eliezar's, whose name she'd almost murmured in the midst of making love to Simon?

At dawn, the moon still shining in a lavender sky, he would drive her to the nearby Nature Reserve — "Sonia, you have never seen anything like this, I promise you." — choirs of rare birds beginning their matins in the haven of marshland, moor, volcanic mud and thermal springs whose vast acreage the lovers entered on foot. It was neither night nor day, but that strange hour when the heavens remind us that the categories of time are human inventions to which the cosmos pays no heed. That morning, my mother was as much in the Delta of her girlhood as she was in this Bohemian paradise, and when she gasped at the sight of Reba and Ovid coming toward her on the path she and Simon were walking, he believed it was the beauty of the place over which she exclaimed, the tears that followed sweet evidence to him that the woman he loved was as moved by this wilderness as he was himself, the mysteries he witnessed here far beyond the range of his scientific training, yet true, he was sure, as all the medical books and biology texts and clinical journals in which his articles appeared.

Overcome, my mother rested on a moss-crusted boulder, Reba and Ovid behind her now, each of them resting a hand so lightly on her shoulders, she might have mistaken their touch for fern fronds or the branches of low-hanging willows wafting in the breeze, or the breeze itself, had not the gypsy whispered her name, had not her mother hummed a bar of the lullaby she'd sung to Sonia as a child.

"Are you all right?" Simon asked, kneeling before the widow, pale now from the power of this encounter. "We can turn back if — "

"Are there pelicans here?" my mother said, grabbing the doctor's hands with the fervor of a patient begging him for a miraculous cure. "Are there?"

"I don't think — "

But there was a white bird riding the mist that lifted now from the bog they faced, wings so luminous they might have been confused with sunlit clouds glowing in the brightening sky, had not the pelican spoken in mid-flight to his earth-bound witness, "Never forget that I love you, *maydele*," and Sonia answering, "I love you, too," and Simon, assuming the declaration meant for solely for him, showering my mother with grateful kisses for the words he had dreamed her saying a hundred times since meeting her, but which she had not uttered until now: oh yes, it was true, Franzenbad's Nature Reserve was a magical place, its powers beyond his ken, unfathomable, divine. Unlike Eliezar, unhappily married in a childless union, the surgeon knew he could never leave his family, that this love he shared with Sonia would always be clandestine, but this trip had sanctified the affair for him, their wilderness embrace a wedding he was certain God had blessed. "I love you, too," he had just heard her say, and what vow promised more?

Sonia Pearl would be Simon Roth's mistress for fifteen years, her life during that entire time as much a secret to me as her past — I would be grown when I discovered the romance — so that in many ways I never knew my mother at all, most of her real self hidden away, undisclosed, a mystery I have pieced together from scattered revelations — Dov's notebooks in her drawer, a letter from Simon that had fallen from her purse, the story she told me just before she died — clues that grow into these tales I write, these genealogical dreams, these family secrets I whisper to you every waking hour, Marcella, every sleepless night.

Does it disturb you to learn that your great-grandmother loved two men already married, Eliezar leaving his wife for her and

Simon taking as a mistress the violinist's widow, fifteen years spent hiding the truth from everyone they knew, adultery turning decent people into consummate liars, as skilled in deceit as confidence artists? Do not judge her harshly, this refugee from the Danube Delta. From the moment in her childhood she saw her father rise as a pelican from a lake of light, calling down his love to her before he vanished into the clouds, concealment became my mother's mode.

Her father's unbelievable transformation, the gypsy Ovid's disguise as a Jewish cobbler, the source of her healing powers, her clandestine romance with Eliezar Pearl, her survival in the waters of Baille Herculanae, her year of amnesia at the convent of the Church with the Moon, her love affair with Simon Roth: oh yes, my mother was in hiding long before we fled from the Nazis to the caves of Koneprusy, living like nomads in the underground grottoes, Prague become a dream to her, just like Tulcea, Baille Herculanae, Orsova and Oradea.

When she told me the story of Dov Landau's disappearance, entrusting to me on her death-bed a fragment of her past, relief so softened her features that she looked like a girl to me when she died. Decades of strain dropped from my mother's face, and she was as lovely as she must have been when my father met her in the Carpathian baths, although even during their brief time together he would see the veil of the past drop over her eyes, some dark loss robbing them of their brightness, her gaze turned inward as if the world before her had suddenly disappeared. How much it had cost her, I suddenly knew, to keep her secrets from me all those years. To be under the same roof as her daughter, yet miss her just the same! How many times did she begin to confide in me, rehearsing the way she would tell me the strange stories of her life only to lose her courage the moment she started to speak? How lonely she must have been! Although we would never live apart, still we were as distant from each other as if one of us had moved to a faraway city and left no forwarding address.

Before I knew that Dr. Roth had been my mother's lover for my entire girlhood, the flat he kept for their meetings as much a home to her as our apartment on Kaprova Street, before I hated him for the years I had been deceived and excluded and cheated, his presence in my mother's life depriving me of any chance for fathering (who might she have married, if not for him? who might have adopted me and raised me as his own?), before I blamed him for every unhappiness between my mother and me, I worshiped him.

He had given Nanna back her sight. Not even my mother had been able to heal my grandmother's stricken eyes, but in five hours of something called "surgery," this man had performed a miracle which others called "science," as if that term could make us all forget the mystery of what transpired in the operating room, the presence of grace that any cure implies. And Nanna loved him so, his "special patient" finding in the surgeon reminders of her slaughtered son, the boyhood schoolmates grown into geniuses whose gifts resided, like my mother's, in their hands.

"Like a member of our family," Nanna liked to say of Simon, never knowing how literal her tribute was.

It would take me months to forgive him for his romance with my mother, and longer still for me to forgive her, but once my rage had quieted, I remembered what he had given us as vividly as what he had stolen, and only then did he become human to me, neither paragon nor pirate, but a complicated man my father's age who had fallen in love with Sonia Pearl the moment he saw her in his waiting room on Karmelitska Street, Prague, 1923.

"Your mother-in-law is not the only one who feels as if she is seeing for the very first time," he would tell the younger widow, and who chooses blindness over sight, who returns to the dark once the radiance arrives?

Here on the verandah where I write today, the flagstones strewn with lilac petals last night's rainstorm flung across the yard, I wait for the story in which the lovers enter their flat on Mozartova Street. First Sonia Pearl, then Simon Roth an hour later, my mother wearing by then her new gown, yellow chiffon with satin-covered clasps. On a table, a vase full of lilacs, two glasses of wine and a platter of cheeses to eat with the bread he has brought. Beyond those few details, this page is blank, my pen poised in wordless air for hours. This is a tale whose scenes you will have to imagine, Marcella, or from which you will choose to turn away, as I do now, closing my notebook like a door I am not meant to enter, or a shade my mother forgot to pull down.

12

THE FIRST THING NANNA did when she came home from the hospital was to pull up all the shades in our apartment on Kaprova Street.

"Your eyes are still sensitive," my mother said. "Too much light can — "

"Too much light?" Nanna was turning on all the lamps in our sun-drenched flat. "My darling Sonia, please believe me, there is no such thing as too much light."

In my grandmother's bedroom, I was unpacking her suitcase for her, and each time I placed an item in its proper drawer or dressing table or chintz-draped nightstand, I was a child winning a carnival toss, the flung ball landing in the right ring every time, the festive bells announcing my unbelievably fortunate streak. My mother made Nanna climb into bed, and I snuggled beside her, her home-coming my grand prize, her recovery worthy of a celebration that lasted for days.

"How many fingers do you see?" and "How many now?" and "Am I smiling?" and "How many freckles on my nose?" and "What color are my socks?" and "Can you read the time on the clock?"

She won that game, and a dozen more, and finally I was truly convinced that Nanna could see everything, especially me, her gaze like a sun in whose light I had thrived, and in whose dwindling fac-ulty I, myself, had seemed to disappear. Marcella, from the day your mother was born, my greatest joy was looking at her, watching for hours my daughter's unfolding just as Nanna had watched my own. If the first miracle of my life was my pregnant mother's underwater survival, the second was surely Nanna's unexpected devotion to the baby she once had chastised my middle-aged father for seeding. My mother loved me, but it was hard for her to concentrate on anything I did: other voices seemed always to summon her attention, her eyes turning from me as if to invisible faces more real to her than my own. But I was always my grandmother's priority; even when her sight was failing, she saw me wholly with her heart. What child can bloom without that loving attention? What life flowers without a witness to that blossoming?

Some nights I cannot sleep, Marcella, wondering if anyone's eyes have rested on you all these years of my futile search. Oh Granddaughter, even though I have never seen you, do you know that I have gazed on your beautiful face every day since I learned of your birth in a Buenos Aires prison, conjuring in my heart your tiny perfection, watching you as Nanna watched me, studying your smallest gestures as if you were right before me, as if it were not thin air I still regard for hours at a time?

After they took our Miriam, after we learned that you had survived, yet all of our efforts to locate you had failed, my husband Jacobo would say to me, "Rachael, please, don't drift off," as if I were floating away in space or wandering like a vagrant through the streets of the city. "I can't reach you anymore."

But I was right here with you, Marcella, the two of us cuddled together in this very chair, as I used to cuddle with Nanna in Prague, you falling asleep on my lap as your *abuela* watched your breath — "The baby is alive, Jacobo!" — rising and falling, rising and falling, rising and falling.

My girlhood was bracketed by wars, though I did not know that the violence into which I was born would return again in unspeakable ways by the time I turned twenty. Who could have imagined Hitler those peaceful years in Prague? In the household of women in which I grew up, no one raised her voice. If my mother seemed abstracted, still she was the gentlest person I would ever know, her temper spent long ago in her fights with Reba, her anger subsumed by a sorrow that softened over the years into a kindly bearing on which everyone remarked.

"To have gone through so much, you would think it would have hardened her."

"Such a lovely woman, in spite of everything."

And Nanna's bitterness had dissolved in her grief like a tarnished coin dropped into acid: not a trace of her rage remained. Even as her sight failed, she faced blindness with an equanimity I did not understand, wishing she would curse the fate she was prepared to accept. I have never forgotten the level tone with which she answered my mother's question:

"What will happen if the operation isn't successful?"

"Then I will be completely blind," she said, as if she were announcing a possible head cold, or bad weather coming on.

Never an argument, never a slammed door, never a hand raised in sudden fury. Except for the months before Nanna's surgery, when I vented on pillows and plates my pain at her condition. I lived in calm repose, my father's beautiful recordings playing in the background like a constant reward for the good behavior of those who had survived him.

When I would tell Jacobo about my life in Prague, how I could not remember a single fight in twenty years, that we had lived together then in an undisturbed harmony for which I longed, he would smile a little and nod and then he would ask me the kind of question I imagine he posed to his patients — their childhoods, too, far behind them, their memories faded photographs he helped them restore, details blurred by time suddenly vivid again, the whole composition altered, the images not what they had seemed.

"Tell me," he'd say, "those headaches you used to get as a girl. What brought them on, do you think?"

"Oh, Jacobo, how do I know? I — "

"And all those mornings you threw up your breakfast?"

"I was a delicate child. I was easily upset."

"Upset? I thought you never were upset. I thought — "

"I mean my stomach was — "

"Ah, but you didn't say 'my stomach.' You said 'I.' 'I was easily upset,' is what you said."

"I don't need this, Jacobo. I don't need this kind of — "

"You have lived in a fantasy all your life, Rachael. It is time to see what's in front your own eyes."

Miriam was still a child then, and Argentina's "Dirty War" still as inconceivable as the Third Reich had been forty years before, but sometimes I think my husband had a premonition of what was yet to befall us, and feared I could not endure it, this future round of catastrophe, these tragedies still to come. Perhaps he was right. I might have gone insane, I might have thought myself a lizard who could live without water in the Chaco's fierce heat or a penguin able to survive a plunge into the glacial depths of Lago Argentino, yes, I might have vanished as Dov Landau did, the day he abandoned his pelican's nest for the Delta's shining lake, yes, once I had the evidence that Miriam was dead and all our efforts to find you had been exhausted and Jacobo would not survive the heart attack that felled him one morning as he prepared to shave (I wiped the lather from his blue face while I waited for the ambulance) and my mother would die six months later, leaving me completely alone in this ghost-ridden house, yes, I might have wandered out of the door one midnight and never returned, had not these tales chosen me as scribe, Marcella, had not they saved me just at the very moment I, too, might have disappeared.

13

SOMETIMES — FOR THE MUSIC, she said, because we were not religious Jews — I went with Nanna to Friday night services in the Maisel Synagogue, a gothic wonder whose ornate ceiling I loved to study from the balcony where the women sat, images from Genesis arrayed above us like a second world of which, I knew, the men beneath us had not an inkling, however privileged their position on the sanctuary floor was supposed to be. Let the Rabbi remove from the sacred ark and carry through the aisles the Torah those below us could kiss, or touch with the fringed edge of their prayer shawls. What were words on parchment compared to the sculpted paradise I tilted my head to enter, Eden emerging out of the void, the Garden flowering, the Serpent lurking behind a twisted tree in which innocent birds still sang?

I remember a fifth-grade field trip, all my classmates Christian girls with whom I felt entirely comfortable, religious differences negligible to me who wrote "Czech" on school forms requesting "nationality," though years later I would learn "Czech" had been crossed out on mine, "Jew" printed there instead, in red ink, by the gymnasium's principal herself.

That earlier day, we were going to Hradcany, the castle district. Mounting the steps of the sight-seeing trolley, in our starched white

blouses and grey plaid jumpers, we looked like twenty young pelicans in giddy escape from the Prague Zoo. I sat beside Maria
Svoboda, a Catholic girl whose long yellow braids I coveted,
though she complained that having her hair brushed was a torture
she would gladly live without. Once, on a visit to her house, she had
come close to cutting off the plaits at the nape of her neck, but I
had imagined grave consequences and pleaded with her to recon-
sider. My hair was straight and dark, and so fine the braids I fashioned looked like skinny worms always sliding out of the barrettes
with which I fastened them. If Maria was going to chop off her
thick yellow locks, I did not want to be a witness to that mutila-
tion. Did I foresee the forced head-shaving of millions of Jewish
girls like me? I screamed at Maria, her scissors poised in her ready
hand, "Something terrible will happen to you!" and though the
clairvoyant insight was a muddled one — Maria's father, a Slovakian
native, had long been a member of the Slovak People's Party whose
leader would gush to Hitler, "My Fuhrer, I lay the destiny of my
people in your hands!" — the horror that gripped me that afternoon would stay with me for days, piles of human hair in all my
troubled dreams.

"Do you go to Jewish church?" Maria said, a tinge of challenge
in her voice.

We were climbing the steps of St. Vitus Cathedral, where she
came with her parents for Sunday mass.

"Sometimes I do," I said. "My Nanna takes me."

She stared at me, as if I looked strange to her, and then we
passed through the massive wooden doors.

Inside Wenceslas Chapel, our teacher was describing the four-
teenth-century frescoes, the stained-glass windows through which
Prague's sunlight poured. Maria crossed herself, curtsied to the life-
size Christ crucified above the altar where she had been baptized.

Then she turned to me again, suddenly angry. "My father says that you — "

How could a man I had never met know a thing about me?

"That I what?" I said, but our teacher was leading us from the sanctuary to the chamber in which the Bohemian crown jewels were on public display. Dazzled by the treasures there, Maria seemed to forget her outburst, I was happy her dark mood had passed, but after that day our friendship cooled and though I never asked her again, I would wonder for years what it was her father had said about me, and what it had to do with "Jewish church," why she had believed him instead of taking my side, and and by 1938 I would understand it all too well.

Nanna had cousins in Lidice, and one Sunday afternoon the three of us took the train from Prague to visit them. From the window, I waved to weekend mushroom-pickers filling their baskets in the wooded countryside and farther on, I watched for deer running through the forests from which the muted explosions of gunshot sounded over the engine's noise, sometimes a flash of light deep in the trees accompanying the rifle's report.

Saul and Belva met us at the station. They were Nanna's age, but looked much older, their lives harder than their city relation who had married a piano teacher from Prague, whose son had become a famous violinist sharing his wealth with his parents. For years, the Lidice cousins had envied my grandmother, seeing her rarely, blaming on her the estrangement she insisted they alone had contrived. After the news of my father's death reached them, they paid a condolence call, followed by visits once or twice a year, but this was the first time in twelve years we had been invited to their home.

The cousins looked alike, short and plump, Saul in the overalls he'd worn all his years as a miner, Belva in a housedress faded from washings in the metal tub they used for baths, still heating water on the wood-burning stove. I gave Saul a hug, and he coughed, a deep rumble in his chest that seemed to mimic the sound of the cave-in from which he was still recovering: I felt the back-brace he wore through his clothes. Belva gave us quick pecks on the cheek, nervously smoothing her skirt after each kiss, as if afraid she was not presentable enough for well-to-do relatives from Prague.

But once we reached the cousins' three-room house in the car they'd borrowed from a neighbor to fetch us from the station, Belva relaxed and Saul, suddenly festive, brought up from the cellar a dust-crusted accordion and played for us the songs of his youth, his singing punctuated by the ominous cough he seemed hardly to notice now, though I found the spasms alarming.

While Saul serenaded us, Belva set lunch out on the wooden kitchen table: pickled herring, sliced tomatoes from the small garden outside, bread still warm from the oven and a wonderful noodle pudding laced with apples and sour cream.

Nanna said, "Belva, the kugel is just like your mother made!" and that began an hour of reminiscences, each woman softening toward the other as the memories collected, and by the end of our meal, they were holding hands and wiping tears from one another's cheeks.

I listened, spellbound. I was so hungry in my childhood for stories of the past, but my mother would tell me nothing, and Nanna memories all revolved around my father, as if his birth had been so central to her life, it had crowded out events which had preceded it, collapsed into a few dismissive sentences ("We were poor people. My brother died from typhus when he was four or five. My mother never really recovered from that.") the years I now could see were teeming with experience, happy as well as sad. Nanna's and

Belva's mothers had been sisters, and the cousins had grown up together not in Lidice, but further out in the countryside, in the village of Zvon, Nanna's father a tailor and Belva's a blacksmith.

"In many ways," Belva said, "Zvon was a paradise."

Nanna smiled. "More than I remembered, if you want to know the truth. More than I recalled."

My mother, Sonia, had been very quiet while the older women had reminisced. She had focussed on her meal as if the tasks of eating — cutting her food, spearing each bite with a fork, bringing the fork to her mouth, chewing, swallowing — demanded all her concentration. Once she began to giggle at a silly anecdote Belva was relating, then cut off her laughter so abruptly, I thought for a moment she had choked on a piece of bread. Even the memories of others were dangerous to my mother, pretending indifference about a past so strangely alive for her, she dared not share it with a soul.

That day I thought: When I grow up, I'll tell my children and my grandchildren everything I remember. I won't leave out a single thing that happened to me. Maybe I'll write a book someday, just for them, and I'll call it "Stories From My Life."

"Rachael," Saul said, "in Prague you probably don't keep chickens, do you?"

"No," I said, and he whisked me out the back door to the pen where a dozen birds waited for the seed I threw them, that day in Lidice, that paradise, that grimy doomed town where twelve years later our cousins would perish along with all of their neighbors, every structure in the village razed to the ground, the slaughter there a Nazi reprisal in which a commandant was supposed to have said, "No one will remember Lidice. It will vanish from the face of the earth."

The hubris of murderers in uniform.

As if anyone can murder memory.

As if anyone can kill the past.

Always, always, the bodies wash up on the shore, or a farmer's plow unearths the bones buried in a mass grave, or a witness comes forth with evidence — "I shared a cell with your daughter Miriam. The day before they killed her, she gave birth to a baby girl."

I learned I was pregnant on the same day that Hitler declared Bohemia and Moravia a part of the Third Reich.

March 16, 1939.

I was twenty-one years old, a student at the Prague Institute of Art and Design, in love with a classmate who lived in a single room on Jindrisska Street, two doors from the house where Rilke had been born. The room always smelled of paint and turpentine, even with the window cracked, and I used to joke to him they'd find us dead one morning from the fumes. Although I still resided with my mother and grandmother on the other side of the city, several times a week I spent the night with Felix, telling my family I was staying with my girlfriend, Ruth, who lived near our school. I never doubted the women knew where I really was and many times I almost dropped the pretext, Felix's name on my tongue, but something kept me from candor and I would summon Ruth again for my cover story.

"Why don't you tell them the truth?" Felix would fume. He was wiry and dark, his black eyes burning. His paintings looked like explosions, whole worlds bursting apart, shards of color spewed across the canvass. "You're an adult, aren't you? You have a right to live your life as you choose. Tell them you don't believe in marriage or God or the bourgeoisie. Damn it, Rachael, you're an artist, you believe in freedom over everything, but you turn into a little girl whenever you talk to your family. What makes you think they'd be so scandalized anyhow? They're modern women, after all, and who knows that they don't have lovers of their own? After all, your mother was a young woman when — "

And I would slam out of his room, catching a tram for the Convent of Blessed Angels, that ancient cloister turned into a museum I said I visited so often to study the fine collection of nineteenth century painting there, but actually it was not the exhibits for which I went. That former nunnery felt more familiar to me than any building I had ever entered, and wandering the rooms once home five hundred years before to Catholic sisters, wimpled and robed, I believed I must have dwelled among them, centuries past. Was my comfort in these stone-walled chambers a memory in which I sought solace when my life in Prague grew too confusing for me to understand? Was the young Jewish woman once a nun in a prior incarnation, my soul nostalgic for that ordered existence hidden away from an unredeemed world?

March 16, 1939.

"Bastards," Felix muttered. "Fascist swine."

On his radio, we had just heard Hitler declare that Bohemia and Moravia were now "protectorates" of the Third Reich, and that night Nanna would return from a meeting of the Jewish Community Council, rumors of massive deportations confirmed. "The Gestapo wants 120,000 Czech Jews immediately — either they buy their way out, or the Germans will send three hundred men a day to Dachau," my grandmother would tell my mother and me. Then her voice would break: "So now it begins for us, my darlings. So now it begins for us."

"Felix," I said, Hitler's radio speech not yet as real to me as the news I'd received that morning at the doctor's office. I stroked

Felix's stiffened back. "I have something wonderful to tell you."

He looked at me as if I were mad. "Didn't you just hear — "

"About myself," I said. I took his paint-encrusted hand and placed it on my belly. "About. . .our baby."

Although his skin was dark as a gypsy's, Felix turned white. For a moment, he could not speak, and I thought he was succumbing at last to the fumes to which he was so accustomed, he said he never noticed the smell. I threw the window open, although it was raining outside.

Finally he said, "Rachael, you cannot have a baby now."

I turned to him. "We don't have to get married, Felix. Really. You're right about marriage, it's — "

He covered his face with his hands. "Didn't you hear the radio? Don't you know what it means?"

"I'm talking about a baby," I said.

"No," Felix said, searching the room for cigarettes. "You're talking about a Jewish baby. If you'd found out you had leprosy today, the news could not have been more terrible."

"We'll go to America, then."

"What 'we' are you talking about? You don't even tell your family you spend a night with me, that you sleep with me in my bed, but now there's a baby, so suddenly you're willing to shock them? That's the 'we' you mean, isn't it, you and your baby? Fine, go to America, take your mother and grandmother with you."

"Felix, I could never leave you behind."

From under his bed, he pulled a wooden crate. He pried it open. The box was filled with bullets, dozens of them. He ran his fingers through the ammunition.

"I'm joining the Resistance, Rachael. In a week I would have disappeared from Prague without a single word to anyone." He hammered shut the crate. "You go to America if you want. But if they want to be rid of me, they'll have to find me first." He put his arms around me, but his eyes were hard as bullets themselves. "They'll have to kill me, the rotten fascist pigs."

14

THAT NIGHT NANNA delivered to my mother and me the news Felix had already intuited: it was time to flee.

My mother rose from the brocade wing chair, and the afghan she was knitting dropped to the floor in a tangle of needles and yarn. On her face, I saw a sad smile, the kind of expression one sees on people at a concert hall when the first strains of a requiem sound: it was as if she were hearing again a wrenching piece of music she knew by heart. In funereal trance, she walked to her room. Nanna, worried, motioned me to follow her. I stood in the doorway, though it seemed to me my mother was unaware of my presence. She carried her tufted vanity bench to the closet, stood on the seat to reach my father's violin case hidden behind hatboxes and a carton of embroidery thread. She lay the leather case on her bed and snapped open the latch. I expected a violin to be inside, but of course there was none, that instrument turned to splinters twenty years before. She noticed me then, and fear flashed in her eyes, as if I had caught her with contraband goods, or in the act of stealing what was not hers. If I had still been a child, I would have insisted she explain to me the meaning of the objects she lifted from the case, studied for a moment, and then returned to that velvet-lined chamber that had been my first cradle. But I was twenty now and knew the language of my mother's eyes as well as I knew Czech and Yiddish. I had read the plea for silence in that frightened glance and given my assent: I would ask her nothing.

Whose opal ring glinted in her palm?

What bed had the coverlet warmed, each crocheted square a single flower, petal knotted to petal, stem to stem?

And Dov Landau's notebooks: years before I had found the volumes she'd accidentally left on her nightstand, and I had examined the books rapidly, not sure when my mother would return from her errands to find me, like a burglar, in her room. Often, when my mother was away, I would enter her chamber for no purpose other than to be in the presence of her secrets, as if by standing in the room where she slept, her dreams might reveal themselves to me, her memories might rise from the bed like a flock of birds hidden under the sheets. But Sonia Pearl's past remained safe from my vigils, and in fact I was relieved that my intrusions, however benign — no rifled drawers, no searched pockets — failed to violate the privacy I resented, yet knew I must honor. I had opened Dov's journals as guiltily as if they were my mother's own diaries, marvelled at the drawings of various Delta birds — in flight, at rest, singly and in flocks crossing a vast paper sky. How intricate the cross-section of a heron's wing! How elaborate the layers of a pelican's nest! I bought my first sketchbook that day, and found in my own hands my grandfather's gift, discovered in my own eye his power to see. For weeks, I drew the pigeons that congregated at the entrance of the Old Jewish Cemetery, and then one day I entered that ancient burial ground whose ghosts my father's music had soothed, and I spent hours sketching the tombstones, each crumbling marker saved from further erosion in the renderings I made. What had moved Dov Landau to make his record of Delta birds? Why did my mother keep his wonderful notebooks hidden away, as if they contained some coded intelligence she had sworn to protect from anyone's eyes but her own?

Now, from between the pages of one of my grandfather's volumes, my mother removed a yellowed envelope. Whose letter had she hidden there? It had been a year since I had found the one from Dr. Roth that had fallen out of her bathrobe pocket — "My darling Sonia," it had begun, and by the time I reached, "Your loving Simon," I had more knowledge than I wanted, more truth about my mother's life than I thought I could bear. Was she holding another letter from her lover? She studied its stamp, ran her finger over it as if reading some vibration the stamp emitted. I could tell from my mother's expression that this was no letter from Simon — she examined the address on the envelope as an archaeologist might peruse unearthed hieroglyphs, markings from another time, a message from a stranger. She took out the page on which Moses Silver had written Reba Landau so long ago from Argentina, and I saw my mother tremble in the presence of the words she mouthed in silence. Then she lifted her eyes and looked at me for a long while. "Pack your things, Rachael. We are going to a place called Bu-e-nos Ai-res. It's far, very far, but at least we can be certain there are no Nazis there."

We left Prague as paupers. Every penny my father had left us paid to the Germans for exit visas, every stick of furniture in our apartment sold to Gentiles thrilled to possess a needlepoint chair, a cherry table, a porcelain vase from the flat where the famous Eliezar Pearl had spent his youth. In one steamer trunk, Nanna packed what remained of our household: clothing, bed linens, towels, her own mother's silverware, a few photographs of my father and a cast iron skillet.

I looked one last time from my favorite window to the cemetery and concert hall below. It was early morning, the sky like the luminous rice paper on which I painted my watercolor landscapes, vistas disappearing even as I fixed them to the page, solid buildings transparent as air, cobblestoned streets shimmering like rivers, trees turned to rising smoke. Goodbye to the twelve-thousand Jewish ghosts. Goodbye to the roof of the House of Artists, my father's music rising like mist from the red tiles, from the opened mouths of the gargoyles just below the eaves.

Kaprova Street, goodbye,

In the kitchen, my mother was weeping. I put my arms around her, and she shuddered against me. Oh Mama, have you said goodbye to Simon Roth and closed up the flat on Mozartova Street and licked the tears from each other's cheeks as Felix and I did last night in his room, the crate of bullets under the bed where we made love for the last time, no matter what we promised ourselves these final hours in Prague, his face buried in my belly, his words to the baby I carried — "Be good to your mother and know that I love you!" — inscribed like tattoos on my flesh?

Kaprova Street, goodbye.

In each empty room, Nanna swept the wooden floors and wiped from sills the tracing of dust in which I used to write my name as a girl. In a month, all the Jews in the provinces would be herded into Prague, and seven families would crowd into our six rooms until the deportations to Poland began, but Nanna cleaned our vacant flat "for the new family," she said, as if normalcy still existed, as if our sudden exodus was a move we had planned for years, this trip a migration we had dreamed about instead of the nightmare it truly was.

"Why are you going to Argentina?" a neighbor asked. "Do you have people there?"

"Oh yes," my mother said. We were waiting for the taxi that would take us to the train station where she had arrived from Rumania with her infant twenty years before, the rest of her family lost in the Jassy pogrom and the "minor skirmish" of Baille Herculanae. "All my relations live in Buenos Aires."

Nanna and I exchanged a glance over my mother's head, the two of us agreeing in silence to leave the sad lie unchallenged. Who could blame Sonia Landau Pearl for a fib in which she invented loved ones waiting for us in that distant country to which we were headed, a faded letter from a stranger our only connection to the port into which we would sail from Lisbon, our life on Kaprova Street vanished forever?

On the train from Prague to Lisbon, I threw up twice. "It's normal to be nervous at a time like this," Nanna consoled, and my mother massaged my stomach still. All my queasiness seemed to move from my body into her fingers, and I wondered if she could tell from touching me that I was pregnant. If she knew, she kept my secret. I would tell her and Nanna both when we reached Buenos Aires, I had decided, morning sickness easy to call seasickness instead on a three-week ocean voyage: who would be surprised at anyone's illness during such a journey, hundreds of us jammed onto a decrepit boat meant for livestock, our food going bad in unseasonal heat, children crying for home and the world turned to brackish water it seemed would go on forever, the solid world lost to us, the earth as we had known it gone for good? Not even at a funeral had I ever seen so many people weeping openly, their tears like tiny samples of the endless ocean on which our frail vessel floated. At night we all descended to steerage where sleep became a public ordeal, moans and curses and nightmare screams rending the acrid darkness for hours, voices and bodies so entangled it seemed we turned into a single suffering nocturnal creature who only at dawn divided again into the separate beings we actually were. Each dawn I climbed the metal ladder to the brine-crusted deck. Behind the clouds that stretched before me like snow-covered celestial Alps, the sunlight burned through each glacial ridge, the sky a giant sea of shining water now, the ocean mirroring that heavenly splendor, the radiance that greeted me so much like the Delta light my mother would describe to me, years later, when she told me the story of Dov Landau's disappearance. No matter how bad the night had been, that first glimpse of the morning exulted me, and I forgot each day what I would soon remember, that we were all penniless refugees, Jews on a freighter bound for Argentina, a world away from the homes we had been forced to flee. By the time my feet were on the deck, I remembered as well my own particular condition, the first waves of morning sickness rising like a portion of the sea I'd swallowed and, leaning over the rail, retched back to the water below.

As you read these words, Marcella, you may imagine that it was your mother I carried within me, a tiny fetus afloat in her own private ocean calm even as the Atlantic roiled, those three weeks of havoc and fear the same peaceful span of time in which your mother's fingers formed, or toes, or heart, her gestation undisturbed by the conditions of our flight from Prague. But no: it was not Miriam I sheltered then, and Felix Levin — "A Jewish baby. If you'd found out you'd had leprosy today, the news could not have been more terrible." — not your grandfather. Felix Levin, my first love: in three months he would die in the Polish forest outside Lodz.

Fifteen hours from Buenos Aires, as I stood in a line for the drinking water poured three times a day into our tin cups, I doubled over in pain so fierce I nearly fainted, the deck shifting under my shoes, the sun's light dimming for a moment in a spasm of wintry darkness that left me cold in the noon's heat. The second pain felled me, and though the strangers at whose feet I landed poured their precious water over my face, and my mother and grandmother raced from the other side of the ship to the spot where I lay writhing, and a man who screamed, "I'm a doctor! Let me through!" took my wrist between his fingers to check for my pulse, nothing could staunch the blood in which the son I would have named Eliezar, after my father, swam from my womb to the world in which he could not live.

My mother, Sonia, cradled my head in her arms, crooned, "Rachael, Rachael, why didn't you tell me?" as if it were a lullaby and I was a child again, not a twenty-year-old unmarried woman who had just had a miscarriage on the lower deck of a Portuguese freighter filled with cargo — two-hundred-and-fifty-four Jewish human beings from Prague — about to be turned back, like rotten fruit, from the Argentinian port to which the ship had been sailing now for five-hundred hours on the open sea.

15

IN EVERY LANGUAGE, the reasons are always the same:

Your passport has expired.

Your visa is invalid.

Your birth certificate appears to be forged.

You have not passed our medical examination.

Your work permit is not in order.

Your name is on our list.

Your name is not on our list.

You have not passed our medical examination.

We have filled our quota for aliens this year.

Additional payments are required.

Entry denied.

Entry denied.

Entry denied.

Oh, Marcella, when our boat turned around in the harbor where we had not been allowed to disembark, a wail went up from the passengers, a heartbroken cry, a moan of such anguish, its vibration must have rattled all the windows in Buenos Aires, shaken the streets from which we had been barred, dimmed for an instant every lamp and sent its residents running for shelter from the quake or tornado or unseasonal tropical storm come to the city this chilly April afternoon, most people still eating their leisurely mid-day meal when the tremors moved from the tenements of La Boca along the River Plate past the Plaza de Mayo to the elegant boulevards of La Recoleta, through the beautiful Palermo gardens, and on to the Parana Delta, orange trees there dropping their unripened fruit into the water below.

Do I have to continue the tale of our journey?

Do I have to tell you about the five passengers who chose to jump off the rail into the Atlantic, rather than return to the deaths the Nazis had in mind for Jews?

Do I have to describe the times others among us broke down on the deck or in the holds below, intelligent adults babbling incoherently or pounding the floor with their fists until their knuckles were bloody?

Do I have to remember the so-called representatives of the German travel agency who met our boat in Lisbon as if we were tourists just back from a pleasure cruise, and how these "travel agents" took us to the train that returned, like a funeral cortege, to Prague where, it was explained, we would have fifteen days to make "proper arrangements" for a second departure, though now we were penniless and could not buy, again, the necessary visas and steamship tickets, did not even have places to stay for the two weeks granted us before a "transfer for those of you still here," to a labor camp in the town of Sered, where, we were assured, with just a touch of malice, "there will be no difficulty when you arrive, none whatsover, no one will turn you away from Sered."?

"Lidice," Nanna whispered to my mother, who passed the same message to me.

Just blocks from our old apartment on Kaprova Street, we were spending the night in the synagogue turned into a makeshift shelter for the now-homeless passengers of our failed voyage to Argentina. From my cot, I stared up at the domed ceiling whose mural I'd loved those Sabbaths I'd sat with Nanna in the women's balcony, just beneath the curved panels on which the world was born out of swirling chaos, Paradise a lush garden through whose glades a hundred animals wandered unharmed and whole flocks of birds wheeled for the first time in the now-illumined sky. Beneath a flowering tree, Adam and Eve embraced. How many days until their banishment? How much time until Eden was a memory too painful to summon, their children saying, "Tell us some tales about when you were young," but neither of the adults able to remember anything, only fierce longing where the stories should have been, only silence when they opened their mouths to speak.

In the morning Nanna died.

Actually, she had died in her sleep, there on the synagogue floor, the steamer trunk beside her like a coffin awaiting her death all the weeks it had travelled with her, to Buenos Aires and back again to Prague, and now — but who knew where we would finally end up, who knew when this wandering would cease?

Did I scream?

Did my mother?

Did the rabbi rush to my grandmother's side, or one of the doctors who had been on the boat with us, or the symphony cellist who remembered my father's appearances with the orchestra decades past?

I remember nothing from the moment Nanna would not stir — only that her shoulder was stiff as stone when I touched it, and her face a motionless mask of sleep — to the day I arrived in Lidice with my mother, the steamer trunk left behind, our only possessions the clothing we wore and the violin case my mother clutched like a second child.

Did we have a funeral for Nanna?

Where is she buried?

Only fierce longing, Marcella, where the story should be. Only silence when I try to speak.

16

IN A TRUCKLOAD OF LANTERNS being delivered to miners in Lidice, I hid with my mother under the canvas tarp. Once the driver's arthritic wife had come to Sonia Pearl for a treatment — "I cannot afford to pay you much, but if ever you need a favor in return, some mending perhaps, or a dress I could make for your daughter, I would be so happy to oblige you." — and now my mother remembered how the woman's husband often took his truck to the town where our cousins lived, our only relations not in Buenos Aires at all, but an hour from Prague in the village toward which we rode.

Under the tarp, it was hard to breathe. The canvas was fastened tightly over its cargo, and fumes from the truck's engine sickened us as well, but I had spotted a small hole in the fabric beneath which we hid, and my mother and I took turns inhaling the spring air through that opening. Once we passed a honeysuckle shrub along the road we travelled, that perfume like all of Vrtba Gardens blooming for us in our hiding place. My mother wept when she smelled the fragrance, perhaps remembering the bouquets Simon Roth used to bring to the flat where they had met in secret for so many years, or the vases of fresh flowers Nanna had always kept on the lace-covered dining room table. Or maybe the aroma itself was enough to move Sonia to tears, a reminder of beauty in a world that had turned so bleak.

Saul and Belva's house was boarded up, abandoned, "Yids" scrawled over the front door. Only years later, once we had made our second journey to Argentina and settled finally into the house I live in now alone, would my mother learn that her cousins had hidden for three years in a neighbor's root cellar, the earthen room not even high enough to allow them to stand. Perhaps they would have survived the entire war in that underground burrow, had not the Nazis extracted their terrible revenge on the entire town, every single person murdered there or sent to camps, every building burned.

Why had we imagined our cousins' lives were still intact, as if their village had escaped the Gestapo's reach, the Jews who lived there somehow safe? "Lidice," Nanna had whispered to my mother on the train that returned us to Prague. "Lidice," my mother had whispered to me, the name like an oath we had all three taken, or a mantra sure to keep us from harm. But who would shelter two Jewish women escaping from the city in a truck full of lanterns, both of us grimy as miners ourselves? When we'd arrived at our destination, and clambered from the vehicle after the driver shook the tarp in signal that it was safe for us to disembark, he had given us one of the lamps, "in case you need it," he'd muttered, thrusting the gift at my mother with one hand and motioning us away from his truck with the other.

Now that our cousins had disappeared, where could we go except to the forest on the edge of the town? I remember the way we paused at the border between paved road and unmarked path, how we seemed unable to move another step, how finally we turned our back on the village and stepped together into the dark woods. For days we wandered that wilderness, eating berries and drinking from rock-bottomed streams, sleeping in the hollow of a rotting elm's trunk. How fast we learned to climb the birches when we thought we heard someone approaching, our legs wrapped around the swaying limbs whose leafy reaches shielded us, but never once did anyone appear, partisan or troop, and what we thought were shots were always natural noises — a tree branch breaking, a boulder loosed from its hillside, our own hearts beating so loudly we mistook that pulsation for some external explosion. Fear is its own assault, and the fleeing refugee is captured a thousand times before any soldier orders "Halt!" and fires his rifle into the air.

"Caves!" my mother said, as if she had just discovered gold along the Berounka River, whose shore we'd followed for hours now, though we could not have said to where, any destination perilous, only this wooded labyrinth safe for two hunted women whose train had left days before for the labor camp in Sered, the Gestapo agent screaming "Sonia Pearl!" and "Rachael Pearl!" to the silent crowd at the station in Prague, vowing "We will find them!" when it was clear we had fled.

A small wooden sign marked the entrance to the underground grottoes. We descended into darkness, and my mother struck a match from the box the truck driver had given her along with the lantern I had tied to my waist with a thick vine. I unknotted the makeshift belt and tilted the lamp toward her: when the flame caught the kerosene-soaked wick, the black cave turned scarlet, the walls of the chamber we entered seemed to pulse blood. In that glowing stone womb, we rested as if for the very first time, our sleep much like an unborn child must experience before she knows the world beyond exists, or suffers through that first expulsion we call "birth" and celebrate in order to keep our grief for home at bay.

I am not sure how long we lived in the caves. Days, perhaps, or weeks. Maybe a month went by before we were found. Without the sun, we had no way to gauge the hours as they passed, and soon time became irrelevant, a habit from another life we had no need of here, in these throbbing stone rooms, these moist tunnels, these narrow pillared alcoves in which we hid. Along the river, we'd found raspberries we'd filled our pockets with, and two dead geese my mother hoisted to her shoulders: we cooked the fowl in the cave, over the lantern's tiny flame. In one of the tunnels, we found a pool for bathing and drinking. Because our appetites had shrunken so, the food we had lasted our entire stay, one bite of goose meat and a few berries all we needed for hours at a time. I think we had learned how to live on air by the time we were found; I think we had learned a kind of alchemy during our underground hibernation.

And what did we talk about, my mother and me, in the grottoes we lived in now? Nothing. We had no conversation at all. Language belonged to the world from which we had disappeared, and here we gave up words like the last loved trinkets Nanna had sold for our fruitless journey to Argentina. We moved from the simplest verbal exchanges — "Eat" or "Wash" or "Rest" — to grunts and gestures our hands could make to an absolute silence in which, nonetheless, we communicated perfectly, our two minds dwelling now in a single collaborative state, the desire to speak become speech itself, the desire to be heard the hearing. We had done more than vanish for awhile from our Nazi enemies; we had gone much farther than the fifty kilometers from Prague a map would chart. We had escaped from History itself, our lives become the lives of the ancient cave-dwellers whose homes we had claimed as the descendants we were, these stony chambers as much our legacy as any ancestral estate we might have sued for in a court of law. In hours, we had tumbled back a thousand generations, time a waterfall we rode past all our pain.

Marcella, believe me: the mute women I am describing, sitting for hours in rocking trance, were not two deranged Jewesses driven mad by their ordeal. We had passed beyond our despair, just as a

Himalayan hermit monk moves out of suffering into a peace he cannot explain, his deprivations so enormous, it seems impossible that they should be the agency of his transcendence.

Sometimes when I cannot sleep, thinking of the torture your mother was forced to endure, I imagine that just at that moment when the pain was so terrible, she was sure she could not survive, a hole seemed to open in the floor of the room where they brought her for her daily beatings, and your mother escaped from her body into that dark refuge. "A cave!" she murmured, and they hit her again, but now she was safe from their blows, now she had truly disappeared, now they could not touch her even as their truncheons landed yet again on her shoulders, her back, her beautiful broken face.

It was raining when they found us, and we could hear their boots sloshing through the mud just beyond our shelter. Together we gasped, the first sound either of us had made for so long, and our silence ruptured like a membrane in which we had been encased. My mother did two things: from a ledge behind her, she grabbed the violin case and thrust it into a crevice in the cave wall she sealed with a boulder; then she blew out our lantern's flame, not even a shadow flickering on the cold stone.

When the blows came, we cried out for each other, "Mama!" a shield I raised in the dark, "Rachael!" a helmet she pulled over her head. Our shouts bounded and rebounded against the rock, a great echoing chorus hurling our names like curses at our attackers, like tribal epithets, like the chants of warriors preparing for battle against invaders. They might have killed us in that cave — how easily bones break against rock — but I think the sound we made frightened them — "Mama!" "Rachael!" — carrying as it did the cries of millions, all those voices born in our own, and how could a single search party vanquish such a multitude in one operation, how could a two-man death squad murder so many on one rainy afternoon?

Surely they meant to return us to Sered, the labor camp to which we had been ordered before our flight to Lidice, and perhaps they might have flogged us in front of the camp population, or hung us from the scaffolds erected for our execution, examples to the others of what would happen to anyone else who tried to escape from any Gestapo command. Perhaps the inmates might have been forbidden to utter a single word to us ever, our shunning the condition that allowed them to live, at least until the transfers began to Auschwitz, where even there an extra day might be secured through a hundred different negotiations, many ignoble, many cruel. Surely if we had survived Sered, we would have been the first names called — "Sonia Pearl! Rachael Pearl! — the morning the first train left for Poland, where Mengele waited to greet us, that infamous finger directing the widow and daughter of Eliezar Pearl to the Zyklon B "baths," whose one-word sign might have reminded my mother of Baille Herculanae and the waters there in which we had been so blessedly protected, so miraculously saved from harm. Within an hour, we would have been ashes taken from the crematorium to the Sola River, the driver dumping his load in haste, lest the wind pick up the gritty powder and blow it, suddenly, into his eyes.

Remember that it was raining when they found us in the cave.

Remember the Berounka River, nearby.

When the jeep into which we had been tossed like two sacks of potatoes skidded in the mud its thick tires turned into slippery craters, and the front of the vehicle suddenly lurched at an angle out of the deepening ruts, the force of that spin loosed the steering wheel from the driver's hands and in his panic to regain control, his boot bore down on the accelerator and we careened into the water just beyond.

I remember the instant we entered the river, the rear seat to which we had been tied lifting out of its track, turned into a boat the current carried away. We could watch the rest of the jeep flip over like a maddened bird in the rain-lashed air, then crash onto the heads of the German soldiers still dazed by the sudden mishap and floundering like children in the swollen Berounka.

We sailed on.

Downriver, my mother moaned, and I tried to turn my bruised face toward her, but the pain in my neck dizzied me. "Mama," I tried to say, and a single tooth fell from my swollen lips into the muddy water on which we rode.

She moaned again, but this time the arm she had tried to raise earlier broke through its restraint, and when she lifted the limb like a victory flag, I could see the jagged end of a shattered bone sticking through the flesh beneath her shoulder. Then she fainted from the effort, her head fell forward on her chest, and I knew that even though this accident had saved us yet again from the Nazis, and my mother had managed to free one badly-wounded arm, still we would surely perish on this improvised raft to which we were shackled, one of us unconscious now and the other praying that the death we had evaded so far would come for us quickly now, no more deceptive rescues, no more miracles that turned into disasters worse than the ones we had just escaped. Then I passed out as well, our little boat riding for hours more the swift current to Plzen, where, in spite of my entreaty, yet another miracle was waiting, one more salvation when the end had seemed so near.

Children found us first. Two young brothers had come down to the docks when the rains abated, shocked to see the Jeep's rear seat floating toward them, carrying its injured passengers into port, our yellow stars still stitched to our soaked blouses. One of the boys tied the seat's rear bracket to a dock post, and stayed with us while the other ran home for help. It was just past dinnertime, and in spite of the German occupation, life in Plzen proceeded normally. Except for the Jews who disappeared each day, nothing much in the town had changed. When the boy burst into the house with the news of our shocking arrival, his father was opening a second bottle of beer from the Urquell Brewery, where he worked as a foreman and kept the German troops supplied with pilsner from the plant: in wartime, who can be too kind to one's captors? He did not like Adolph Hitler, and he had wept last year when he'd heard on the short-wave Chamberlain's betrayal of the Czech nation, but now that the Germans had taken over, wasn't it important to stay in their good graces? His wife disagreed. She was a very religious woman, in fact devout, and it seemed to her wrong to befriend the Nazis, when it was a known fact, she was telling her husband at the very moment their son arrived, "that something terrible is happening to the Jews."

Who can account for that confluence, the wife's declaration and the son's summons — "You have to come quick! They're hardly breathing!" — and the husband putting down his beer to follow the woman and child through the cobble-stoned Plzen streets, past St. Bartholemew's Church where the couple had married and baptized their boys in the font at the feet of the Gothic Madonna, across the bridge to the Urquell Brewery, beyond the railway station to the docks where two Jewish women, beaten almost to death, bobbed on the back seat of a Nazi jeep dredging crews would find one day on the bottom of the Berounka River?

Because Kurt Svoboda worked in the brewery, he knew all about the nine kilometers of medieval underground corridors one could enter at Perlova 6, though visitors only saw one small section of the complex beneath the town. Once intended to be refuges during military sieges, some of the tunnels were still used by the brewery to store kegs of beer, and Kurt had a map of the labyrinth on his office wall. He descended often to the supply rooms beneath the streets of Plzen to fetch his gifts for the Germans, and sometimes his boys came along to chase each other through the endless hallways that stretched, he joked with them, "around the world three times."

The Svobodas brought us here to heal. How they managed to carry two injured women from the docks where we were moored through the center of town to Perlova 6 without being questioned by a single Occupation soldier is a mystery, and how they were able to transport to our "hospital" two cots, blankets, a kerosene lamp and a bucket we used for a toilet remains a riddle as well. When did a brewery foreman learn how to set a bone? Is it any more implausible than the ride we made down the river, tied to the waterborne seat of a Nazi army vehicle from which we had been magically ejected and carried to Plzen?

Who would have believed that our capture in the Koneprusy caves should result in a second underground hideout, this one to be our home for more than four years, the "room" we lived in walled from view by a fortress of beer kegs, one on the bottom tier movable, a door through which our rescuers could enter and leave, though my mother and I never dared use that portal ourselves? They brought us food and water. They brought us books. They brought us rat poison, but we were never free of the rodents for more than a few days; I still carry the scars of their teethmarks up and down my arms. They brought me a sketchbook and charcoal, a tin of watercolor paints. They brought my mother yarn and needles with which she knitted and unravelled and knitted again the same afghan a hundred times; sometimes she could not sleep and she would work on the blanket in the dark, her needles clicking, clicking, clicking all night like crickets I remembered from the world outside, where people still sat in their yards on warm evenings, where children still captured fireflies in jars.

One day my mother asked me for a piece of drawing paper. On the page, she drew a map of the caves where she had hidden my dead father's violin case behind a boulder in a crevice just large enough for the battered leather box. That weekend, the Svobodas took their boys on a long Sunday drive along the Berounka River, and delivered to us the following morning the family treasures Mititei had rescued from Baille Herculanae so many years before, carrying them with her to the hospital in Orsova where I had just been born.

Beneath the boots of an unsuspecting Gestapo patrol, my mother opened the case she had brought with her through so many exiles now, so many flights. She unfolded the coverlet Reba had crocheted in Tulcea, and lay it like a cloth over the table at which we ate. She tied a length of yarn through Ovid's opal ring, and slipped the necklace over my head, a gift I recognized as a talisman though I knew nothing then about the gypsy who had been Dov Landau's closest friend. She placed her father's leather-bound notebooks on the shelves Kurt had made from several two-by-fours tiered on empty kegs, and though it would be many years before she would tell me the story of his Delta disappearance, at last the volumes I had paged through surreptitiously were there for me to study freely: hundreds of drawings of wilderness birds so perfectly scaled and minutely detailed, I could feel wings fluttering across my cheek, an egret's heart pulsing against the finger I lay on its feathered breast.

In one of the notebooks, I found Moses Silver's letter from Buenos Aires, which I read myself for the first time, and I would have ripped it to shreds had my mother not saved it from my hands. I demanded: why would she still want to keep a message that had brought us so much pain? Did she even know if this Moses Silver was still alive? Did she still imagine our salvation lay in that distant city to which we had already sailed once, my baby aborted on the ship's deck, Nanna dead in the Prague synagogue shelter to which all the passengers had been forced to return? If we had chosen New York or Montreal or Havana or Shanghai, we might all be together, making a new life, my son six months old and Nanna bouncing him on her knee. But my mother pressed the envelope to her lips and said, "My mother Reba would be alive today if she had gone to Argentina thirty years ago," the letter I read as a message of doom still, for Sonia Pearl, directions to Paradise. ("It is far, very far, but at least we can be sure there are no Nazis there."). I softened. It was not Moses Silver who had turned us away. It was not a populace which had never even known that our boat had arrived and departed again, millions of good people there who would have surely sheltered us. A few petty bureaucrats had decreed our fate: would I hold an entire city responsible for that? My mother needed an oasis of which she could dream — so many places now had turned to dust for her — and she had chosen Buenos Aires, where her mother's admirer had settled. Who was I to steal her fantasy away? "Mama," I said, groping for one of the few Spanish phrases I knew,

"Siento mucho. I am very sorry," and from her hand I took the letter I might have destroyed and placed it back in Dov's notebook, for safekeeping.

And what of the violin case, emptied now of its cherished possessions? It rested now at the foot of my mother's bed, and sometimes, when I started to weep over the days, the months, the years of dark silence in which we were forced to live like criminals in prison, when we were guilty of nothing at all, she would lift the lid of the case as if turning on a radio or placing the arm of the phonograph on a favorite record, she would begin to hum softly, and the first strains of my father's music — Mozart or Beethoven or Liszt or Bach — would fill our hiding place with a glorious sound that only we two fugitives — "Sonia Pearl!" "Rachael Pearl!" — could hear.

17

JACOB SILVER WAS FLUENT in Spanish, which he had learned the year he had lived in Buenos Aires as a boy, his father an attaché in the Polish embassy there. "He used to sing my mother Ladino love songs in their bed. I come from a line of great romantics, you know." Jacob spoke English, French and German as well. At home, of course, he had conversed with his family in Yiddish and in Polish with his colleagues at the Warsaw Hospital for the Insane, just finishing his residency there when the ghetto gates locked and the daily deportations began.

During his three years in Dachau, he gave language lessons to the other inmates in his barracks. "It was very important," he told me, "to keep the mind active and focussed on something beyond the horror of the camp." Sometimes a man would die in the midst of nightly instruction ("We were all on the verge of starvation. Many suffered from typhus as well.") and the group would move immediately from their conjugations of irregular French verbs to the chanting, in Hebrew, of the prayer for the dead. Those who had lost their faith gazed at the corpse in respectful silence that had nothing to do with God. "Then two of us would carry the body outdoors and we would resume the lesson. It kept many of us from madness, I think, and even from suicide. Often we wept during the class, but we always continued the session. We were even grateful for tears. We knew it meant our souls were still alive."

He was crying when he told me this, and I wiped the tears from his cheeks with my fingertips.

"And you, Rachael? You and your mother alone all those years, never a speck of sunlight to warm you. What did the two of you do to keep your sanity?"

I smiled at him. "My mother knit the same afghan two hundred times. I made a thousand drawings of beer kegs. And we listened to music that did not exist."

We were sitting on a wooden bench outside the British army barracks in Brno, a Czech city three hours from Plzen and hundreds of miles from Dachau's German site, two survivors in a Displaced Persons Camp discovering — under the full moon, in the spell of peonies and lilacs sending their perfume through the barracks' barbed wire fence — that their bodies as well as their souls were still alive (Jacob's hand moving under my skirt, my hand touching his thigh, a kiss after which I can only say, Marcella, the sky filled with stars not there before, thousands of planets born in the heat of our embrace).

"Rachael," your grandfather whispered to me, "I have the keys to the major's Jeep."

"I don't under — "

"So we can go for a drive. Two hours, he said."

"My mother — "

"She's sleeping already. She won't even know you're gone. Will you come?"

At the car's side, I froze.

"I can't," I said.

"This isn't the Gestapo, Rachael. We're not inmates here."

I had not yet told him about the caves beyond Lidice, the beatings there, the crash in which we rode the back seat to which we were bound down the Berounka River and I prayed for the end of miracles at last, for who could survive any more reprieves like this, who could endure such terrible blessings any longer?

"I can't," I said again, but Jacob Silver took my trembling hands in his and kissed each finger, the ritual of tenderness chasing my fear out of my body, over the fence, a dybbuk flying off into the star-soaked sky.

Even when we drove through the gate of the barracks, I did not scream, though I would not have been surprised to hear gunshots aimed from the tower, and the soldiers' "*Schnell!*" sending the dogs after the car Jacob had surely stolen.

But no gunfire sniped at us, no dogs barked at our wheels, no German voices split the air. A man and a woman were taking an evening drive through the Brno countryside in a borrowed Jeep. Could that be true?

"I knew the major's brother at Oxford, before the war," Jacob said, as if he realized my confusion. "'I hadn't realized you were a Jew, old chap,' that's what he said when he recognized me here. 'I'm a Jew, all right,' I told him, and I showed him the numbers on my arm. 'No doubt about that.'"

We rode through the moon-lit farmland, both of us dressed in the DP uniforms that hung from our gaunt frames — oh, Jacobo, you were so handsome, not even Dachau had managed to steal your elegance! — the hair I had managed to keep long all the years of hiding clipped short as a boy's by the British, both of us reeking still of the disinfectant they doused us with each day, but what two movie stars were ever more desirable than we were to each other the night we took the major's Jeep to the Macocha Abyss, that lime-stone canyon on whose grassy lip we made love for the first time? When at last we rose, and gazed together into that gleaming rift, it was as if our passion itself had split the earth apart.

Later that night, back in my bunk, I menstruated for the first time in over four years: I folded the stained sheet and put it in the duffel bag each of us had been issued by the British, that muslin

now a flag I wanted to keep, a banner proclaiming my second liberation from the Nazis — the first from the underground corridors
of Plzen, this one from the deck of the ship on which the baby I
would have named Eliezar, after my father, drowned in that sudden
hemorrhage, so much blood I would not pass another drop until
tonight, my parched womb a river now, a spawning field, a future
home for your mother whose parents would soon sail away on *The
Pelican*, a British freighter bound for Buenos Aires in the summer of
1946.

18

DID WE SAIL ON MY grandfather's pelican wings to the harbor for which we had always been destined? How else to explain a freighter dubbed for the Delta bird who spoke to my mother in Dov Landau's voice?

And what accounts for my Jacobo having the same last name as Moses Silver, who had written to Reba from the very Buenos Aires where, twenty years later, my husband would spend his most memorable childhood year?

And the Latin word for "silver?" *Argentum*, for which the country itself is named.

And the Rio de la Plata, where *The Pelican* docked? "River of Silver," Jacobo announced, as if the entire estuary belonged to him, as if he had come at last to his rightful home.

My mother had not read a palm in decades, but when she learned in the Brno barracks of her new son-in-law's Argentine past, she turned his hand over and claimed that the text of Moses' letter was inscribed verbatim on Jacobo's flesh. "It can't be true," I insisted, but she read aloud from his skin as if the letter were there before her, and although it is possible she had memorized the lines, still I believe she saw the words as she claimed, the *fusgeyer's* proposal to Reba from his South American refuge — "Already I have a job in a meat-packing plant. I would make a good husband to you, and a good father to Sonia, and I will wait forever for you to arrive." — inexplicably penned on the Polish psychiatrist's palm.

147

For awhile we lived in two rooms in La Boca, a poor Italian neighborhood popular also with artists, dancers and starving political
pamphleteers.

Jacobo studied day and night for the medical boards that would
allow him to practice in our new country, a small stipend from the
Jewish Welfare Fund all we had to live on those first months in
Buenos Aires. Every morning my mother and I bundled up in our
second-hand winter coats and walked from our barrio tenement to
the little markets along the waterfront. We practiced our Spanish
with the vendors there, repeating our fractured versions of the
names for food we had learned in class the prior evening, shocked
to realize we had come home with goat's meat, or frog, or peppers
so hot the smell of them alone sent us for water.

Would we ever learn how to eat like long-settled *porteños*?
Would we always be strangers, fumbling for words, pointing like
deaf-mutes to items whose names we could never remember?

Soon enough we would cook like natives: brewing mate, rolling
out the dough for meat-filled *empañadas*, boiling milk and sugar and
a square of dark chocolate for the rich *dulce de leche* I spooned on
toast, dripped over fruit, ate by the spoonfuls as my pregnancy
advanced. My mother and I wandered the city, memorized maps,
eavesdropped on guides leading boy scout troops through the
ornate hallways of the Casa Rosada, then across the Plaza de Mayo
to the Cathedral, where we stared with the children at San Martín's
tomb. For a few pesos, we rode the tour bus through Recoleta
Cemetery, the rich buried in fancy crypts and fabulous marble
mausoleums; I remembered the twelve-thousand tombstones in
Prague, the graves there stacked like tenements collapsing in disre-
pair. Once we went to a symphony orchestra matinee in the Colon

Theater; I closed my eyes and pretended we were back at the House of Artists, Nanna and Sonia crying because the music reminded them of my missing father, his violent end the last one they thought we would have to bear.

How hard we worked, my mother and I, to be at home in Buenos Aires. Refugee, survivor, immigrant, greenhorn: so many words in this world for "stranger." So many words for "lost."

In the afternoons, we napped, my swelling belly a pillow Jacobo rested on, the heartbeat of our unborn daughter drowning out for him the screams from Dachau where his whole family had perished, all his focus on the future now, his child to be born as an Argentine citizen, the ghosts of his dead like ashes he had scattered to sea from the rail of *The Pelican*.

But in the other room my mother, Sonia, called out in her sleep for her vanished loved ones — Dov, Reba, Ovid, Eliezar, Mititei, Anna, Saul, Belva, Simon Roth. Once, while she chanted that litany, Jacobo said, "We should decide on some names for the baby, I think," but I was afraid to speak my favorites aloud for fear they would enter my mother's dream: "Miriam" or "Eli," before even arriving, joining her list of the disappeared.

Marcella, by the time your mother was born, we had left La Boca for a quieter neighborhood north of the shipyards and the smoky tango bars of San Telmo, and when Miriam was ready for school, we moved here to San Isidro's tree-lined streets, the slate-tiled foyer of our spacious stucco home as big as both of our La Boca rooms together. Jacobo saw more and more patients in his office downtown and lectured as well at the medical school; my mother had stopped having nightmares; my watercolors sold well in a good

Palermo gallery, and Colonel Juan Domingo Peron entered the second term of his Presidency still a popular leader (though the peso was losing its value, and inflation was so terrible even the wealthy were worrying now, and Peron was still so despondent over Eva's death he was developing ulcers, some said, and drinking too much even for a man famous for his indulgences. Who could blame him for his despair? some countered later. Wasn't the Vatican considering Evita's canonization at the same time the military was planning its coup against her husband in 1955? She had a miraculous power to heal, her faithful insisted; the President might not have been all that he claimed — what about the secret police, the stories of torture in certain prisons, Swiss bank accounts in spite of his populist speeches? — but Eva Peron was truly a saint).

One balmy November Sunday, in 1955, while families watched the televised soccer games some joked were the true Argentinian religion, or picnicked in Palermo Park on the shores of the boat-filled lake, or strolled after Mass beside the elegant storefronts of Calle Florida, two generals forced Juan Peron from the Casa Rosada without firing a single shot. What did he think, *El Presidente*, lying on the floor of the limousine in which only a day before he'd been transported like royalty on his daily visit to his embalmed wife's crypt? Did he imagine for himself a firing squad or a slower death in a torture room? Or did he know the chances were good — as they were — that he would be in Panama soon, sending out change-of-address cards to the Italian clothiers who made his suits?

No one would know for a day that Peron had been deposed, most people at work or school when the generals went before the cameras with their announcement declaring "a brief state of emergency," curfews, armed soldiers on the streets watching rooftops for snipers.

Hearing those words — emergency, curfew, soldiers command-ed "to shoot on sight those who would violate the peaceful transi-tion" — my mother rushed to her room, returning again with the violin case she would hold on her lap for the next twenty-four hours, refusing to eat or sleep, the sentry of San Ysidro awake in a chair, waiting for worse news yet to come, waiting for the signal to flee. Tomorrow Jacobo would give her a tranquilizer, and the day after that Peron would be under house arrest, and the day after that Miriam would return to school, where her teacher would write on the blackboard the names of the new leaders of Argentina.

How many times would those names change in the next eigh-teen years, until Peron's unlikely return from his exile in Madrid? How many juntas, how many short-lived civilian regimes, how many coups and counter-coups, how many riots and demonstra-tions, how many bombings and kidnappings and executed corpo-rate executives discovered in the trunks of their Mercedes sedans?

And the worst of it still to come.

Sometimes, Marcella, I remember your great-grandmother Sonia the day we learned Peron was overthrown, how she sat vigil all those hours in the parlor, sure we would leave by morning for convent or caves we would hide in for years, or else escape over the border, making our way through Bolivia, Brazil, into Venezuela where a ship would be waiting for us in Caracas, bound for New York or further north, perhaps some island off the coast of Maine, a village in the Canadian woods. How many routes did she map out those hours she sat in the darkness? Did her father offer his wings again, did he hover over the red-tiled roof waiting for us to mount again his white-feathered back, did he leave in the morning through gold-laced clouds from which he called "Goodbye, good-bye?" to each of us by name?

"A stress reaction," Jacobo said of her refusal to sleep that night. "Completely understandable. An anxiety attack, a minor delusional episode." (She had whispered to him, "I heard the Gestapo!" when he returned from the hospital the following day).

If only we had fled, I once told Jacobo. If only we had listened to her. If only we had taken Miriam and gone away, far from Buenos Aires where once my mother had believed that "at least we can be certain there are no Nazis there." Years later the same archaeologists who dug up our daughter's bones from a secret graveyard in La Plata would discover the remains of Dr. Josef Mengele, the Auschwitz "Angel of Death," nearby. Perhaps they were his wings, and not Dov Landau's, flapping over our house the night of the coup; perhaps it was Mengele's voice ("I heard the Gestapo!") who called out our names in the dark.

A year later, 1956. My mother takes the subway from San Ysidro to the Plaza de Mayo, where she walks up the stairs of the Municipal Building to the Department of Vital Statistics, Moses Silver's letter to Reba Landau in Sonia Pearl's pocketbook. There she tells a clerk the story she has not told me: how, in Tulcea, she had heard Moses' group singing in the square, how the next morning she left with the gypsy and her mother to follow the band to America, how at Baille Herculane Reba declared, "This is as far as I am able to go," and several months later the letter from Buenos Aires arrived.

The clerk has come from somewhere herself — Italy, perhaps, or Poland or Wales. "I'll try to help you," she tells my mother, and several hours later it is confirmed: he had waited forever, a full three years, and then died of consumption before he turned thirty. No known survivors, the records say. My mother puts the letter back in her purse and sits for some time in the Plaza de Mayo, speaking to no one, pigeons congregating at her feet. She listens to music no one else notices: a band of *fusgeyer* singing only for her. Isn't that Ovid approaching now from the Casa Rosada? Isn't that Reba on a distant bench? Soon it will be dark. My mother rides the subway back to San Ysidro, and that night she adds Moses Silver to the long list she keeps on her bedside table: names of loved ones for whom she lights candles on the anniversaries of their untimely deaths.

19

MARCELLA, I HAVE NOT been able to write for days.

What has become of the feverish scribe who found in her own imagination the buried chronicle of generations, who exhumed for you the vanished history of disappearances and death squads and unmarked graves? Didn't I record the journey of our family as if I had witnessed myself each drama, each scene, each unfathomable surprise? Didn't I set down the dreams and secrets of lost relations, as if they were whispering in my ear as I wrote, as if they gave me their stories like ghosts convened at a seance? Yet now that these tales approach the present, now that the action concentrates in the very house where I am struggling for words — no more escapes routes, no more sudden flights to towns with strange names, no more places to hide — the same empty page mocks me each morning with its single notation, copied from the registry of an obscure La Plata cemetery: "NN," some clerk wrote down to account for the arrival of yet-another body the local police had instructed him to bury after dark. "Identity Unknown."

Oh, granddaughter, grief blankets the landscape I am struggling to recall, and the details of your mother's short life vanish before me like photographs lost under gray volcanic ash. Numbed by disaster, Memory forgets her own name, wanders the once-familiar streets of the past, an amnesiac lost in the rooms of her very own house. What was it I meant to tell you about my Miriam? What vignettes slip like treasured heirlooms from my hands into the grave where they discovered the bones they said she had become? Skull, ribcage, pelvis, femur, fibula: where is the flesh-and-blood daughter I bore?

Disappeared, disappeared, disappeared.

But didn't my own mother, Sonia, find her lost memories the night of the fire at the Church with the Moon? In that story I discovered a reason for her silence, and a cure for it as well. Be my cure, Marcella, reading these tales in a future I enter now, just at the moment you reach that place in the narrative when I confess "how the details of your mother's short life vanish before me like photographs buried under gray volcanic ash."

"But I need to know everything about her!" you scream. "Do you think I have been reading all of these pages just to be robbed of her again? You must tell me what you remember!"

"Skull," I whisper. "Ribcage, pelvis, femur, fib — "

But you say, "*Abuela*, do I look like her? Do I look like my mother?"

This is why imagination is a miracle, Marcella: in a future I may not live to witness, the granddaughter I may never find takes my hand and places it upon her face. Don't you? Against my palm, the familiar planes of cheek and nose and brow, the beautiful fall of silken hair, the temple's pulse I touched a thousand times in Miriam, who rises from the gurney now where they assembled her skeleton, the daughter I bore alive again in the daughter she bore, both of them vanished, yet both of them here with me in San Ysidro, where I have been keeping a vigil, first for Miriam and then for Marcella, both still lost to me, both here at my side.

Beneath "NN" I correct the record: "Miriam Silver Rojas, 1949-1976." Tombstone inscription, courtroom testimony ("After that day, I never saw my daughter again."), the next tale's first line. Upon this tear-blessed page, I am giving birth again, these days of painful labor finally culminating in a delivery of memories real as

that first birth was: head, shoulders, arms and hands, torso, legs and
feet. "A girl," the doctor announced, and I said, "Miriam," and in
answer — as if acknowledging her own identity, as if already aware
of the name she would have in this world — your mother let out
her first living cry.

What soothed her during those colic bouts, those infant nightmares, those days of new-born misery for which even a mother has
no name? Miriam travelled miles on her father's shoulder, and I
rocked her for hours at a time, and my mother massaged her tiny
contorted limbs. But still she wailed, oblivious, it seemed, to any of
our efforts to ease the mysterious pain against which she protested.
From the flat downstairs, a sleepless neighbor banged on the ceiling
with a broom, apologizing the next morning for "losing my temper like that at a helpless infant, poor thing." I feared the obstetrician had overlooked some grave but obscure malady, some obstruc-
tion or growth — surely these weeks of suffering had some physical source for which there was a cure — but the doctors reassured
us Miriam was perfectly healthy. Then the stump of cord fell off, I
immersed her for the first time in a basin of warm water, and my
daughter sighed like a wanderer returned after long exile to a
beloved home.

    What else is healing, if not the memory of once-known peace
restored again to form, some ruptured balance righted, some vanished map retrieved? Your mother looked at me as if to say, "At last!"
and I wonder now how deep the history was into which she sank
with such relief: the uterine pool from which she'd only weeks ago
been expelled, the Baille Herculanae bath in which my mother hid
those last hours before my birth, the Danube Delta lake into whose
depths Dov Landau disappeared? Soon she would swim in the Mar

del Plata sea, and the alpine-like lakes of Bariloche, and the private swimming pools of San Ysidro, so happy in water Jacobo called her "Little Fish" and scattered the ashes of her reclaimed bones — skull, ribcage, pelvis, femur, fibula — in the River Plate, at the spot where *The Pelican* had docked twenty-nine years before and we had disembarked, safe at last from the Nazi nightmare, half a world away from Europe's blood-soaked ground.

"Little Fish," her father called her. And "Penguin," because she loved to imitate the way the sea-loving birds waddled from the beach to their cliffside nests the summer we visited Peninsula Valdes to see the whales. And "Mermaid" when she paraded through the house in bathing suit and flippers, even though there was still snow on the ground outside. Can I count the number of trips we all made together to the Palermo Park Zoo, where Jacobo shot rolls of film of Miriam feeding the sea lions, calling out to the dolphins, waving hello to the otters sunbathing on rocks beside their tended lagoons? If Dov Landau turned into a bird when he died, I am sure his great-granddaughter found her way to water from her La Plata prison long before Jacobo delivered her ashes to the river's current.

Did that dust, so like the baby powder I smoothed on her infant skin after a bath, travel upstream to Tigre, the town at the mouth of the Parana Delta, where Miriam begged us to move the first time she saw the stilt-raised houses at the edge of the canals where people tethered the boats they used instead of cars, and children went to school on floating busses that travelled the Delta's watery maze, town held to town by graceful wooden bridges arching over myriad streams and creeks and riverlets into which the Rio de la Plata had been transformed?

We spread a blanket, I remember, underneath a willow tree in a waterfront Tigre park. Although she usually stayed at home when we went on excursions, my mother had come with us that day, and I can see again how she walked with Miriam to the edge of the bank where the sunlight sequined the water from which it seemed the two of them had just emerged, their skin and clothing turned like the stream's surface to scallops of light. Was my mother thinking of Tulcea, of that other Delta in which her father had changed from man to bird before her eyes? Was my daughter imagining herself beneath the tiny waves that lapped at her toes, her earth-bound body loosed at last to its rivered home?

"Why can't we live here, Mama?" she cried. "Why? Why?"

If I had been able to read like a palm the Delta map Jacobo had unfolded, a thousand tributaries spreading across the surface of the page, perhaps I would have seen how soon her child's plea would find its terrible fulfillment: tragedy under the second finger, loss under the third, the life-line broken in half.

"Lunch is ready," Jacobo called to them a moment later. Together my mother and child moved again up the grassy slope to our picnic site and they shed their scales behind them, a radiant trail whose brightness thinned and finally vanished into the solid ground on which we waited.

Little Fish, Penguin, Mermaid, Miriam: do you remember the daughter you left behind on land, the child who swam from your body into your murderer's arms? In the sea you live in now, sing out her name — Marcella! Marcella! — and maybe she will hear you when she floats into dream, maybe she will recognize your call in her own unfathomed depths, maybe she will answer one day — Mother! Mother! — and begin the search that will lead her to these stories I write now as evidence that you once were alive, that your name was Miriam Silver Rojas, that you gave birth to a daughter in a prison in La Plata three months after you disappeared.

In San Ysidro, my mother liked to say, "Now we all have room to breathe," and I realized how constricted life had been for her in the tiny La Boca flat, and even in the larger apartment where Miriam slept in a crib in her grandmother's room, the older woman insisting, "A married couple should have some privacy, after all." After Plzen and Dachau and the DP camp and *The Pelican's* refugee-jammed decks, who would think we would even remember privacy? But we did. Isn't that how we survive the horrors of history — holding in our minds those days we lived in dignity, sheltering our souls in the refuge of those memories? Think of my mother opening my father's violin case during our years beneath the streets of Plzen, filling the tunnel in which we hid with music she remembered him playing for her in Baille Herculanae.

By the time we moved here, to San Ysidro, we had enough money to buy a fine phonograph, and Jacobo found some of my father's records at a music store on Calle Florida, and Miriam loved to dance on the polished tile floors to the virtuoso's performances. "When I grow up," she liked to say, "I'm going to be a ballerina and my grandfather will play for me." In the parlor after dinner, my mother would settle herself in her favorite chair and Jacobo would position the phonograph arm and Eliezar Pearl would serenade her again, as he had done in person at the Hotel Roman years before, as he had done later in the tunnels under Plzen, as he did now in in a Buenos Aires suburb where the dead violinist waited for his granddaughter Miriam to join him on stage, my child whirling and whirling and whirling to the music of eternity.

Once I remember Jacobo picking her up from the Oriental rug, where she had fallen in a dizzied heap, and Miriam pretending to be unconscious or worse, her father carrying her motionless form through the house and singing a parodied lament for his limp and silent girl. Then suddenly, her shouts of laughter and his dramatic outburst: "So the *senorita* is alive after all! Thank goodness we didn't give away her toys!"

From the yard where I was fixing the vanishing sunset to a sheet of rice paper, I heard their voices and shuddered. In my trembling hand, the brush slipped, the sky's red glow turned into a gash that bled across the ruined page. I knew Miriam's "revival" in her father's arms was just a playful skit, yet still their game chilled me, and several times that night I slipped from our bed to my sleeping daughter's side, needing to see the rhythmic rise and fall of her body in the house that had blessed us with "room to breathe."

"You must not project your own fears on to her," my husband instructed me. "Either she will grow timid and anxious, or else she will resent you for hovering so much that she will turn into a real rebel."

Did I hover? Did I project on to her the memories of my own wartime girlhood, those European traumas a scrim through which I watched my Argentine daughter's life? Or did I feel History sliding toward us again like the forbidding glaciers of Patagonia, mountains rent and canyons collapsing into themselves and bodies of water split in two by the force of implacable ice? Did I sense the ground shifting beneath our very house before the signs of disaster registered, before the earth gave way?

"I will try, Jacobo," I promised him, but even as I spoke I rose from the sofa and peered through the French doors that led to the yard. There Miriam played with school-friends on the dappled lawn, and I wondered if my husband knew that I was checking on her safety even as I made my promise to him, that I was holding her in my anxious gaze even as I said I was letting her go.

On our tenth anniversary, Jacobo took me to dinner at a French restaurant down the street from the Colon Theater, where we had been to the symphony. Across the linen-clothed table, I held his hand, thinking how far we'd come from the DP camp where we had wed, our wedding dinner rations we ate from tin bowls the American army had donated to the survivors housed in the Brno barracks. Yet still I felt our well-being fragile as the crystal goblets the waiter filled with fine champagne, and when Jacobo offered a toast to "our wonderful life here," the tears I could not restrain came from fear as much as gratitude, a grave unease that laced my love for husband, child, mother. He left his chair to sit beside me on the upholstered banquette.

"Rachael, it is all behind us now," he said, as if another government had not fallen just last week, as if the Buenos Aires Herald was not running a series of articles about Nazis sheltered since the war in cities and towns all over Argentina. "You must not live so much in the past."

Oh Jacobo, it was not the past I feared, haunted like your patients by losses from which they struggled to recover, wakened at night by memory-tortured dreams in which they thrashed like prisoners of time itself. It was the future that frightened me, some inkling I had of ordeals yet to come, some foreboding I could not shake. Perhaps I chose watercolor as my medium because it was a project of the moment, quick glimpses of beauty before the darkness fell.

We drove home through the city's wide boulevards filled with people travelling from cafe to cafe, tango bar to jazz club to shops opened past midnight for Buenos Aires' nocturnal crowds. Perhaps the whole city suffered as I did from premonitions it tried to forget in insomniac revelries. By Buenos Aires standards, we lived a staid existence — visiting occasionally with friends, seeing a film or a concert from time to time, most evenings our lights out when others were just heading downtown — but now I wonder if during those uneasy decades before "the Dirty War" began, every person in Argentina wasn't breathing in the air of portent, wasn't drinking from the waters of impending catastrophe.

When Miriam was sixteen years old, she brought home a copy of Eva Peron's memoir, *La Razon de ma Vida*. My Life's Cause. "'I remember I was very sad for many days,'" Miriam read aloud to us, "'when I discovered that in the world there were poor people and rich people; and the strange thing is that the existence of the poor didn't cause me as much pain as the knowledge that at the same time there were people who were rich.'"

My daughter's face was glowing, her always-lively eyes burning now like smoldering coals. The swimmer and the dancer and the actress and the straight-A student had found another passion now, this one full of danger, I knew. ("Shall I give you fire?" Evita had asked the crowds. "Shall we burn down the Barrio Norte?") Were the walls shaking as Miriam read? Were those flames I saw flashing through the draped windows? Did I hear the faint thud of distant explosions each time she paused? No, no: only her mother's heart knocking in its house of bone.

Jacobo looked up from his medical journal. "That woman was not stable, Miriam. Grandiose and paranoid, probably a borderline type. And Juan Peron is a fascist. We're lucky to be rid of him. Why do you want to bring such madness into this house?"

Behind their voices, my father's sweet Mozart, bizarre background music for the first skirmish in what would be a full-blown war in time.

"You're just afraid you'll lose all this," Miriam shot back, sweeping her arm like a searchlight from one end of the room to the other. "You tell me who the fascist is around here, you — "

Now Jacobo was on his feet. "Are you actually lecturing me on fascism?" he yelled. "Do you know what these numbers mean?" He drummed his fingers against the tattoo on his forearm. "Did you forget your father was in Dachau, and your mother and grand-mother lived like animals underground for years? Do you think I raised you to — "

"This is not Europe! This is Argentina! I was born here, remem-ber?"

And then she was flying up the stairs, the room to her door slamming like a gunshot fired above us.

Later Jacobo sat on the edge of his daughter's bed and had what he told me was "a good discussion," but I knew the truce between them would never hold. The man who feared I lived too much in the past had discovered how much a refugee he still was himself — "Do you know what these numbers mean?" — and our daughter had declared herself *porteño* — "I was born here, remember?" — and oh Marcella, how clearly I did remember, how clearly, all that night my belly contracting in labor-like pains and this time I was delivering my grown child into the world, into history, into the very future I had feared for so long, here at the front door now, knocking and knocking and knocking, calling out my Miriam's name.

20

GRADUALLY THE PICTURES of movie stars on your mother's bedroom wall gave way to political posters, *La Prensa* clippings, quotations from Evita and Ortega Y Gassett and Che and Ghandi and Martin Luther King. Three times a week she took the subway after school to the barrio where she had been born, tutoring La Boca's children in the basement of Our Lady of the Flowers Church. On Saturdays she travelled to demonstrations in the Plaza de Mayo where Peronists of all persuasions gathered — trade unionists, students, Communists, right-wing merchants, housewives, leathery-skinned gauchos. farm workers selling sugar cane from the backs of dusty pick-ups they drove from Jujuy to the capitol. Sometimes the party-like protests turned grim — tear gas and mounted police and men in expensive suits taking photographs. Once I found her in the bathroom washing a friend's blood from her jeans. "It looks worse than it is," she said, seeing me pale. "I mean, he's fine, he didn't have to go to a hospital or anything." And every few weeks Jacobo's restraint gave way — "Are you mad, Miriam? Have you lost your mind? Do you have the slightest idea how dangerous your — "and her "I'm sorry I didn't turn out to be the coward you'd hoped for!" Then the slammed bedroom door, his coded knock, the tentative reconciliation.

"Jacobo," I wept one night, "I can't stand the fighting anymore. Please. My heart breaks every time the two of you — "

"Am I supposed to stand by while she — "

"She cares about the poor," I said. "Is that such a terrible thing?"

Was that really my own voice speaking on her behalf, the child whose breathing I still listened for in the dark? Was this really Jacobo raging at his "Little Fish" whose spirit he'd warned me not to thwart? Perhaps in every family alliances shift, attachments prosper and wane, the embattled embrace and the inseparable break from each other with a violence commensurate to the strength of their prior bond. Perhaps any issue might have been the one to pull Jacobo and Miriam apart, to bring my daughter and me closer together. Or perhaps the very fear he'd so skillfully counselled me to relinquish had taken up residence in his heart instead, foreknowledge a kind of psychic infection passed like a fever between us, his symptoms full-blown just as mine abated.

"My God, Rachael, the next thing I know you'll be marching with her in the Plaza de Mayo and I'll be filing writs of habeas corpus when they arrest you both!"

Yes, yes, yes, I would march in the Plaza, but not by her side, and not for twelve more years, not until she disappeared one day and never returned. And the dozen writs of habeas corpus we filed on her behalf with the court? I still have the clipping — June 14, 1980 — from *La Capital*, a Rosario newspaper quoting one of the ruling generals: "In this type of struggle, the secrecy with which our special operations must be conducted means that we cannot divulge whom we have captured and whom we want to capture; everything has to be enveloped in a cloud of silence."

Habeas corpus: you shall have the body.

Did he actually think mothers would be silent while their children vanished from the world? Did he really believe fathers could be stilled by a murderer's decree? And didn't he know the clamor the ghosts of the disappeared would make, night and day the cacophony growing, twelve-thousand spirits determined to be heard, their terrible symphony filling the Argentine air, that orchestra of wails and moans and curses and screams, that rattle of bones rising finally from rivers and sea, breaking at last though the bulldozed earth?

From Buenos Aires, the flatlands of the Pampas fan out for hundreds of miles, and when the wheat is up, the landscape turns from tilled ground to a golden sea which only the horizon interrupts. Windmills pumping water to the surface of this dry region seem to become lighthouses, and in the distance the round hills of Cordoba loom like whales. If not for the barbed wire fences separating pasture from planted field, or the occasional stand of eucalyptus trees lining the *estancias'* winding driveways, or the rare glimpse of tiled ranch-house roofs behind a bank of bougainvillea, Jacobo might have confused the car he'd been driving for hours with *The Pelican* whose voyage he was just now remembering, and the steering wheel might have turned into the ship's rail he'd grasped eighteen years before. During these months that he and Miriam had been warring, memories returned in fierce and unpredictable bursts of experience so vivid he felt like an amnesiac reclaiming the banished knowledge of decades, though he had always believed himself conscious of his past without being at its mercy. He was a psychiatrist, after all. Wasn't it his work to help his patients extricate themselves from long-ago traumas still tormenting them with nightmares, ill health, addictions and phobias and compulsions? Didn't he spend hours a day with people suffering from the aftermath of accidents and injuries and abuses so terrible his awe for the powers of endurance grew with each case? A whole phantasmagoria passed through Jacobo Silver's professionally-decorated office downtown: survivors of incest and battering and desertions and rape and, more and more, death camps in Europe (these seemed to be turning into his specialty, patient referring patient until a third of his caseload were refugees like him from Dachau, Auschwitz, Treblinka, Belsen). He was writing articles now on the long-term effects of Gestapo torture; just last week he'd delivered a paper on the subject at a medical convention in Santiago.

Then why was the eminent psychiatrist pulling his car off the highway and crawling into the back to lie under a blanket on the floor? Because the gaucho on horseback trotting over pastureland toward an injured calf near the road turned suddenly into a German commandant bearing down on Jacobo, the lasso in the rider's hands now a whip whose lashes the Jewish doctor knew too well (weren't his back and buttocks already infected from last week's session under that leather switch?). He lay for an hour on the car's floor, and then the episode passed and he rose, disheveled and sweat-soaked, the gaucho and calf now vanished, the flash-back abated, and perched on the fencepost beside which he'd parked, an oven-bird, *hornero*, named for its nest which so resembled the earthen ovens of rural Europe. For a moment the man and the bird gazed at each other, as if in acknowledgement of some mutual secret, some terrible shared understanding, and then Hornero lifted its wings and flew off, its shadow moving like a dark thread, a rift, across the pale grass sea of the Argentine pampas.

When Jacobo and Miriam battled, my mother drew into a silence so deep, I feared she might never utter a sound again. I remembered the months we'd hid in the Koneprussy Caves, how speech deserted us in that ordeal, and I knew how much she must be suffering now by the fact that she never spoke a word about the angry scenes that seemed to come more and more frequently between father and daughter, between husband and wife.

Did my mother remember her own feuds with Reba, the harsh

words they would later regret, the plates smashed to pieces and the down pillows ripped apart in rage? Did she think about the times her husband, Eliezar, had wept in her arms during the years his mother had forbade him to visit her in Prague, how her conciliatory letter had come just days before the bombing raid in which he would perish without seeing her again? When it seemed that only magic could bring us together — Jacobo sleeping in his study now, Miriam sullen for days at a time, my tearful pleas to both of them dismissed and my mother stricken again with nightmares of the war — she awoke in the midst of one such dream to Dov Landau's presence, the sheet in which she enfolded herself becoming his wings, the whirr of the ceiling fan changing into his voice which whispered instructions to her for the very plan she had been considering herself for weeks.

She rises at dawn, just as her father did the day he made his final voyage into the Delta wilderness. In a picnic basket, she packs several sandwiches, an apple, a ripe pear, a thermos of papaya juice she drinks for a digestive ailment. While she works, she sips her morning cup of mate and swallows the dozen vitamins she learned to take so many years ago at the Baille Herculane spa. Jacobo has been trying to prescribe medication for her high blood pressure and occasional angina attacks, but my mother refuses; the mestizo maid next door brings herbs and promises special Indian prayers in exchange for palm-readings the first Tuesday of every month. Once the maid drops a vase she is dusting on her big toe, and my mother amazes her by healing the injured foot with her hands. "Just like Evita," the maid declares, making the sign of the cross. "Did you know she was a healer like you?"

It is early December of a particularly warm summer, and my mother wears a flowered cotton shift and her grass-stained canvas gardening shoes. She carries the picnic basket outside, stopping at the closet by the back door for the straw sombrero she uses to shade herself the hours she spends weeding in her beloved flower beds and the vegetable garden just like the one she helped her father tend in Tulcea. Before any of us in the house wakes up, Sonia Pearl lets herself out into the dew-drenched yard.

But it is not for gardening that my mother has prepared herself. True, she has gone to the shed behind the garage for a pruner and a pair of shears and a wheelbarrow good for transporting compost from its cage to the various cultivated sites in the yard. This morning, however, her tasks are of a different kind. She cuts a dozen willow branches, a pile of fern fronds, bamboo stalks she breaks into thirds, handfuls of sawgrass and the pieces of a fallen eucalyptus limb she would have kept for kindling fires next winter, had not this project taken precedence. Now the wheelbarrow is heaped with her harvest. Now she is ready to build her nest.

Yes, Marcella, the story I am telling you is true, for who could invent the moment one discovers one's own mother squatting like a bird at the base of the blooming magnolia tree, her uncoiled white hair flowing like plumage to her waist, her hands open-palmed in her lap to to catch the petals drifting from the flowers overhead, her face transfixed in an alert repose as indifferent to me as it was focussed fully on some sight or sound beyond my senses' range? I screamed for Jacobo, and both he and Miriam tore across the grass from the house. When they saw my mother in her roosting position, father and daughter gasped lungfuls of air, as if suddenly the atmosphere had altered and they had entered a territory in which not even the simple act of breathing could be taken for granted; in this new gravity field, my husband and child clasped hands, and I took Miriam's too, and in our re-established connection, the three of us knelt down as one at the foot of my mother's nest. If you had seen us that moment in our supine postures, you might have thought us worshippers at the base of a holy shrine, or pilgrims arrived at the location of a miracle toward which they have journied for months or years. "Mama?" I said, and Miriam whispered, "Can you hear me, *Abuelita*?", and Jacobo said, "We must bring her inside." Together we lifted my mother from the nest and carried her like a wounded bird to her room. She neither spoke to us nor resisted; in fact, her body seemed to lighten as we approached the house in which only hours ago she had stood in the kitchen like an ordinary woman, though perhaps for Sonia Pearl that was always a masquerade.

When she was sleeping deeply from the sedative Jacobo had given her, we returned to the yard in which she had acted out this inexplicable drama. What had possessed her? Was she senile now? Was this a breakdown, dementia, a madness for which there was no cure? These questions plagued us all as we approached my mother's amazing construction, but the closer we got to it, the calmer we seemed to grow, almost reverential. The magnolia tree had dropped more petals which formed around the nest a luminous circle behind which we stood as if it were an intentional boundary, a kind of fence around a ceremonial site.

"It's a work of art," Miriam said.

"Her father loved birds," I said. "I have seen his drawings."

"We have all been going mad," Jacobo said, pulling us each closer to him, "and now we will all recover."

Although we were not religious people at all — "cultural Jews," we considered ourselves, "Jewish humanists," "assimilationists," "non-observers" — still for a moment we bowed our heads and in unison spoke the word with which all prayers close: "Amen," we said, "amen, amen."

Then we entered the circle of blossoms, and branch by reed by delicate frond, we unwound the beautiful filigree of my mother's inspiration, we disassembled the nest in which, for a morning, she had become once again her father's girl — "Never forget that I love you!" As we emptied onto the compost heap the wheelbarrow in which we had piled the materials of her construction, it seemed as if we were emptying ourselves as well, months of rage and contempt and regret and spiralling fear flung like refuse upon the transforming mound.

21

MY MOTHER INSISTED she had no memory of having built a nest in our backyard, and perhaps the sedative Jacobo administered fostered her forgetfulness. But in the remaining years of her life — ten more until Miriam's disappearance, and six beyond that terrible blow — it was always to the site of the nest that she retreated, setting her canopied lawn chair on the spot where we had found her roosted that day, turning the chair toward the gardens whose vegetables she claimed grew better if she sang to them certain gypsy songs she'd learned as a girl in the Danube Delta.

I would be lying if I claimed that from the day of my mother's nesting, all the strife in our household vanished. Marcella, these stories may be laced with improbable mysteries, but who would believe a family — even one in a fairy tale — cured forever of its conflicts and pain? Still, all of us were humbled by the strange events of that morning, and by my mother's complete overnight recovery from what Jacobo later told me he'd feared was a total breakdown which would require years of treatment in a psychiatric hospital.

My husband returned to our bed.

Miriam took down the Peronist posters that so offended her father, and for the months until she moved from our home to the university where she would begin her pre-law studies, she spoke little about politics, the fiery dinner-table speeches of the past years replaced with conciliatory chatter about courses she would take her first term, and dormitory regulations, and clothes-shopping we

172

would have to do "before I leave," she'd say, though the campus was only an hour's drive from San Ysidro, thirty-five minutes by subway.

I began sleeping through the night again, regained the fifteen pounds I'd lost during those months of chaos in the house where we had "room to breathe," and stopped carrying tissues for the daily tears I'd come to think inevitable. Once again I spent the mornings working on my delicate watercolors, the dramatic contrasts of the Argentine landscape turned to a subtle play of shadow and form, the famous hard light of Buenos Aires muted to perennial opalescent dawn.

And once again my mother listened in peace to her beloved recordings, the music of my father's violin like a balm in which our wounded family bathed.

Just weeks before, yet another military dictator had taken over the Casa Rosada and declared martial law "until the current crisis is over," and Juan Peron was quoting Lenin in manifestoes smuggled out of Spain, his old hero Mussolini denounced and the youthful brigades of the Argentine left encouraged to "bring the people's revolution to the streets," those young rebels never imagining that their leader would repudiate them as soon as he returned from his exile abroad. It would be Peron himself who would mandate the secret arrests of hundreds, and after his death, twelve-thousand more would disappear before the "dirty war" of his successors was over. But in those last months in our house until Miriam moved to campus, none of us spoke a word about the latest political turmoil, and which of us could have foreseen the murderous purges still years away? We devoted ourselves to conciliation, our new-found domestic harmony a difficult score we practiced constantly like the dedicated members of a string quartet about to tour the capitols of Europe, or make our debut at Carnegie Hall.

From the Universidad de Buenos Aires, Miriam rode the subway most Sundays to join us for dinner. She was excited about her pre-law studies, already working part-time for a group of attorneys who called themselves the Legal Institute for the Poor, cases referred to them by sympathetic priests who knew the unlisted number to call when one of their parishioners needed legal advice or representation. "Mostly," Miriam told us one day, "I type up writs of habeas corpus for the lawyers to take to court. Poor people get arrested for anything these days. If your shoelace comes untied, they'll charge you with vagrancy. What they really want to know is whether anyone in your family is a Peronist, or a Montenero, or ERP, or — "

In mid-sentence she stopped, as if Jacobo had interrupted her, but he had not said a word, the force of his silence enough to unnerve her, to stir her memories of earlier battles at this very table.

The Dachau survivor looked up from the drained cup of expresso whose oily residue he'd been studying as if it held the prognosticatory power of tea leaves. Jacobo had tears in his eyes. "We do not want you to be harmed in any way," he said in a husky whisper, "but we — I — respect your dedication."

Little Fish.

Miriam.

NN.

For years she had waited for him to soften, to see her side, to offer support. Now she was crying, too, leaving her chair to lay her head on her father's lap, and I was the one instead of Jacobo stifling the words of terror and prohibition: Much too dangerous! You must not! How could we bear it if anything ever? How, how, how?

As if in answer, an elegy rose from the stereo in the parlor, my father's lament consoling me with its beauty even as those sorrowful measures seemed to confirm the fear that had seized me once more that evening.

In spite of the terror that lived in Jacobo and me like parasites whose attacks we could never predict, we remembered the years of embattled estrangement from which my mother's bizarre reproach — an old woman making herself a nest outside the house whose conflicts she could no longer endure — had rescued us all, and a thousand times we repeated to Miriam and to ourselves Jacobo's declaration: "We do not want you to be harmed in any way, but we — I — respect your dedication."

Now she was a lawyer with her own tiny apartment in San Telmo, two rooms above a bakery on one of those winding cobblestoned streets lined in the summer with artists selling their paintings or offering on-the-spot charcoal portraits to monied weekend strollers, the cheap drawings luxuries now in the country's mad inflation. On her salary from the Legal Institute for the Poor, Miriam bought a few pieces of used furniture and a second-hand car she drove to court, or to the prisons where more and more of her clients were detained without charges.

Habeas corpus.

You are ordered to have the body.

She still came for dinner on Sundays, and avoided political discussions, and danced in the parlor when my mother played Eliezar Pearl's Hungarian rhapsodies, the violinist's granddaughter doing a kind of Argentine tango to his gypsy-inspired songs. When she disappeared, I would remember the way she'd lunged and arched and raised her hands in frenzied clapping and collapsed in laughter at our feet, and I wondered if the energy we'd taken for Miriam's high spirits wasn't a kind of hysteria in the face of dangers she foresaw more clearly even than her worried parents, some part of Jacobo and I still riveted on the past, on our vanished European world, on the flumes of smoke behind our backs.

22

AIRPORTS SMELL LIKE BATTLEFIELDS.

Burning diesel acrid as gunpowder, curtains of singed air rising from the hot tarmac, near-sweet fumes of puddled oil and the stench of scorched rubber: who is ever really surprised when the sirens wail, the ambulances streak across the landing strip, the fire trucks converge and the medics pull the victims from the mangled plane?

All the same it was a terrible shock to discover that Ezeiza Airport had turned into a war zone on June 20, 1973, the day that Juan Peron returned from his exile. Perhaps, Marcella, you have already learned in school how a hundred thousand had mobbed the terminal, pushing toward the gate where his jet was expected, spilling out onto the loading docks and lining the runway on which they believed his plane would taxi. In fact, at the news of the huge and volatile crowd, the leader's plane was diverted to the Moron Seventh Air Force Base, and no one in that waiting army of civilians would lay eyes that day on their beloved Peron.

Who struck the first blow?

Which faction insulted another, hurling an insult fifty yards like a winged projectile that gathers momentum as it travels?

Who fired the first shot from a loaded revolver hidden in a pocket or boot or a holster under a jacket on whose back the name of a neighborhood soccer team was cheerfully emblazoned?

In the melee that turned so fast to pitched battle, dozens dead and hundreds lying injured where they fell, who knew enemy from friend, who knew which arm was raised to murder and which arm was offering rescue when everyone chanted the same warriors' oath — "Peron! Peron! Peron! Peron!" — even as they struck each other down in the airport where they'd come to welcome together this man meant to save them from this very fratricidal fate?

When the telephone rang, my mother was napping and I was rolling pastry dough in the kitchen.

It was Jacobo calling from the hospital where the casualties were filling the emergency room, lining the corridors on blood-stained stretchers. "He isn't back in the country for five minutes and already there's disaster. They want me on duty all night to talk to the families," my husband said, "when I'm half-crazy myself, checking every gurney for Miriam. Did she say she was going to the airport, Rachael? Did she? Did she say — "

But I had dropped the receiver to the floor and stumbled to a chair where, to keep from passing out, I dropped my head between my knees and held my ice-cold face with floured hands. By the time the fainting spell had passed, Jacobo had hung up on his end. In the bathroom I searched for a bottle of aspirin in the cabinet over the sink, and in the mirror caught sight of my flour-streaked brow, cheeks, nose and chin: I looked like a woman readied for a tribal dance meant to keep the evil spirits at bay. Then tears cutting vertical streaks through the white mask. "Please, God," I prayed, though I am not a religious person. "Please let her be all right."

If your mother were still alive, Marcella, she would have told you herself of those hours at Ezeiza when the crowd of which she was a part exploded, I remember her saying later, "like a human bomb," and she would detail for you the brutality she witnessed — "I saw a man smiling as he choked another to death" — and the courage — "An old woman leaped like a cat onto to the back of a boy who had just drawn a gun from his coat" — and then she would lower her voice in the manner of one about to share a secret, or relate to another an event of such gravity that only a solemn whisper will do: "It was the worst day of my life, and also the best."

"Why the best, Mama?" you would say, "if such bad things happened?"

"Because I met your father there," your mother would murmur. "That's why, my angel. Because in the midst of all that madness, I fell in love."

And you would say, "Show me his pictures, Mama. Show me his pictures again," Miriam picking up from the table beside the sofa where you cuddled with her the album she had prepared for you "to look at until he comes back," she had told me six months after his disappearance, a week before her own.

Oh Marcella, a person reading these pages might claim I have written for you a chronicle of despair, but think of all the love stories flourishing here in the presence of calamity:

Reba and Dov.

Reba and Ovid.

Sonia and Eliezar.

Sonia and Simon.

Felix and me.

Jacobo and me.

Miriam and Carlos.

On the charred ruins and the boxcar sidings and the barricades that litter these tales, imagine the names of those couples etched within hearts like ancient hieroglyphs the centuries preserve. When you have finished reading these tales, perhaps you will rest your own head on the shoulder of a dear companion, that bond part of your legacy, Marcella, tenderness and passion and joy — "Because in the midst of all that madness, I fell in love!" — family treasures offered to you as surely as jewels whose value increases each time one generation passes them on to the next.

"Tell me the whole story, Mama," you would plead with her. You are sitting beside her in this room where I write, your father's album of photographs in your hands like a book you are asking your mother to read. "Tell me exactly how it happened that day."

And so she does, the next tale in this narrative Miriam's as well, her voice as I imagine it speaking through my pen to you, who receives it as if it were truly your mother creating for you the memory of your parents' meeting, that singular event in each person's life in which one's private cosmology originates, in which the star bearing one's true name — Marcella, because it sounds like music — explodes.

"It began like a holiday," she tells you now. "In the morning I woke to carnival music beneath my window, and cars already clogging the streets, and the sidewalks filled with people hurrying to the subway, which was free today for the trip to Ezeiza. I had not been sure I would go myself. I was not the Peronist I was as a teenager, though I did think it was good for Argentina that he was returning. Maybe now the chaos would end, maybe his compassion for the poor would bring some real change. Still, when my friend Graciela had asked me if I was planning to be at the airport, I'd told her, "Graciela, I have retired from demonstrations," and we laughed, because here I was only twenty-five years old and I'd been to so many rallies and marches, I could talk like an old woman about 'retirement.'" In truth, I had decided that I was worth more as a free lawyer than a jailed protester, and I had stopped going to public events in which there was a good chance of violence and arrests. And of course my parents and grandmother were very relieved, for which I was happy, though it was not for them that I had made this tactical choice.

"But when I looked down on that celebration, I knew I would have to join the crowd heading for Ezeiza. Oh Marcella, the crowd! By the time we reached Retiro station, tens of thousands had amassed, the avenues of Buenos Aires like funnels down which people poured — rich and poor, men and women, rightists and communists, union organizers and college professors — everyone flowing together because of one man in whom all of them believed: Peron! Rich women from Palermo in high heels and dresses and new wool coats they'd bought on Calle Florida; barrio boys in rope-belted dungarees and moth-eaten sweaters dug out of Recoleta dumpsters; dust-swathed ranch hands riding miles on mules from their *estancia* shacks; students wheeling through the throng on English racers they'd chain to bicycle stands at the station's entrance; shopkeepers giving away fresh oranges and hot *empañadas* and finally yielding to the excitement themselves: 'Closed for the Day,' the signs read on the shuttered doors; 'Viva Peron!' Who could remember inflation or bribes or broad-daylight abductions or amputated ears sent through the mail or torched shantytowns to which no fire trucks sped? It seemed we had all just risen from a terrible dream, these last years of chaos, and we were rushing by the thousands in a roused state toward the agent of our awakening: 'Peron! Peron! Viva Peron!'

"If you had gazed down on the airport from the sky, I think we would have looked like lava pouring over the roof of the terminal, the high metal fencing, the parking lot asphalt, the grass slopes, the landing field. Truly, Marcella, in a crowd like that, one feels as if one has lost the boundaries of one's particular body, that one has melted into the man in front and the woman behind and the shoulders on either side could be your own or another's, it becomes difficult to know whose limb belongs to whom. So when I say that I heard a gunshot, I could not even be sure if my own ears or another's had registered that popping noise, if my voice or another's screamed 'Get down! Get down!', if I had already squatted or was pushed to the ground by others, if I yelled, 'Run!' or heard that call from someone still standing, beneath whose stampeding feet I might have perished had not a stranger lifted me like a fallen sack and carried me with him on his galloping escape from the battling mob that festive crowd had now become, carried me with him over the tarmac through the terminal to the lot where he'd parked his motorcycle on which we sped through back roads back to the city, my eyes closed against the gusts of wintry air, my arms around a stranger's waist, my body pressed to his back as if in intimate embrace, my mind filled with images I'd recorded like a wartime photographer on the front.

"At a red light, he said to me over his shoulder, 'Where shall I drop you?'

"'Where are you going?'

"'To my office to file a story.'

"'You're a journalist?'

"'I am.'

"'For what paper?'

"He told me. I said, 'That's the only paper worth reading in this whole damn country, and it's one block from my own office, so we're going to the same place. And thank you for saving my life!' I said, screaming the last words over the din of his revving motor into his helmetted ear.

"Marcella, I did not even get a good look at his face until we arrived on Belcarce, but by that time I was already in love with your father. Who can explain how such a thing happened? All I know is that it did. Later I told him that and he said, 'You certainly took your time, didn't you? I fell in love with you at the airport. You think my heroics were strictly altruistic?'

" 'Well,' I said, 'for two people who claim to abhor the reactionary agenda of romance, we have gotten ourselves into a beautiful mess, haven't we?'

" 'I agree with you that it's beautiful, Miriam,' he said, lifting my hand as if it were the most fragile piece of crystal and kissing each finger, one by one. 'But I don't think it's a mess at all.' "

Granddaughter, forgive me for silencing your mother here.

I could write forever in her voice, until I, too, believed it was truly Miriam recording her memories for you and for me, both of us giving ourselves up to the fiction of her presence here on these pages when the truth we must face resides in all the stories she will never tell. Let her fall silent suddenly, in the midst of her narrative, in the pause between one sentence and the next, in the moment it took some morgue clerk to enter "NN" in his official register.

These glimpses I give you of your mother are my memories, my inventions, my inspirations, and if they help you imagine her as she was, I am grateful to whatever the power is that impels me to write these stories, each morning my wavering resolve to complete this project somehow renewed by the time I have finished my breakfast, the despair to which I wake each morning staved off each time I pick up my pen and begin.

Between each line, be sure to read the one fact I must not obscure:

No Name. NN.

Miriam Silver Rojas.

Little Fish.

Beloved daughter of Jacobo and Rachael Silver, granddaughter of Sonia Pearl, wife of Carlos Rojas and mother of Marcella.

1949–1976.

23

As it turned out, they had heard of each other, the attorney for the poor and the journalist for "the only paper worth reading in this whole damn country," a leftist weekly whose staff Carlos had only recently joined, the Legal Institute for the Poor on his list of contacts to cultivate, someone there surely a good subject for a story, a profile, an in-depth interview.

"The only article I'll help you with," Miriam told Carlos, "is one you write about the barrio I serve. Come with me one day to Villa Francisco, if you want stories. People there will talk to you for hours, believe me. They are not afraid. What else can they lose?"

Villa Francisco is one of the shantytowns, over fifty of them, that ring Buenos Aires. From high-rise apartments and office buildings and elegant hotels advertising the panoramic view from rooftop restaurants, *porteños* and tourists alike look down on a necklace of slums, cardboard shacks and burned-out cars reclaimed as shelters: the desperate resourcefulness of the poor. Raw sewage runs in gullies down dirt roads, and all day women scream at barefoot children, "Don't play in the water, *bambino*, it will make you sick!," but still the stench of diarrhea and vomit is so strong, people there say you can find the encampment easily: "Follow your nose!" they tell you. "Follow your nose!

"You know what Evita used to say to the poor?" Miriam said. "'Shall we burn down the Barrio Norte? Shall I give you fire?'" She was leading Carlos through the maze of structures so flimsy it seemed the slightest breeze would topple the entire neighborhood, roofs of salvaged tin clattering like pot lids to the littered ground. "Now they have no advocate in the Casa Rosada. Peron's in bed with the military and Isabelita redecorates."

Children came from all directions, tugging at their clothes. "Money?" they asked the visitors. "*Por favor?*"

Many knew Miriam by name, and greeted her as if she were a relative returning from a trip. "Did you bring us presents, Senorita? Can we ride in your car like last time? Is that your husband?"

"No, no," she said, blushing. "He is a friend."

(Later Carlos would tell her, "You remember the first time I went with you to Villa Francisco and some kid asked you if I were your husband? I nearly said, 'Not yet, but I will be.' Pretty self-confident, wasn't I?"

And Miriam would smile. "My grandmother would tell you it's all inscribed on your palm. It has nothing to do with self-confidence. We were destined, she would say. How does your male ego like that explanation?")

Walking through the mud two days of rain had made of the road, puddles so big children sailed paper boats across the "lakes" and waded up to their knees in the brackish pools, the couple came at last to the shack Miriam decided to visit first, its cardboard walls kept dry by a huge tarp no doubt filched from someone's docked sailboat. Through the curtain of oilcloth passing for a front door, she called, "Maria! Are you home, Maria?" and a woman, nursing a baby, appeared.

When Maria Ortiz saw Carlos, fear flooded her face and her smile of greeting vanished.

"He's a friend," Miriam said. "*Compañero.* A writer. I hoped Miguel would talk to him. Please trust me, Maria. You know I — "

For a moment, the woman looked into Miriam's eyes as if they held information words could not convey, and when Maria seemed convinced that Miriam's silent speech confirmed her utterance, Senora Ortiz welcomed the two of them into her home.

Inside, newspaper insulated the walls and someone had made a floor of splintered planks of wood made to fit together like pieces from several puzzles, but there were gaps between the planks and Carlos saw a rat burrow into one of the holes. Nearby a pot simmered on a kerosene stove and half the floor was taken up by a mattress covered with a new quilt Miriam had bought for the family. Maria gestured for her guests to sit on the bed, and pulled the single rusted folding chair closer.

"How is Miguel?" Miriam said. "Is he home today?"

"Working, thank God," Maria said. "If they had kept him in jail, I would have had to — " she pointed with her chin to the bed on which they sat — "do something for money. I told Miguel, 'Look, if I don't eat, my milk *doesn't come*,' but he said he would kill me if I sold myself again. So it is a good thing some day work came through. because otherwise — "

"Maria, I brought some papers for you and Miguel to fill out. To qualify for food assistance. I know you don't read, but Miguel — "

"He knows a few words — "

"When the social worker comes on Wednesdays, ask her to help him fill these out. Or Father Amaya."

"Father Amaya, *si*," said Maria. "He does everybody's papers here. Put them under the quilt for now."

Then the baby was crying, refusing to nurse.

"I think he's sick," Maria Ortiz said. She began walking back and forth in the tiny space with the wailing infant, her shuffle so labored it seemed that she, herself, were ill.

"Maria," Miriam said. "Can I do something? Can I drive you to the clinic?"

"I don't go to the clinic anymore. You wait for hours and every-one there has fever and cough and the baby gets sicker than before. I will take him to my friend Dolores, she will give me Guarani medicine."

"You are sure?"

She was trying to feed the infant again. "Yes, yes. I go to Dolores tomorrow."

Miriam and Carlos rose.

"Tell Miguel I am glad he is free."

"This time he is," Maria said. "Next time who knows?"

"I was glad to meet you, Senora Ortiz," Carlos said, but Maria did not take notice of them anymore. She was singing to her baby, a song about golden fields and heaven and angels with beautiful wings.

Outside again, Miriam said, "Do you know what Father Amaya calls this place? He calls it 'the village of tears.'"

And then she was weeping, Carlos offering her his handker-chief.

"What happened to my toughness?" she said. "I'm usually so strong."

"You are very strong, Miriam," he said. "I wouldn't have the courage to cry myself."

They would marry five months later, and a month before the wed-ding, Jacobo, my mother and I drove to La Plata to meet Carlos' mother. He had shown us a picture of his parents weeks before. "When my father died ten years ago, my sister and I feared for Mother. She was the perfect Latino wife, you know, completely devoted to her husband and children, and now what would she do with herself? Claudia and I were seventeen and eighteen already, about to go out on our own. Well, she fooled us, and herself as well, I think. She began to volunteer at the hospital, in the pediatrics ward, telling stories to the children, the way she did for my sister and me when we were small, and soon she had a title — 'The Story Lady' — and a whole new identity in the world. She's there four, five days a week. She likes to joke with me. 'Carlos,' she likes to say, 'a journalist can only write from the facts. I take over where you leave off, I'm like a Borges for the little ones!' "

She had invited us here for dinner, the two families together for the first time in the small bungalow the widow lived in alone, now that her son had moved to Buenos Aires and her daughter gone to America to study archaeology "so she can come back here to dig up dinosaur bones," Nidia Rojas told us, rolling her eyes over Claudia's eccentric ambitions, never fathoming the grim and practical task toward which her child's talents would turn.

"When she and Carlos were children and their father was still alive, he used to take them every weekend to the Museum of Natural Science here. Every weekend. Do you remember, Carlos? You were not so enthusiastic, but Claudia was entranced from her earliest years. She was always in the backyard with her little shovel. 'You'll dig up my flowers!' I used to scold her, but Emilio would tell me, 'Nidia, please, let her play. It's a sin to punish curiosity.' A philosopher, Emilio. Not for a living, of course. He was an electrician, that was his work. But he loved that museum. For him, it was like church, I think."

"I wish we could have met him," Jacobo said. "And I look forward to meeting Claudia at the wedding. I have always been a bit of an amateur archaeologist myself. And Freud, you know, used it as his metaphor for psychoanalysis, so I'm already in the field, so to speak."

And so the dinner table talk continued, each of us contributing slivers of family lore like shards we'd found at the site of one excavation or another, placing the fragments on Nidia Rojas' handembroidered white cloth, that ceremonial linen we did not realize would become a shroud, that feast a funeral, that laughter tears I mix into the ink with which I write these tales, Marcella. Yet even in my grief, I feel again the gaiety of that evening as I reconstruct it for you, and in the fact of your existence I find my consolation. Isn't it true, granddaughter, that in every word you utter all our voices rise again in unison — "To the future!" — and defy the terrible events we could not know our toast announced?

Later, in the fever of memory that grief becomes, I would remember how quiet my mother was that night at Nidia Rojas' home, quieter even that usual, as if she were focussed on some other drama entirely, not the festive banter and the nostalgic anecdotes tailored to the occasion. Who would have thought to recall at that table our flight from Baille Herculane, or the months of hiding in the Koneprussy Caves, or our first failed migration to Argentina and Nanna's sad death, or Jacobo's ordeal in Dachau in which all of his relations perished? Perhaps my mother was lost in those memories Jacobo and I could gladly forget for those few happy hours; or perhaps she, too, fixed on the future, her vision not the bubbly one we saw at the bottom of our hoisted glasses of champagne, but one she discerned from the palms she read covertly, her eyes not really shut in fatigue, or the aftermath of the flu from which she was still recovering, but lowered just enough to allow her to glimpse one person's upturned hand, then another, until by the end of the evening she could have drawn a map of the years ahead, each one's destiny tied to the others, each one's fate wedded to the next, a secret circle of sorrow only Sonia Pearl perceived that night.

"Nanna," Miriam said toward the end of our dinner. "You have hardly eaten anything. Perhaps your stomach is still upset? The flan will go down so easily, and soothe you as well. Try a spoonful, you'll see it agrees with you."

"Ah, sweetheart," my mother said. "This is not a night for you to worry about an old woman's digestion." She smiled at her grand-daughter, but pain clouded her eyes, and years later when I recalled that look, I suspected it was not over her own health that my moth-er had been suffering. Once I asked her, long after Carlos and Miriam had disappeared, if she had foreseen their tragedy that night we had celebrated their imminent marriage.

"When I was a girl," she said, in one of her rare references to her childhood, "a gypsy taught me that no matter how much one sees in a palm, God sees more."

"I didn't think you believed in God, Mama."

"And what if I don't? Do you think God cares about what I believe and don't believe?"

We laughed together, and then we wept.

And wept.

And wept.

24

ALTHOUGH IT WAS SMALL, Miriam and Carlos had decided to live in Miriam's San Telmo flat, Carlos moving out of his furnished efficiency downtown and arriving one day on Belcarce with a rented truck loaded with his belongings — boxes of books, mostly; an iron skillet; a typewriter; some Indian pottery from Jujuy and a twisted three-foot limestone spire mounted on a block of mahogany.

Days before their first anniversary, I visited them. "You know, Carlos, each time I've been here, I've admired this sculpture," I said, tracing the curves and hollows of the stone's contortions. "Who is the artist?"

Carlos grinned. "God," he said.

"I'm serious."

"So am I. I found this on the ground when I was hiking in the Valle Encantado. Have you been there? Incredible formations, for miles. It's like being inside a cave full of stalactite, except here you're out in the open, surrounded by these stone totems. My sister told me the Indians who used to live there believed the formations had once been people who were frozen in place by an angry god. One spire, actually, is called God's Finger, and let me tell you, it is menacing."

Miriam laughed. "That's because you have a lot to be guilty about. Your wild bachelor past."

"Really? Is that so? And here I thought I was having a metaphysical experience."

"Please, Carlos," Miriam teased. "Not in front of my mother!"

"Oh!" I said in mock irritation. "So you think I am that old-fashioned, do you? Please remember I am a bohemian artist, as well as a suburban wife and mother. Which reminds me — "

I reached into a shopping bag beside the chair in which I sat.

"A gift for my daughter and son-in-law," I said.

Miriam unwrapped the watercolor I'd made for them: a painting of the jacaranda tree blooming outside their window, yellow blossoms massed against a blue Buenos Aires sky.

"Mama, how lovely!"

"What a wonderful present!" Juan said.

"So you can remember how beautiful the flowers are when winter comes again," I said.

Winter would never come again for your father, Marcella. And before the next cold season arrived, your mother would also disappear, allowed to survive just until your birth — "The baby is alive, Jacobo!" — which I would learn about years later, beginning the search I will soon recount to you in the final pages of these stories. If I were a religious woman, I would call them *God is still angry*, that finger of rock pointed at your parents' murderers in a verdict no pardon can ever erase, no amnesty ever subvert, no government ever set aside "for the sake of national unity and reconciliation."

Miriam went to the kitchen for a hammer and nail, wondered with Carlos where the best place for the picture would be. She drove the nail into the wall and hung the framed watercolor, tilting it this way and that until she was sure it was even. Suddenly a huge explosion — a car bomb on the waterfront, we'd learn later, and seven dead on the docks — shook the building and the painting of the tree fell to the floor, glass shattering at our feet.

"Stay inside!" Carlos yelled, as if we were children who might get hurt, while he himself was the invincible elder. He grabbed a notebook from his desk and slammed the door behind him.

Miriam said, "Don't worry, Mama, I'll sweep it up," as if the broken glass were the reason I had turned white as snow, trembling like a woman chilled — in the middle of summer — right to the bone.

At home that evening, before I could even recount to Jacobo how close to us the violence had come this time, he was pounding the kitchen table with rage over news a patient had brought him that day: another Jewish cemetery desecrated, and a synagogue in Corrientes riddled with bullets in the middle of the night.

"We have to face it," Jacobo said. He was sitting now, his face in his hands, on the verge of weeping. He looked so stricken, as if his most cherished friend had deserted him, as if he had been betrayed by a beloved. "Nazis are in this up to their eyeballs. I always knew Peron was an anti-Semite, but since his death the worst elements, the very worst, are taking over. I tell you "— his voice broke —" I wouldn't be surprised if we wind up with camps again, the whole nightmare. The Jews who were born and raised here, they refuse to believe it could happen in this country. I used to deny it myself, didn't I? Not anymore. Only survivors understand."

I sat down beside my husband and stroked his face. "Jacobo, sweetheart, you know what you tell me when I get frightened like that? You say, 'Rachael, it's behind us. Europe is behind us.' Do you hear me, Jacobo? Your own words. I am giving you back your own words, darling."

"And Miriam on the other side, with the Marxist maniacs, with the — "

"She's not, she's not. You're — "

"I'm what? You don't think she knows Montoneros? You don't read your son-in-law's articles?"

"He's a journalist. A journalist talks to anyone."

Jacobo wiped his eyes with a napkin. He shook his head. "No. No. Not in Argentina in 1975. If he wants to stay alive, he does not talk to 'anyone,' Rachael."

"Do you remember when you told Miriam how proud — "

Just then Jacobo raised his hand to me in a silencing signal, and I looked from him to the doorway. My mother stood washed in the rose-tinged light that turned our house, at dusk, into a series of watercolor tableaus — I had done dozens of still-lifes at that time of day, trying to capture the transforming glow, but this was the first time I understood why its beauty moved me so deeply. Although her expression was sorrowful, it seemed as if my mother herself were emitting that opalescence, her own aura made visible. No less than the sun's unextinguishable splendor, this was a radiance so essential, so primary, I knew in a sudden wordless awe that it would outlive her body, that no earthly force could ever truly threaten the muted power of that illumined field. Just looking at her calmed me. Yes, I rose to comfort her and put my arms around my grim-faced mother stricken once more by the peril that pursued her family from one end of the world to the other, but in truth it was that light that embraced me, that turned us both into beings whose mystery can never be contained in the mere vessel of skin and bones we take to be ourselves.

Skull, ribcage, pelvis, femur, fibula: do not think that is all that remained of your mother by the time we found the unmarked grave where they believed they had disposed of her.

Who can bury radiance, Marcella?

Who?

"Mama, please, please, don't be frightened," I crooned into her ear. Although I was the one offering the solace, she was patting me on the back in a gesture of maternal concern, the two of us swaying together in that hour of illumination that always precedes the night.

On the day the doctor confirms she is pregnant, Miriam leaves her office early and walks to the market in La Boca where she buys ingredients for paella and a bottle of wine and pastry from her favorite bakery. Carlos likes to tease her about her cravings for sweets: "When we find out you're pregnant," he'd say, "the sugar cane growers will celebrate!" At a flower stand she chooses lupine, asters, baby's breath. "Big storm coming," the vendor says, wrapping her flowers in tissue paper. She looks at the sky, heavy purple clouds spreading like bruises to the horizon; wind makes tiny cyclones of the dust at her feet. By the time the bus drops her a block from their apartment, it is raining and the gusts turn her umbrella inside out as soon as she manages to open it, the inverted spokes thrust suddenly upward like a ring of broken bones.

Still, the weather does not disturb her, nor the ruined umbrella. The flowers are soaked, but intact, even the fragile baby's breath; in the sink, she shakes the water from the bouquet, then fills the vase and arranges the assortment. Carlos will laugh at the phallic lupine spears, the round aster blossoms. "I wish your father could see this," she imagines him saying. "A psychiatrist's dream come true."

While she shells the shrimp for the paella, she rehearses a dozen different ways to tell him the news they have hoped for months to hear. She naps while the fragrant stew simmers, and when she wakes she showers and puts on a caftan Carlos particularly likes, its sleeves and hem embroidered for her by an Indian woman whose son Miriam has represented many times in court. At work, she wears her long hair braided, the plait coiled and pinned at the nape of her neck. At home, she undoes the braid and lets the crinkled mane flow down her back. "You look Inca," he often tells her, running his hand across her high cheek bone, down the length of her black hair. "A beautiful Inca woman."

How long does she wait for him to come home?

Until the candles burn down to the rim of their hammered brass holders?

Until the paella is cold and the bread she's warmed in the oven like stone to her touch?

Until there are no more friends and fellow reporters and names she barely recognizes next to numbers he's scribbled into their book left to call? "I was wondering, Hector, if Carlos mentioned where he might be this evening. It's not that I'm worried, exactly, but it isn't like him to be this late and not. . ." and "This is Miriam Rojas and I thought you might know where Carlos. . ." and "Yes, I am trying to locate Carlos Rojas and since he has recently been in contact with you, I hoped you could tell me where. . . ." and hanging up several times after dialling us in San Ysidro because she is not yet ready to panic, imagine the worst, give in to the terror that keeps her from eating a single bite of food that night.

At two a.m., she will tell me later, she drinks half the bottle of chablis from a water glass she fills three times, then falls asleep on the sofa, dressed in the hand-embroidered caftan the Indian woman had promised would bring good luck each time it was worn. "In our tradition," the woman had said, "stitching is sacred. The designs are like prayers, and you see this bird here I put on the left sleeve? This is the bird of eternal life. It reminds us how the soul flies from the body after death and lives forever with God."

"Such a beautiful symbol," Miriam had said, and the Indian woman had answered, " 'Symbol,' that is a white person's word. For us, it is the actual thing. For us, it is what it is."

When Miriam wakes from her wine-induced stupor at five in the morning, and Carlos has still not returned to their apartment, "I prayed he was with another woman," she will confide, "but I knew the truth. I sat down at the typewriter and started to make out a writ of habeas corpus — I'd done hundreds already, for others — but I couldn't finish. I don't know how long I sat there, frozen like a statue. By seven, the phone was ringing and ringing — "Is he back?" "Did he call?" "No word yet?"

Yes, yes, one word, of course there was one word, Marcella, though it would be weeks before any of us were willing to say it aloud: *desaparecido.*

Disappeared.

Disappeared.

Disappeared.

Every day Carlos' mother went to church in La Plata and prayed for some word of her son, and every day Miriam went to the central courts building to file yet another writ of habeas corpus on Carlos' behalf. Scores of people waited in line; the *Buenos Aires Herald* reported the daily disappearances, the unmarked Ford Falcons into which victims were being dragged in broad daylight now, out of homes and classrooms and cafes and parks where children knew to turn away from the abduction scene as if it had not really happened at all.

"No such person is being held," the police told Miriam again and again. "We never issued a warrant for the arrest of this person."

"He was kidnapped from a bar called El Nido where he was having a cognac with a journalist from America. If you don't have him, why aren't you investigating his kidnapping?"

"We have taken the information."

"You have taken my husband!" she screamed at the officer. "You have taken the father of my baby!"

What Nidia Rojas screamed at God, I do not know. A sister in Mendoza wanted her to move in with her, but Maria insisted she

had to remain in La Plata "in case Carlos tries to call me," just as she
did when I suggested that she join us at our house in San Ysidro.

"Carlos would not want you to be going through this all by
yourself," I told her.

"Oh, I am not by myself," Maria Rojas said. "The Blessed
Virgin is with me."

When she offered that response to her archaeologist daughter,
whom Maria had begged to stay in California "so I know at least
one of my children is safe," Claudia said, "Does the Blessed Virgin
cook for you and take you to the doctor when your angina flares
up and put her arms around you when you need to cry, Mamita?"
When the priest who had baptized both children called Claudia to
report that Maria had "broken down" in the chapel, blowing out all
the votive candles people had lit for their loved ones that day,
Carlos' sister was on the next plane to Buenos Aires. And three
months later, when Maria Rojas died in seven weeks from uterine
cancer the doctors had believed she would survive, Claudia told the
surgeon, "You don't understand a thing. My mother did not die of
cancer, she died of grief. They took her son from her, her little boy!
Do you think it was an accident the tumor was in her womb?"

Years later, standing at the site of the grave from which she had
helped exhume her own brother's bones, Claudia Rojas would tell
me, "When I came back from the States, I knew he was dead as
soon as we touched the tarmac. The Indians would say his spirit
came to meet my plane."

"What would you say?" I asked.

She bent to the excavated ground, ran her fingers through the
dry dirt as if it contained some further evidence the team of scientists had not discovered in their countless siftings of the earth.

"I would say that those were Carlos' bones we found here, but
that those bones were not Carlos."

We had not yet found your mother's grave, Marcella, but I would remember those words when we did: these are Miriam's bones we have found here, but these bones are not Miriam.

Skull, ribcage, pelvis, femur, fibula: yes.

But who can kill radiance?

Who?

25

"TELL ME," THE JOURNALIST from New York said yesterday, here in this house where she had come to interview me, "how did you women first get the idea for the weekly marches in the Plaza de Mayo?"

"It was not 'an idea,'" I told her. "It happened on its own."

I told her how the military government, besieged by pleas for information about those who had vanished, designated ninety minutes on Thursday afternoons for dealing with "the current hysteria," ninety minutes allotted to our "unrealistic requests during a state of national emergency."

This was April, 1977. Miriam had disappeared over one year before, Carlos seven months earlier.

I told the American journalist that while we waited outside for the office to open its doors to the few of us who could be seen in an hour and a half, and waited until the "closed" sign was posted and those remaining cheerfully instructed to "try again next week," as if we had missed a sale or a sold-out concert, we walked.

I told her we were used to walking, after all.

Didn't we walk half the nights in our homes, stalking the dark rooms like nocturnal animals searching for food? Didn't we walk the long corridors of hospitals, peering in rooms where a child might lay wounded, a beaten son comatose, a tortured daughter amnesiac and mad? Those were the terrible scenarios for which we hoped — at least if we found our babies there, we could nurse them back to health, we reasoned — and even those hopes were futile. Didn't we walk, like women in a trance, the familiar routes our children had frequented, retracing their steps from home to office or campus to favorite cafe to tango bar to shops they liked on fancy Calle Florida or the outdoor stalls of the San Telmo bazaar? Didn't we think we spotted the vanished one a dozen times a week, our slow pace turning to gallop only to discover yet another mistake, a mumbled "Excuse me, I thought you were — " and then the tears stinging our eyes and exhaustion upon us. Oh yes, I told the woman from New York, day and night we mothers walked and walked and walked, the Plaza de Mayo just one more place for us to measure off the endless miles of our pain.

Soon others were joining us, as if we had actually planned demonstrations Thursday afternoons in front of the Casa Rosada. Women who had been afraid to report a disappearance drew strength from our presence, came in spite of a husband's injunction "not to tell a soul what has happened," in spite of a sibling's terror that "if we file a report they'll come after the whole family." Women who had already given up any hope that their children might be found left the beds to which they had withdrawn like invalids, dressed again for the first time in weeks or months and joined our growing number "to make them tell us something, even the worst." One week someone wore around her neck a picture of her daughter glued to cardboard, and the following Thursday dozens of us arrived with our own missing children's photographs next to our bosoms like the babies we had nursed decades ago. "And white scarves on our heads, like Senora Conti always does," someone suggested, dozens of us donning them the subsequent week, the simple garment like the hooded wimples of nuns and we the women of a particular order: call us the Sisters of Sorrow, the Sisters of Unspeakable Pain. Soon the dozens we were turned into hundreds, the weeks turned into years, and and some of us disappeared like our children, and we walked in every kind of weather, we walked when we were sick and when we were healthy, we walked like the silent mourners in a funeral procession for which we were constantly rehearsing, we circled the plaza enough times to walk around the world.

The Sisters of Sorrow.

The Sisters of Unspeakable Pain.

Madres de la Plaza de Mayo.

"You were such heroic women," the journalist from America said. "You helped bring down a despicable government, you raised the world's consciousness, you risked your lives every time you marched."

Telling her just this much of the story had exhausted me, and the interview had barely begun.

"I don't know about heroics. We were mothers," I said. "Mothers. That is the important thing to remember."

I looked down at my hands and they seemed to have aged in the time I had been speaking. "I must lie down for awhile," I told her. I gave her documents to read while I napped: testimony, depositions, copies of legal decisions. I gave her albums filled with photographs of Miriam as a child, a teenager, a bride. "I must rest."

In an hour of half-sleep, the last day I saw Miriam returned in a shower of images, meteor-bright and brief as those shining flares that flash for a moment in the night sky, then vanish even as we gaze. Once, when she was very young, I took my daughter to the planetarium. In the high-domed hall, our seats tilted back like beds, the lights went out, Miriam reached for my hand in the dark and the ceiling above us opened to heavens pulsing with so many stars, it seemed we must be dreaming this glittering landscape. A disembodied voice, soothing and deep, described the constellations whose immutable beauty, he said, "humans have been studying since the beginning of history." Then what streaked suddenly across that fixed field, what bright object broke loose from its moorings, lifted and fell in a fatal arc? Miriam lurched upright, her gasp the only sound in that stilled auditorium, the rest of us mute witness to that star's doomed flight.

Oh daughter! Where is the invisible announcer to help me understand your disappearance?

And where is the science that makes sense of that fateful day's memories, scenes that glow and plummet, glow and plummet, glow and plummet on the ceiling over my bed?

Morning in the kitchen. March 3, 1976. Miriam stirs the polenta she makes each day "for the baby," and the steam turns to ringlets the strands of hair not caught by the barrette at the nape of her neck. In the sunlight, she looks like a woman in a Reubens painting, ample and healthy, no sign of the terrible strain she carries inside her like a twin to the child due in two months. Of Carlos she says only, "I refuse to believe that he is dead," though each week of his absence confirms the fear none of us will utter. Days ago a colleague called to tell her bodies had been found at the city dump, and one had been identified as a reporter at Carlos' paper. "Tortured," Miriam told us, trembling "Tortured and killed."

Yet this morning she has recovered from that latest blow to her hope, and I even hear her humming as she cooks.

"You always hated breakfast," I say, kissing her on the cheek.

"And I still do," she says, putting her free arm around me. "What we mothers do for our children." She winks at me, grins. "If they only knew."

I get down three cereal bowls from the cupboard. Jacobo has already left for the hospital, but my mother is up — we hear her footsteps above us. Sometimes she sleeps until noon to make up for the hours she spends in the dark, awake, listening for danger. Jacobo suggests sedatives, but she refuses. How can she maintain her vigil if she is groggy, drugged? Last night I dreamed of us in the Koneprussy Caves, how she always divided our foraged food into three portions, allotting me two.

At the table, we all eat polenta, drink coffee, spear with a fork pieces of melon my mother has cut into cubes. This is one of those rare hours when all of us are able to pretend together that nothing terrible has befallen our family, a moment of mutual denial, a shared fantasy of well-being.

Think of my mother pretending to hear my father's in the tunnels of Plzen.

Think of my grandmother Reba making love with her vanished husband, Dov.

"Today I'm meeting Claudia for lunch," Miriam says. She and Carlos' sister have grown close since Maria Rojas' death. "My appointment's at two. When I'm finished, I think I'll walk over to Papa's office and come home with him."

"If you feel up to it," I say, picturing the long hike she plans to make through Palermo Park. "You can always take a taxi if you get tired."

"Don't overdo," my mother says. "Be careful."

Miriam smiles and rolls her eyes. "Cluck cluck cluck," she says. "Cluck cluck cluck."

From the bathroom where she readies for her appointment, I hear water running in the tub. I am upstairs, making beds, taking down curtains that need to be washed. Later they will flap like white flags on a backyard clothesline. In the hallway, taking sheets from the linen closet, I listen for a moment to the sounds of Miriam bathing, the tiny splashes reminding me of the first time I immersed her in water, how her wailing ceased and her tense limbs relaxed in a kind of bodily sigh of relief, how all through her childhood bath time was her favorite hour. Little fish, I whisper through a sudden sting of tears. Little Fish.

"Let me drive you to the subway," I tell her.

Eleven now, and she is putting on her coat, a putty-colored trenchcoat she cannot button anymore — she ties the sash gently across her baby-swelled belly. I hug her, fix her crooked collar, look upon my daughter's lovely face and lower my eyes quickly, so she will miss the worry I know has risen in my gaze. Whenever she leaves the house now — at least, Jacobo reminds me, we convinced her to leave the apartment and stay with us here in San Ysidro — I have to fight my urge to pull her back inside. "Mamá," she told me once, "I don't want to frighten you more than you already are, but you know they are taking people out of their homes. In front of their families. There are no safe places anymore in Argentina."

"What are you saying, Miriam? My God, you're pregnant. You think they would — "

"I refuse to think about it at all," she said. "It's not good for the baby for me to be upset. Okay?"

Well, Marcella, they did not take your mother out of her home, in front of her family. No, they waited for her outside the office of her obstetrician; they allowed her the time for a third-trimester pelvic, and only when she had dressed again and paid her bill and taken the elevator down to the lobby did the men in the unmarked Ford Falcon kidnap the woman who could no longer button her coat. "First I thought they had taken me because I was Carlos Rojas' wife," Miriam would tell a cell mate who survived to report the conversation. "Then I thought it was because of the work I had done as a lawyer. But finally I understood: they took me because I am pregnant. Do you see? My God, Beatriz, they took me for the baby!"

At six, Jacobo comes home. I hear the door shut behind him. From my studio, I holler, "What did the doctor say?"

"The doctor said, 'Hello, is anybody home?'"

"No," I laugh, walking from the room at the rear of the house where I paint to the front foyer. "I meant Miriam's doctor. Where is she? Outside with Mama?"

"I haven't seen her," he says.

"But she came home with you."

"No," he says. "She didn't. I haven't seen her at all today."

We are staring at each other so hard, it seems we are keeping each other erect with our eyes.

"But she said she was — "

"I am telling you, Rachael, I — "

"Claudia," I say, on the way to the phone in the kitchen. "Claudia will know. They had lunch together."

Claudia Rojas tells me, yes, Miriam planned to walk to her

father's office after her doctor's appointment at two. Is anything wrong, she wants to know. Is anything wrong?

"Yes," I answer, though Claudia is saying, "Rachael, I can't hear you. Rachael?"

Yes, yes, yes, I keep telling her. Yes, something is wrong.

And then the telephone hitting the floor as I fall.

"Mrs. Silver, are you all right?"

Outside my bedroom door, the journalist from New York tapped lightly, called to me. For a moment, I thought it was Claudia, whose voice on the telephone all those years before — "Is anything wrong?" — played in my head over and over like the recording you hear when you have not hung up the receiver properly.

"Yes," I said, opening my eyes, the images of the last hour dissolving in the dazzle of afternoon light that danced on the far wall. "I'm fine. I was just getting up. Thank you for waiting."

"What I'd like to focus on," she said, once I had joined her again in the parlor, "is how you discovered that your grandchild was alive, and what followed from that."

Telling her about the disappearances and how we mothers bore our losses had forced me to bed. No matter that I had narrated those events a hundred times, sworn under oath to the truth of my account, talked to reporters and college students and American congressman come to verify with their own ears the charges of the Madres of the Plaza de Mayo. Each time I recounted that terrible time, exhaustion followed. Sometimes I fell ill, attacks of fever and chills lasting all night, or a deepening cough that racked my ribs and left me voiceless, unable to speak a word for days. "No more speeches!" Jacobo implored, and after he died, my mother Sonia begged me to leave the recounting to others less frail. "Words," she would tell me, her own silence about her past not yet broken. "What can words do for anyone?"

What do they do for you, Marcella, these words I leave you as a legacy, these words I spill like precious coins into your hands?

"Yes," I said to the American journalist, feeling revived, able to go on. "I will tell you the whole story. In the summer of 1979, a woman called me from Mendoza. . . ."

26

IN THE SUMMER OF 1979, a woman called me from Mendoza. "My name is Beatriz Vargas," she said, "and I was in prison with Miriam Rojas. Do you know her mother, a Rachael Silver?"

How many messages like this had I taken for others, here in the Madres' office where I came every day now? Sometimes a caller had hopeful news — "Yes, he was still alive when I left there, and in good enough health." Sometimes the word was bleak and foreboding — "I do not think she can stand many more beatings in that place. I do not think she can survive much longer." And sometimes the voice on the other end of the line offered only "He's dead" or "They shot her," and then a survivor's sobs overtaking speech.

"Rachael is good on the phones," other Madres would say. "She stays calm, and she knows the right questions to ask."

It was how we divided our work in those years: figuring out each other's strengths, matching them up with the tasks at hand. Some wrote press releases and letters to foreign officials; some delivered dispatches to newspapers and wire services and embassy maildrops; some visited the homes of released desparacidos, hoping for more clues about the thousands still missing; some toured the morgues together, teams of mothers looking for the bodies with torture marks; some kept the files updated and orderly, grief's archivists typing our anguish onto three-by-five cards we ordered by the gross. Some, like me, answered the phones, learned to tell quickly a crank call from a lead, a bad lead from a good one, an informer from a friend, speaking to all in the circumspect manner of one under surveillance, listening closely for the faint sounds of the tapping device.

"You are not a detective," Jacobo said once about what I had undertaken. "A person needs training — "

"I am a mother," I said. "Who trained me for that?"

"Yes," I said now to Beatriz Vargas, "I am Miriam Rojas' mother. Is she — "

"Can you come to Mendoza? I would rather speak to you in person and I am not able to travel myself." Then an address in the faraway city, and a plea: "I have cancer, Mrs. Silver. You must come soon."

"I will be there tomorrow," I told her, my heart already flying out of my body, on its way before I even placed the receiver back in its cradle, rose from the desk, took a few steps and stumbled, tears blurring my passage, my famous calmness gone now that the message was for me.

I am Miriam Rojas' mother. Who trained me for that?

I arrived at Mendoza at dusk, and rode in a taxi from the airport through the vineyards to the address Beatriz had given me. I had told Jacobo and my mother that my trip was Madres business, and they were used to my travels beyond Buenos Aires to help mothers organize in the towns and cities of the other provinces. Why did I keep the real reason for this journey a secret from my family? In my work with the Madres, I had seen too many eyewitnesses recant, grow confused, suddenly forget the information they had offered themselves; I had seen families paying money to impostors who knew nothing at all about the one from whom they had claimed to have messages; I had seen parents lured to cafes where they waited

for hours for "a friend of your son" or "your daughter's comrade"
who never arrived. How did I know what awaited me in Mendoza?
The cliffs of the Andes shimmered in the distance. In the fading
light, grape leaves turned silver, fields became lakes, vines like water
snakes writhing for miles. On a different errand, I might have found
the spectacle beautiful, wanted to paint that earthen sea, but I carried foreboding in all my cells now and nothing my eyes beheld
looked lovely. If bodies had risen from that terrain, I would not have
been surprised; if bones had floated up from the vineyards, I would
have stopped the cab to gather them, a harvest I dreaded and prepared for each day.

We were in the city now, destroyed once by earthquake and fire,
rebuilt low to the ground to withstand natural disasters, street after
street graced with rows of overarching trees and every few blocks,
a well-landscaped plaza in which lovers embraced and parents
played with their children on the grassy esplanades and elderly
Mendocinos walked their Pomeranians. Such harmony here: the
orderly architecture, the tended greenery, the citizenry enjoying the
mild twilight hour. Who would suspect that Mendoza, like all of the
country, was still under curfew law, and thirty minutes from now
the parks would be deserted, cafes shuttered, people and cars vanished from sight? The disappearances would soon cease — a country on the brink of economic ruin finds it hard to maintain the
apparatus of terror — but in the morning someone still might be
found dead at foot of the statue of San Martin, the thumbs of the
victim's bound hands tied together, a death squad's signature everyone recognized now in Argentina.

And I knocking on the door of a woman who claimed to have
shared a cell with my daughter, who I had last seen three years ago,
the shape of her shoulders as I hugged her that day like a phantom
limb an amputee feels for the rest of her life — the pain of what
has disappeared, the throb of absence in my arms.

I rang the bell at 44 San Juan, and it seemed that a ghost opened the door: a woman white as the moon and entirely bald, so that she looked like a moon herself whose face might be as much an illusion as the features we think we see in that celestial globe. And so thin. A cotton robe hung on her body like a cloth draped over a leafless tree. Only her eyes looked living to me: black and burning beneath that bleached mask her skin had become.

"I am Rachael Silver," I said.

"She looked just like you," Beatriz Vargas said, and my heart broke on the past tense, one word like a driven stake from a dying stranger who lacked the strength to shake my hand.

Miriam was dead — "We heard the baby cry, and five minutes later they wheeled Miriam covered with a sheet on a gurney right past the cell so we would see her. 'Here's the Jewish whore,' the fat one said. They lifted up the sheet to show us her face and when I reached through the bars to touch her cheek, one of the monsters brought down his club on my fingers. Laughing, all three of them. But I got a look at her before they hurt me, Mrs. Silver, and she was peaceful, very peaceful, because she was out of her pain now — oh, they hurt us so much those months — and she knew her baby was alive before she died."

In the parlor, Beatriz lay on the couch and told me the story of Miriam's death and your birth, Marcella — "The baby is alive, Jacobo!" — and tears rolled down the wasted woman's face. I did not cry. I sat on a chair like a stone, like Carlos' unmoving Finger of God pointed forever at the ones who murdered my daughter and then stole you from us, and though it is many years now since that evening in Mendoza I listened like a statue, some piece of me still remains in that seat, frozen, my rage eternal, my grief intact, a rock-hard witness to the truth.

"When did they release you, Beatriz?" I said when I could finally speak.

"A year later. When I got sick. A healthy woman delivers a child and they kill her. Another gets cancer and they let her go. They are insane, Mrs. Silver. They are not human beings."

"Where is the — ?"

She put her hands on her womb. "It started here," she said, still weeping. "At first I thought I was pregnant, but I knew that was impossible. I think I wanted to be Miriam, to bring her back to life again in me. A lady in my cell, she said it was the Immaculate Conception again and started to pray to me, on her knees, as if I were Mary. You go crazy in there. Finally they took me to a hospital, in the middle of the night, and did tests, x-rays. Then they took me back to the prison. They kept me there until I was so sick that nothing could. . . . And then one day they let me go. They brought me back here to Mendoza, to my mother's house, to die. Do you know what I said when they pushed me out of the car? This is what torture does to you, Senora: I said, "I bless you for this from the bottom of my heart." "If you knew my name," I said, "why did you wait — "

"My mother could not endure anymore, Mrs. Silver. Please understand. I was frightened they would find out I had talked to you and come for me again. Or for her."

"Then why now, Beatriz?"

"I could not die," she said, "without telling you the story."

She closed her eyes, and I saw she had no lashes. Even a newborn has lashes, I thought. Suddenly she became like my own child to me and I lifted her frail and broken hand. Without even realizing what I was doing, I turned it over and looked at her palm.

Tragedy under the second finger. Loss under the third. The lifeline broken in half.

"Ah," she said, trying to smile, "I think I know my fortune already."

"Thank you for calling me," I said. I kissed the papery skin I held. "And thank you for touching Miriam's face."

"I have made a room ready for you," Beatriz said, "if you would like to stay here."

"Your mother may not — "

"She is staying with my sister tonight. She said to tell you she is sorry, but she is afraid. She knows you are active with the Madres, and — "

"I would be pleased to stay here," I said, and we sat together for a long time in the dim house, silently now, waiting for the day's last light to withdraw.

I lay awake all night, hearing Beatriz' story over and over again like one of my father's recordings when the needle on the turntable sticks. "She was peaceful, very peaceful," Beatriz' voice chanted to me, and just when that phrase had nearly lulled me into something like sleep, the woman's narration began once more: "We heard the baby cry, and five minutes later. . . ." At two a.m., as if an infant had called in hunger or distress, I reached for the pillow beside me and held it against my chest until dawn. No, Marcella, it was not you I pretended to cradle that long night at 44 San Juan. It was your mother, a grown woman murdered in a prison cell become again my baby Miriam screaming for me in the dark. Her little head of curls, her heaving back, her tiny legs drawn up in pain. Whose tears soaked the pillow case? Who wept, inconsolable, for hours? Who?

At dawn I sank into a sleep so deep, I dreamed Miriam's whole life, years turned to minutes, memories compressed like diamonds min-

ers exhume from the depths. I saw her freed from her imprison-
ment the instant you were born, leaving her own body along with
her child, both of you delivered from the ordeal of the past months.
"Oh Mama!" she said, greeting me as if I had come to visit her in
the hospital maternity ward, her room filled with flowers, her baby
at her breast. "Isn't she wonderful? Isn't she dear?" Some healing
began in me then, I see now, and continues today in these tales I
mine. Perhaps, Marcella, it is not just for you that I set them down;
perhaps these stories are waking dreams I chisel and polish with my
pen, each one a prism whose beauty I discover as I write.

In her stucco-walled kitchen, Beatriz Vargas was squeezing
oranges. Coffee brewed on the stove. She was stronger than she'd
been last night, and there was some color in her cheeks, not that
white pallor from which it had seemed life had already deserted
her. We embraced as kin, her ruined body familiar to me now, the
hours we'd spent last night like years of bonding coming to an
abrupt and grievous end.

"Beatriz," I said, "I would like to help you in some way. Medical
bills, perhaps, or — "

"Oh, I would never take money from you, Senora!"

"Then something else," I said. "Not payment, Beatriz." Tears
sprang to me eyes. "A gift from a mother."

She put her hand to her heart, as if receiving my affection there,
releasing her own to me. "Could you drive me to Cacheuta? To the
hot springs there? I would like to go once more. Would that be possible, or must you get back to — "

"Of course I will take you," I said. "Of course."

I called the airport to book a later flight home. I called Jacobo's
answering service, leaving a message about my change in plans.
Soon I was helping Beatriz out of her wheel chair into her car —
she lay on the back seat on a bed I fixed from pillows — and

putting the wheel-chair into the trunk, and driving into the desert with the woman who had touched my dead daughter's cheek ("She was peaceful, very peaceful.") before the guard brought his baton down on Beatriz Vargas' outstretched hand.

West of Mendoza, the irrigated green oasis gave way abruptly to the fault-line's true face: parched desert soil stretching to the Andes, and thousands of bright-colored boulders flung, it seemed, from another universe to this barren field. I drove for an hour through that rock-filled scrub, and though the road we travelled was well-paved and level, Beatriz moaned as if the car were climbing up and down the mammoth stones, the tiniest pot-hole crater for her, the slightest rise a cliff. Several times I stopped to give her water and suggested that we turn back, but she was adamant: "Cacheuta," she said. "Just this last time."

Finally, we approached the town. At a filling station, a silent Indian pumped gas and stared at bald Beatriz, prone on the back seat with her eyes closed, so still I know he feared her dead.

"She is very ill," I said. "We are going to the hot springs for treatment. Can you give me directions?"

With his leathery hand, he pointed ahead, crossed himself and gave me my change without speaking a word. In the rear-view mirror I saw he watched in mute attention as we proceeded to the spa.

"I frighten people," Beatriz said. "They will stare."

"Then I will stare back," I said, and we both laughed, the sound of mirth bubbling up unexpectedly like the steaming springs I saw now here between two cactus-like shrubs, there beside a boulder behind which the great Andes cliffs rose like the stone wings of a mammoth bird.

Now the red tile roof of the lodge appeared, and soon the building came into view. In front of the wide veranda, several busses were discharging patrons, and on the porch, uniformed attendants brought glasses of mate to robe-swathed visitors between treatments. A nurse came to help Beatriz into her wheelchair and rolled her up the flower-edged ramp. People did stare — Beatriz was right — but I thought the looks were more like wonderment than aversion, that a woman so clearly near death would still venture out to a place like Cacheuta: she changed the spa from a kind of hospital for ordinary ailments to a shrine that day, dying as much a miraculous event as a curse to be feared, a sacrament as much as a sentence some capricious jailer serves. ("Here's your Jewish whore," he'd said, and smashed his baton across Beatriz' fingers).

Now we were moving through the portals beyond the doctor's office — "Not long," he'd warned. "In your condition, not more than ten minutes, Senorita." — to the gravelled path leading to the springs. At the lip of a rock-bordered pool in which several others already soaked, Beatriz Vargas rose from her wheelchair and dropped the terry-cloth robe she was wearing to the ground, let the slippers fall from her feet. She was emaciated, her bones visible through her translucent skin, and I could see the scars on her back from beatings in the prison. She moved forward a woman walking out of her stricken body, discarding it as one would a dress that no longer fit, and stepped unaided into the steaming baths. If the other bathers stared, it was because they were transfixed, as I was, by her dancer's grace, by the uncanny agility of an invalid suddenly empowered, freed from her pain. Had she lifted her arms and flown toward the peaks beyond us, who would have been surprised? But she continued her descent into the water instead. Soon only the back of her bald head was visible, a luminous crystal ball I might have been able to read if I had been a gypsy like Ovid — "How can

I find Marcella?" he would have asked, gazing into that living globe like a scientist staring into a microscope, waiting for the signs to appear like cells suddenly visible on a translucent slide.

In ten minutes, I called to Beatriz Vargas. She floated on her back to the pool's side. Her fingers fumbled for the rail by the stairs, her legs buckled in the effort to stand, she choked on a mouthful of the steaming metallic water. A white-haired woman still immersed saw Beatriz' plight, and together we lifted her to the chaise from which I'd watched her beautiful swim. Whatever strength had powered her was gone. I covered her with her robe. She lay exhausted on the chair, her breathing rapid and thin. She whispered, "I told you the story. I came to Cacheuta. Now I can die." Then the woman from Mendoza closed her eyes and a final shudder passed through her like a gust of wind, and Beatriz was gone. I touched my fingers to her cheek, kept my hand on her face until the doctor, breathless, arrived at her side.

"Too late," he said, shaking his head, lifting the stethoscope from her stilled chest. "Are you her mother?"

I closed my eyes, as if in prayer. ("At first I thought I was pregnant, but I knew that was impossible," she'd said. "I think I wanted to be Miriam, to bring her back to life again in me.") Then I lifted my gaze to his and answered his question.

"Yes, yes, I am her mother," I heard myself say. "She looked like me, you know. She looked like me."

27

JACOBO DIED IN 1983, the year democracy returned to Argentina. At least he had been able to witness the disgrace and resignation of the junta after the country's defeat in the Malvinas. Although most people supported the war against England, the Madres had opposed it: were more of our children to die for a regime that refused to account for thousands and thousands missing at home? "You know why we're going to war, don't you?" Jacobo had said the day we learned of the invasion. "Because the people are finally ready to throw the military out. Not because of the disappearances, no. Because the butchers have wrecked the economy, that's why *Porteños* are out in the streets."

He died in the summer, for which I was grateful. Jacobo hated winter. Once he tried skiing at Bariloche — he loved hiking those mountains in warmer seasons — but even those magnificent Alpine-like slopes failed to capture his interest in July. "I just don't like the cold," he said, and later he told me it always reminded him of his time in Dachau, how once a man in his barracks had amputated his own frost-bitten toe with a rock he'd honed into a primitive scalpel. "Then he put his bloody foot into his shoe and went out on his work detail, not even limping, but the dogs smelled the blood and the guards let them. . . ."

So I was glad he had died in the summer, and fast, a heart attack in the kitchen, my husband crashing to the floor like a felled tree, a wistful look on his face as his breathing stilled. When he collapsed,

I screamed his name, but it was as if I had called out in the depths of a forest, my voice reduced to whisper, swallowed up by those towering woods. I knew he was dead even before the medics arrived, bursting into the house as if an emergency existed for which their services were needed. "He's gone," I told them, refusing to rise from Jacobo's side as they listened for vital signs, tried to resuscitate him, worked with the fierce, detached speed of all specialists of crisis. "I'm sorry," one of them said to me finally, giving me the news I had already given him. "He's gone."

That was a Saturday. My mother had eaten breakfast with us, then gone with a neighbor to the outdoor market in San Ysidro plaza. She wanted to make us a special Rumanian eggplant dish whose recipe she had only remembered the day before, after so many years of forgetfulness. "This was my father's favorite dish, when I was a little girl," she'd said. More and more the past was returning to her as a kind of rescue, I thought, from the pain of the present. Sometimes I'd hear her talking to her husband Eliezar as if he were right in the room with her; sometimes she'd write her mother Reba a letter and ask me to mail it when I went downtown. "Make sure it has enough postage," she'd instruct me. "Baille Herculanae is very far, you know." More often, she knew the years she yearned for were vanished now, and she did not often have the consolation of an old woman's confusion. But songs came back to her, and jokes, and recipes like the stew Dov Landau loved, memories arriving out of the air like a flock of birds landing in her garden, or flying into her bedroom window while she was asleep. She returned from the market just in time to see the attendants carrying the stretcher out of the house, the white sheet already drawn over Jacobo's face. My mother dropped the bag of produce she carried, eggplant and tomatoes and onions and eggs exploding on the walk like the volley of artillery she'd heard decades before, in that

Transylvanian resort town where so many would perish. "My God, my God, it never stops!" I heard her cry, the meal she had wanted to cook us turned to wreckage at her feet.

Now Jacobo lay in the closed casket on which I'd draped the afghan Miriam had crocheted for our twenty-fifth anniversary. She had not made us a present since the days of her childhood, when she was always presenting us with drawings and painted clay pots and the pipe cleaner animals Jacobo had kept on a shelf in his office until he died. I had placed one in his pocket before they'd closed the coffin's lid: a pelican Miriam had made after seeing such a bird at the zoo, mesmerized by the dives of the bird into the water for fish it stowed in its bulging pouch. That night Jacobo had told her the old legend about how, when no food can be found, pelican mothers feed their young with their own blood.

"I don't think the babies like the taste of it." Miriam had said, grimacing.

Jacobo had laughed. "Probably not, but they love their mothers for caring about them so much."

"Like when I have a cold and Mama gives me 'the concoction'?" she said, meaning the herbal remedy the Indian maid next door had taught my mother how to mix.

"Exactly, exactly. Like when Mama gives you 'the concoction.'"

Then he'd told her how he and I and my mother Sonia had come from Europe on a ship named for that very bird, how he had wept when *The Pelican* docked in the Buenos Aires harbor, dropping its anchor in the River of Silver and releasing its refugee passengers like a flock of new-born fledglings to the Argentine shore.

The next day our daughter made her first pipe-cleaner animal, the same hand-fashioned pelican I buried with Jacobo, who would have given his own blood, a father's blood, every drop of it, if that offering could have saved Miriam's life.

Now one of his former patients — an inmate at Treblinka during the war whose son, like Miriam, had died here in one of the
three-hundred-and forty-six "detention centres" the now-deposed
military government had created with their Nazi "consultants" to
advise them — limped to the podium from which the rabbi had
called him forward. From the chapel's private anteroom reserved
"for immediate family," I sat with my mother and Carlos' sister
Claudia, watching the man named Reuben Levi search in his pocket for the envelope on which he'd written his notes.

"I want to say goodbye to Dr. Silver," he began. "And to pay my
respects to his widow and mother-in-law as well."

I touched my hand to the black ribbon of mourning the rabbi
had pinned to my dress, rending the grosgrain with one slight slash
of a razor and uttering in Hebrew the prayer that confirmed the
words with which Reuben Levi had just addressed me: "widow."
Yes, my hand remembered, this was the truth. Miriam was murdered and now Jacobo, too, had disappeared into the province of the
dead.

What Reuben Levi said about my husband I do not know,
though my mother told me it was a beautiful and moving eulogy,
and Claudia said she'd wept at his words. In my mind, I had travelled again to the River Plate, standing beside Jacobo that sun-
soaked day he had taken the ashes of Miriam's recovered bones to
the water and sent them into the current, our Little Fish released to
the element she loved best, returned twenty-nine years after her
birth to a larger womb in which her spirit could swim and swim
and swim.

I wanted to loose Jacobo's ashes into the water as well, father
and daughter making their way together back to the sea which had
brought us here from Europe all those years before. But I remembered him telling me once that even if he was not an observant Jew,

not "a believer" at all, still he wanted "a Jewish funeral" — the rabbi chanting the kaddish, the mourners travelling in cavalcade to the cemetery where he would be buried in the earth in a plain pine box — to honor the millions who had perished in Europe "for the crime of being Jewish," he'd said, "and nothing else."

"Here's the Jewish whore," the guard had said to Beatriz Vargas.

"I always knew Peron was an anti-semite," Jacobo had said, "but since his death, the worst elements, the very worst, are taking over. Whatever they do, they will do twice to a Jew. I tell you, I wouldn't be surprised if we wound up with camps again here, the whole nightmare."

The whole nightmare.

Yes.

Except for this miracle, which I proclaimed with the fervor of a Biblical herald — "The baby is alive, Jacobo!" — and in which I continue to believe years after Beatriz Vargas told me the story of your birth, even though it is true I have not found you yet and may die myself without ever seeing your face. Although it is part of the nightmare that they stole you at birth from us, the fact that you survived, were spared your mother's terrible fate, and have grown into the young woman reading these pages I write now, discovering finally who you really are and how we never stopped loving you, the family you were not allowed to know — that is still a miracle to me.

Do you look like your mother, Marcella?

Do you look like your mother?

Because it was drizzling, a tent flapped in the wind over Jacobo's gravesite. Following the pallbearers who carried the casket from the hearse, my mother and I walked the petal-strewn path, Claudia behind us with friends of Miriam, and scores of mourners after them. Like a ridge of black hills suddenly altering the flat horizon, umbrellas ringed the coffin. I sat between my mother and Claudia beneath the canvas shelter, Jacobo in the pine box before us. When the *kaddish* began, I remembered how the rabbi at our wedding in the DP camp had mistakenly chanted that same prayer for the dead. Oh Jacobo, here we were again under a canopy, your funeral a sad reprisal of that earlier ceremony. Who could have imagined the sorrow we would have to bear in the years that followed? I cried your name — "Jacobo!" — and this time my scream could have woken the dead, but you did not stir from your final rest, darling, you slept on, and then the sound of creaking, like a bed, as they lowered you down for all the nights to come.

I remember Claudia Rojas calling us the day Miriam's grave was discovered, six archaeologists digging up the ground behind the police barracks in La Plata, sullen uniformed officers watching the scientists perform the court-sanctioned task at one more unmarked site — "Sometimes," Claudia wept one evening at our home after several weeks of solid work, "it seems they have turned all of Argentina into a giant burial mound!" The day she learned the La Plata exhumation contained her sister-in-law's remains, she waited for the team's pathologist to show her the evidence the skeleton revealed: yes, this woman had given birth to a child — "You can see how her hip bones moved to accommodate delivery." — and the infant was not among the corpses the dig had unearthed.

"Beatrice Vargas was telling the truth, Rachael," Claudia said. "Miriam did have her baby in detention, we have the evidence now to prove it."

Evidence of death, evidence of life, both truths contained in those bones spread out in anatomical order on a white-sheeted examining table, Jacobo and I brought to the tiny room in the hospital basement where the team's pathologist had analyzed and catalogued and reconstructed the skeleton he said was our daughter. I stroked the crown of the skull as if it was actually Miriam lying there before me — injured, perhaps, in an accident or stricken with a terrible illness — and I here at her bedside, crooning to her as if she were a child again. Overcome, Jacobo turned away and wept against the wall.

Skull, ribcage, pelvis, femur, fibula.

And you, Marcella. ("You can see how the hip bones moved to accommodate delivery.") And you.

The Madres would work without me now. From that moment on, I belonged to another group of women: the Abuelas de la Plaza de Mayo, dozens of grandmothers searching for children kidnapped from their cribs or born in the camps — "The baby is alive, Jacobo!" — only to disappear again into the homes of strangers for whom the truth was not part of the adoption procedure, for whom the identities of their new babies' biological parents was a mystery better left unquestioned, or a knowledge to be concealed.

"NN," the lawyers handling the adoptions wrote on the forms in the space for the names of the birth mother and father. "NN."

Find your own papers, Marcella, and change the lie to the truth. Cross out "NN" and write in its place "Miriam Silver Rojas" and "Carlos Rojas," and attach that document to these stories I leave you and never let anyone tell you again that you were abandoned without any identification, left in a dumpster to die or placed at the door of an orphanage that took you in, a foundling, an unwanted infant given to parents who raised you, thank God, as their very own.

Tell anyone who insists on that version that you now know

what happened. Tell them you know who you are. Tell them you know that first they took your father away, and then your mother as well, who delivered you minutes before she was killed — "Here's the Jewish whore," the guard said to Beatriz Vargas. Tell them your mother would have named you Marcella "because it sounds like music," she had decided the day before she disappeared. Tell them your grandmother, Rachael Silver, your mother's mother, your *abuela*, looked for you ever since the day she learned of your birth, and left you a book of family tales that ends with the story of that love-driven search.

Like census-takers assigned to Hell, the Madres canvassed cemeteries and prisons and hospital wards, every province of pain a potential address for a missing daughter or son. Are you there? we screamed to the ghosts and the inmates and the patients for whom visitors were not permitted: Are you there? One by one we would learn the truth, and almost always it was sorrowful: unmarked graves and bodies thrown out of airplanes into the sea and corpses left on the porches of parents who opened the front door for the paper and found their dead children at their feet. Or just the hands in a bottle of brine, like pickles left by a neighbor as a token of good will.

But now I roamed another world, Marcella, one in which nobody seemed to be suffering and death was a rumor best dismissed. Schoolyards, zoos, playgrounds and parks, movies theaters and confiterias where parents bought laughing children pastries and fruity sodas they slurped through straws. Sometimes, in a pediatrician's waiting room, a feverish boy or a sick little girl reminded me that pain existed in this world, too; then I would be ashamed for feeling relief at the sight of a stricken child. How far I had journeyed from the years of Miriam's youth, when I was a mother like the ones I trailed now on their normal errands, their carefree excursions, their unremarkable daily itineraries I shadowed like the spy I had become, now that I knew you were alive.

Once I believed I had found the couple who had adopted you, a wealthy Palermo businessman and his wife, and I followed them one afternoon to the private school their daughter attended, Jorge and Alicia Morales on their way to a student talent show in which their Anna would play *Au Claire de la Lune* on the piano. From the rear of the auditorium, I watched Jorge and Alicia move forward a bit on their seats when Anna's name was called, and then the girl appeared in a spotlight, illumined and revealed. How much she resembled Miriam to me! How like Carlos she moved! I might have run to the stage and claimed her there, but we *Abuelas* always reminded each other of this: gather all the evidence and bring it to the lawyers, but never disclose yourself beforehand. Why risk restraining orders, or getting arrested for invasion of privacy, or — worst or all — alerting the adoptive parents in time for them to flee with the grandchild for whom one has searched for so long? I left the school as their Anna began her performance, the delicate notes surely the work of a talent, obviously the descendent of the famous violinist, Eliezar Pearl, whose records my mother listened to every night after supper in the house this girl was stolen from before she had even been born.

I arrived in Palermo the following day, introducing myself to Alicia Morales as a maid who'd been sent by a cleaning service to this address. I wore one of my mother's housedresses and a moth-eaten sweater I kept in my studio and scuffed oxfords on my feet. From my pocket, I pulled out an official-looking card on which the family's street and house number had been written in pen.

"I am so sorry," the woman said, smoothing her blonde hair

from her brow. "There's been a terrible mistake, I never called
for — "

My eyes filled with tears. "I must have work today," I said. "My
husband is sick and the medicine costs so — "

"Well," she said, examining again the business card I had handed her. "Look. It's obvious this isn't your fault. We're having a party
this weekend, and I could use some extra help getting ready. All the
silver needs to be polished, and maybe you. . . ."

She rattled off tasks and I agreed to them all — "Oh, Senora,
yes, I do very good pressing." — and five minutes after my arrival,
I had been hired by the woman who would have slammed the door
in my face, had she known who I actually was and why I had come
to her home that morning.

All day I worked, Marcella, waiting for you to return from
school. In the hallway I dusted the frames of pictures that tracked
their daughter's life from infancy on: I peered into those images of
Anna Morales for distinguishing marks — was there a mole like the
one on Miriam's shoulder? did she bear Carlos' single dimple? was
her nose a little off-center? were her bottom teeth crowded together? I could see none of those clues in the photographs, and the
striking resemblance to my missing daughter and son-in-law I'd
seen in Anna the day before faded some now, much as the auditorium spotlight had been replaced by a muted sixty-watt bulb in the
hallway's overhead fixture.

At noon Alicia Morales called from the kitchen where she had
been making *empañadas* for the upcoming party. "Senora Garcia!"
she hollered. "Come join me for lunch," and I lay down the rag
with which I was shining the bronze bucket beside the living
room's fireplace. She was fixing us platters of fruit and cheese and
slices of bread warmed in the oven.

"Will you drink *maté*?" she asked. "Or coffee is here in the pot,
if you'd like."

"*Maté* is fine," I said, unsteadied by her hospitality. I knew it was unusual for maids to be treated like guests in one's home, and either Alicia Morales was strikingly kind, or suspected that I was no maid at all. Had she seen me staring at Anna's pictures upstairs, or entering her room to sit for a moment on her bed, my fingers lifting the edge of her quilt as if it might fall apart at my touch?

"So," the woman said, "your husband is ill?"

"Yes," I said, "a very bad heart. The doctors — "

But in the midst of my response, the phone rang, Anna's school calling Senora Morales.

"Yes, yes, straight to the hospital!" I heard her insist. "I'll meet you there!"

Then she was grabbing her purse and a canister of medication from the cupboard over the sink. "Our daughter has asthma," she said, her eyes brimming. "She's adopted. Just last year we discovered her birth mother had been an asthmatic from childhood and died of the illness herself. It frightens me so, every time Anna has an attack." She looked confused, as if she had suddenly realized she'd confided in a stranger, and then I saw her accept her need for a moment of closeness in the face of her fear. "But you have a sick husband, so you know of such things." Then she lay some money on the table — "in case you finish before I return" — and rushed from the house. I heard her car backing down the driveway, the rumble of tires on gravel like her child's wheezing breath.

I knew Alicia Morales was telling me the truth — a mother knows another mother's alarm, recognizes that unmediated terror at the news of a child's plight. "Her birth mother had been an asthmatic from childhood on, and died of the illness herself." In the stranger's kitchen, I wept. Why did I think I would ever find my granddaughter? How many leads like this one had led me in so many circles I seemed to live now in a constant state of vertigo, always on the verge of falling, always on the edge of collapse?

"You will exhaust yourself with this obsession," Jacobo would tell me. "It has taken over your entire life."

"Do you want me to give up searching?" I'd cry.

"Do you want to lose yourself in the process? There are many ways to disappear, Rachael. Many ways to disappear."

I left Alicia Morales' money in her house in Palermo, where sometimes the daughter she called Anna woke in the night gasping for oxygen.

In San Ysidro, my mother liked to say we had "room to breathe," but no child filled her healthy lungs with that air now, no granddaughter sang her true name — "Marcella, Marcella, Mar-cel-la!" — like a song. That night I dreamed of Miriam underwater, submerged for hours on a single breath, her stolen infant in her arms and both of them waiting for me to signal them that it was safe to rise again, to surface once more to the land.

Oh, I could make a book from the dreams of these past years, my sleep a mirror of my waking life, painful and driven and never at rest. Perhaps Jacobo was right, that I had become obsessed with my search. I knew how he worried about my health. Once I had found him alone in his study, weeping over a picture he kept of me on his desk. I took him in my arms. "What is it?" I asked, and he answered, "I am so afraid for you, Rachael, so very afraid. If you keep on like this, I don't know what will — "

But how else was I to find you, Marcella? ("You can see how the hip bones moved to accommodate delivery.") Every morning I woke to the scene of your birth in that torture camp, your moth-er's murder ("My god, Beatriz, they took me for the baby!"), and then her new-born daughter driven to some secret address in an unmarked Ford Falcon just like the one in which Miriam had been abducted months before her death. Every morning I flung myself across the hood of that car and screamed to your kidnappers, "Give me my grandchild!" but the driver laughed as he gunned the engine, the car's sudden speed pitching me to the side of the road as you vanished. If I did not devote myself to every clue, respond to every intuition, follow dreams like roadmaps into the city where you might be hidden from us, who would?

Easier to tell my heart to rest from its throbbing work.

Easier to tell my blood to cease its flow through the body's rivered maze.

Easier to tell my cells to slough off the knowledge they carry like invisible oracles, to forget the secrets with which they have been entrusted.

"Mitochondria," the geneticist from California said, as gently as if she had spoken the name of one of our lost grandchildren.

"Mitochondria," we repeated in a choral hush so much like a prayer several of the women took out their rosaries, and Liliana Schell murmured a blessing in Hebrew, here in a basement conference room of Durand Hospital where we had come to hear the story for which we had waited so long.

The American scientist lifted her poster boards to an easel, and began a narrative as spellbinding to us as the tales we had all told our children long ago, before they had disappeared.

"In every cell, there is a special form of DNA, different from the DNA found in the chromosomes. It is called mitochondria, and it is inherited from mothers, generation after generation, disappearing only when a woman fails to produce a daughter to pass it on to her children, and those daughters to theirs, and so forth. No two families have the same mitochondria. If a sample from a child matches a sample from any maternal relative, that is absolute proof of identity. Absolute proof. Incontrovertible evidence. If I took a drop of blood from one of you and isolated the mitochondria, when you looked at it through a microscope, you would be seeing, in a very real sense, every maternal ancestor you ever had, and every descendent. So we can use this procedure as evidence in court, to prove grandpaternity of the children you've found. And we can establish a genetics data bank, so that even after you're dead, a grandchild who uncovers the truth of his or her birth can determine, with complete finality, who his or her real family was, simply by matching mitochondria samples. Your blood is your legacy, then. A few drops of your blood. Am I explaining this clearly enough? Do you have questions?"

Because we were in the basement, Marcella, the room did not have any windows, and the overhead fluorescent fixtures were the only mechanical illumination. Then what brightness seemed to rise from the floor as Dr. Clare spoke, cones of radiance pluming upward, bodies of light adding their presences one by one to the gathering of women in Room 36? Did anyone else see the spirits that joined us that afternoon? Were they our dead daughters and sons, come to hear the scientist explaining the mysteries of yet another invisible world? I never discussed what happened with the others — you are the first one to know what I witnessed — but I cannot believe those beautiful visitors intended that I alone should be graced by their presences. Surely each woman knew when the light of her own lost child leaned against her as if in embrace, and then vanished again, the room dimmer now, the radiance ebbed.

I would remember that light as I sat at my dying mother's bedside, listening to her tale of Dov Landau's disappearance, how she tracked her missing father into the Danube Delta and saw the pelican he had become fly away into a luminosity she had never before described to a soul.

Weeks later, in a special waiting room at Durand Hospital, I would think of that magical bird when it was my turn to have Dr. Clare prick my finger, collecting on a slide the specimen to be stored for you in the National Genetics Data Bank like food from your pelican grandmother, sweetheart, food for Miriam's daughter, my dear one, these tales of your family I am just now completing already created, already recorded, already passed on from Reba to Sonia to me to Miriam to you, Marcella, in just a few drops of my blood.

DATE DUE

OCT 0 2 1999		
OCT 2 2 1999		
OCT 3 0 1999		
NOV 1 2 1999		
GAYLORD		PRINTED IN U.S.A.